Rise

A Novel

by Leslie McCauley

2019

Cover design by Mark G. Maxwell

ISBN: 9781701626089
Imprint: Independently published

Prologue

I wake with a start, "He's here! He's here!" I scream. My own piercing voice brings me back to my room. Yes, my room. With canary-colored walls and my white comforter, with tiny daisies embroidered delicately on the edges. It's twisted around my body, but I am safe. I am home.

Beads of sweat kiss my brow and as I wipe it clean with my shirt sleeve, my breathing begins to steady. What is this the fourth or fifth night in a row? I thought these nightmares were gone. Well, for at least a short time they were. It's just because of tomorrow, that's all. The anniversary of the day that would forever change my entire life. I have got to sleep!

With the hairs on my neck still standing, I slip out of bed. My bare feet hit the cool hardwood floor of my bedroom. I look at the bedside clock, 2:15 a.m. Yeah, that sounds about right. Next to my clock is my favorite picture of him. I flip the frame down on its face. Why do I still have that right there? As a reminder of the good, the bad, and the piece of my heart still longing to be filled. I should put it away, but I can't bear it. I will someday when I've moved on. "Someday" I whisper to myself.

I make my way down the hall, passing the full-length mirror behind the bathroom door. My hair is a mess tangled and sticking up in all directions, which might be sexy had I not slept alone again. My long, dirty blonde hair sits straight, just grazing my collar bone. My eyes look sunken and dull. Not quite the sparkling hazel that they used to be. No; just dull, like me.

I wander to the other end of the house to the kitchen. The moonlight shines brightly through the French doors and illuminates the dark granite kitchen island. As I sit at one of the bar stools, I am reminded of the last day I saw him. The man who haunts my dreams. Will I ever feel safe again? Will I ever be safe again? I shake my head as I will the dark thoughts to go away. It helps for a moment, but it's fleeting as I know they are never far. I need a distraction.

I grab what's left of a bottle of merlot from the wine rack.It's not much, but it'll do. I pour a small glass and make my way to the living room. My house is a small two-bedroom and one bath ranch. It's a cool ivory brick with dark red shutters. It's not much, but it's cozy and it's mine. I pick up the remote, sink into the old Lazy Boy, and click on the television. Luckily, I don't have to worry about waking anyone. I haven't lived with anyone since Evan... But I don't want to go there, not now.

I taste my wine, a small sip. Mmmm it warms my throat all the way down into my belly. Sleep, I hope this helps me sleep. After a few more sips and channel surfing, I settle on an infomercial talking about the latest exercise craze. The overly enthusiastic voice of the man selling me, well, crap, is buzzing in my ears as my eyes finally begin to drift. My mind slows and I succumb to sleep....

Chapter 1

An Old Friend

I start my walk home from work taking the same route I've taken every day since beginning my new job. I finally feel like I have come into my own. That I'm "grown-up". I have been hired at a small newspaper as a photographer, just fluff pieces mostly and high school sports, but it feels so rewarding seeing "Photo credit: Nettie Madison".

My full name is Antoinette. A name I was graced with after my grandmother, but all my life, friends, and family have called me Nettie. I grew up not five miles from here, and I am so close with my family that I never wanted to go far. Small town Ohio. It never bothered me, and it never even occurred to me that I could leave. This was home.

Many classmates of mine couldn't wait to move to a big city but not me. I like the quiet. I like that everyone knows everyone, although that can be a good or bad thing. But we take care of our own. We support one another when it's needed. I feel lucky to have grown up here. I feel lucky to have such a supportive family and friends.

It's raining lightly but not enough to need an umbrella. Even the smell of the rain hitting the warm pavement is comforting. Summer in Ohio is hit or miss. It could be a hundred degrees or cold enough for a sweater. Today would be one of those perfect days if it weren't for the rain.

About halfway to my place, I run into an old friend from high school, Sam. He and I still see each other from time to time because he lives not far from me.

Sam was never overly popular in high school, but he was always kind and friendly, one of those friends who could make you laugh when you were having a rotten day. Now he works for a local construction company and generally keeps busy, from what he tells me. Although now that I think of it, he appears not to have been doing much work because his clothes look fairly neat, which is not typical, with the exception of his work boots.

Normally, Sam's scruffy blonde hair has bits of dirt and drywall dust lying on top of it. His jeans are typically torn and dirty with remnants of past jobs he's done. He's a good-looking man. He has a medium frame, but because of his job he has muscular shoulders and arms. He is very cute. I had never really given it much thought

2

until now. He's wearing a pair of dark washed jeans and a plain light blue t-shirt that highlights his steel-blue eyes. I've known him since he was a lanky, knobby-kneed little boy.

He greets me kindly and asks if he can walk me home. I'm grateful for that. It's just beginning to get dark; the air has a slight chill. The walk isn't a long one, but it's good to have the company. We laugh and chat it up, making small talk and then gossip a bit, too.

He's like a nosey girlfriend. I swear he knows more than I do about the people in this town. I guess construction workers gossip as much as the old ladies at the beauty salon. I haven't seen him in a few weeks, so he has a lot to say.

"Last time we went out you were supposed to buy me a drink for kicking your ass at pool!" He boasts.

"I don't know I think you cheated! You said you never play, and I think I was hustled!" I say in my defense.

As we approach my house (MY house, not my parents' but mine. Gosh, that is a great feeling.), I invite him in.

"Well, I have beer in the fridge if you want to sit on the back patio and visit? I mean I don't want to have any debt, of course." I smile a big-tooth grin. I have always thought of myself as awkward.

3

This has, in turn, made me very outgoing. No one seemed to find me attractive in high school, so I was always goofy and fun in an attempt to make up for what I thought I was lacking in looks. I suppose I have grown into my own now. Sam laughs and shakes his head.

"Of course, I want you to be debt free. I'msure the guilt of owing me consumes you," he says with sarcasm. I unlock the door and wave my hand for him to enter.

"Ladies first," I say as serious as I can.

"Very funny, Nettie! You better watch it!" He pokes at my side as he glides passed me into the house.

"You can leave your shoes on, we'll just go straight back to the patio. Just let me put my camera and bag down. Go ahead and make yourself at home. There are a few beers in the fridge." I walk into my room and put down my things. It is a complete and total mess in here. Clothes are thrown all over the floor. Dirty or clean I don't know. Argh, I have to get this place in order tomorrow! I make my way back out to Sam and he is sitting on the patio smoking a Marlboro Red.

"You are still smoking those things?" My entrance startles him.

"Jesus you scared me! Yes, I'mstill smoking them and mind your own business! You used to smoke in high school and college if I remember correctly!" he says with a matter of fact attitude.

"Yes, I did but I quit, that's the difference. Most adolescents smoke because they are stupid and don't know any better." My hand on my hip now scolding like he is my child. "You are technically an adult! You know better. And your dad is a doctor for Christ's sake!" I'm giggling now but really, I'm serious. I hate smokers. It's a nasty habit and I know. It took me a long while to quit. I'm one of those annoying reformed smokers. Smokers hate me! "I'm just busting your balls, Sam. Did you get a beer?" I look around and don't see one.

"No, I wanted to see what you were having?"

I open the patio door. "Let me check what's in the fridge." I walk back into the kitchen leaving the patio door ajar so he can hear me. As I scan the fridge, I notice there is not much to choose from.

"Bud light or a Great Lakes?" I shout.

"Great Lakes would be great," he giggles. "Thanks." I get him a beer and reach for a Bud Light myself. The Great Lakes must have been leftover from a party. I don't remember buying it. Opening both the bottles I stroll back out to join Sam.

"Thanks again," he says softly as I hand him his bottle.

We both sit in the mismatched, hand me down patio chairs that face the back yard. I am lucky to have found this house when I did. I had just been hired and it was a foreclosure, so I got it for an amazing price. I would have never been able to afford it otherwise. My backyard is just big enough with trees surrounding so that I have privacy. Two willow trees sit opposite the house which is my favorite part. I feel like I'm in the country even though it's only blocks from the main part of town. I haven't had a chance to plant any flowers yet, maybe over the weekend, depending on the weather. I like to say I have more of a black thumb rather than green because for some reason plants don't care much for me.

It's quiet for a beat and it almost feels a little awkward. Sam shifts in his seat looking a bit weary as well. I wonder if he is nervous. Why would he be? He takes a long drink of his beer. After what seems like forever, he takes one last drag off his cigarette nearly burning his fingertips, smoking it to the brown filter. He then leans forward and flicks the butt into my yard. How rude! I think but don't say anything. I'll get it tomorrow.

"Well, what should we do now? I guess you could repay your debt?" he whispers. Something has changed, his eyes, they look almost eerie or dark somehow. I have known him for so long but now that I'm thinking of it, I don't think we've ever been completely alone with one another. That's strange. We have always been with other friends. The thought sends a chill up my spine, why is that? I feel uncomfortable in the way his demeanor has shifted from a friendly face to this intense almost spooky look, that I have never seen before. I try and brush it off.

"I thought that's what I was doing, the beer right? I only owed you one drink," I hold up a finger.

"Well yeah, but given the fact you have been sending me signals for the past, God I lost count of how many years and finally you've invited me in alone, I don't want to miss my opportunity to get out of the friend zone," his smile is almost grimacing now. Is he serious right now?

"Huh? Oh, Sam, I didn't mean to give you the wrong impression. I, I mean I see you as a friend and always have. You know? We have been buddies since we were kids." I sound so unsure of what I'msaying. This is so uncomfortable. The last thing I want to do is hurt his feelings.

"Oh," his face turns red. "Oh my God, I'ms so sorry if I misread things. ...I... oh what an idiot! I'm mortified!" he buries his face in his hands and begins to laugh. "Oh, what a fucking moron, of course, you don't see me that way. You are HOT, and smart and talented and I'm just, well... ugh... Why would you?!" HOT? what? Is he insane!?! Well obviously, he believed I wanted this to be more than a friendship, but why?

"Oh, Sam it's okay, I didn't realize you, I mean you never said anything to me. Let's just forget about it." He still appears stiff and uncomfortable.

"Yes, please can we? I'm humiliated. Please don't tell anyone." I nod my head and gesture to locking my lips in secrecy.

"No of course not, I promise." I take a deep breath as he lights up again. "Another beer?" I say hoping to make him and myself for that matter more comfortable.

"Sure, please."

We sit for a bit longer enjoying another beer, but there's obviously still tension there. The alcohol helps to relax the situation a bit. Before I know it it's almost nine-thirty. For me, it's almost bedtime. I don't make it much past eleven unless I go out with friends. Sam noticing my infatuation with checking my watch, stands politely and says, "Well, I think I better get going. I gotta be up at five for a job tomorrow." I stand and follow behind him.

"Sure, I should get to bed myself I have a busy day tomorrow too. Work and getting this place cleaned." I shrug not quite knowing what else there is to say.

Once we arrive at the door, he reaches out a hand to shake mine.

"Really a handshake? Are you afraid of me now?" I ask.

"No, I just didn't want to embarrass myself twice in one evening," I smirk and nod in agreement shaking his hand back. Wow, this is weird, awkward… strange.

"Ok," I say breaking the tension. "Maybe I'll see you around then."

"Yeah, I'll see you around, um again sorry for before. I, ya know just, forget about it please," he looks embarrassed again.

"Forgotten," I say firmly. He begins to leave and turns back briefly for a small shy wave. I wave back and close the door. I stop and stand there for a moment trying to process what has just

happened. What a strange night. I don't even know how he ever had

that impression of me. Well, it's over now, he gets the picture. I kinda

feel bad that I never noticed it before, that he liked me like that.

I clean up the beer bottles and decide to pick up the cigarette

butts in the morning. I'm tired and want to take a shower before bed.

I have a few events tomorrow to photograph so at least my day won't

be too dull. I go into my room and grab a pair of panties out of my

top drawer and scoop up my sweats from the night before off of the

end of my bed. My bottom drawer houses my most comfortable t-

shirts, all worn and soft. I choose the basketball tee that I have had for

years. I am not a cute PJs kinda gal. I dress for comfort not for show.

I make my way to my bathroom and flip on the shower.

Checking to make sure the temperature is ok, I undress and carefully

climb in, closing the curtain behind me. I reflect on my day and the

conversations with Sam. Had I led him on? Did I flirt or make him

feel like my intentions were for a romantic relationship? Nothing

comes to mind that could be construed in such a way. The water feels

perfect blanketing my body. I feel so worn out today, I can't wait to

dive into bed. Maybe the beer has made me sleepy. I wash fairly quickly not worrying about my hair as I just washed it this morning. I shower quickly, so quickly in fact that my new razor gives me a painful nick or two. I flip the shower off and steam has filled the room. I wrap my robe around me and dry the dampened ends of my hair with a hand towel.

I continue with my bedtime routine in record time. I cross the hall to my bedroom and flip on the light. My mess of a room is staring me in the face yet again. How did I let it get so bad? I 'm not much of a housekeeper, I know. I will make it a point to clean tomorrow, especially if I get the shots I need early. I need to make myself some sort of schedule to keep me on track for Christ's sake. I am so all over the place.

I make my rounds through the house making sure that the front and back doors are locked, and dead-bolted then head off to bed. As I lay exhausted in my oh so comfortable bed my body begins to melt into the mattress, and it isn't long before I'm asleep.

Chapter 2

The Beginning of the End

CRACK! I feel rather than hear the crash that has demanded me from sleep. A raging pain burns and hisses through the side of my face. FUCK! Something just hit me. Confused I try to focus my vision and see a blur of a man on top of me. I try to get up, but I am pinned by his body. He is sitting on my knees, so my legs are immobile. My wrists are pinned by his elbows and he has both hands on either side of my head fisting my hair. "Ow fuck!" I scream.

"I know what kind of games you play," he hisses through clenched teeth. It's dark but I know before he even speaks who it is. I can smell the cigarettes on his breath. And the booze, not beer, whiskey maybe? He obviously didn't go straight home when he left.

"Sam STOP!!" I don't even recognize my own voice I sound almost childlike. "Why, why are you doing this? You're hurting me!" I begin weeping. I have never been in a situation like this before, ever. You talk about the "what if's" in life and this is one of them. What would you do? Fight back? Scream for help? Until you are there, in that moment you have no clue. What do I do? I feel like I'm outside

of my own body with no control over what happens next.

"You know why Nettie. You know I have wanted you for

years. Don't play fucking dumb! And earlier well I thought you were

just being coy until you didn't say any more about it. No one

humiliates me like that you FUCKING BITCH!" he screams so loud

into my ear that it immediately begins ringing. Oh shit, what is he

going to do? I already know the answer to that question. I just hope

I'm wrong. "You will get what you deserve, WHORE! You can't treat

people like shit and get away with it!"

Treat him like shit?! Is he insane!? I have never been anything

but nice to this man. He was my friend, I thought. "Don't please, Sam

don't," I plead. "I'm sorry if I made you feel embarrassed. Sorry if I

gave you the wrong impression," sorry my ass, I think. It's the only

thing I can think of to try and calm him down.

It doesn't help. It almost fuels his rage. "Oh, baby," he

seethes. "go ahead and beg all you want. It just turns me on more," he

runs his nose up my neck and into my hair smelling me as he does. I

think I'm going to be sick. This isn't happening please God, this isn't

happening. Wake up Nettie, wake up! I do the only thing I can think of and scream, I scream for my life thrashing underneath him. Scream in hopes someone, anyone will hear. He will not do this to me! Pain radiates from my scalp as he rips a chunk of my dirty blonde hair from its roots. I can feel the warmth of blood run down the back of my neck.

I open my eyes and my hair in his hand. He smells it once more before placing it quickly into his jacket pocket. I try for a moment while his arm is off of mine to break free, but he is too quick, too strong. He has both of my hands above my head now, held by one of his large calloused, disgusting hands. Oh no, his other hand is free. I scream again as he slams his hand over my mouth stifling the noise.

"You fucking do that again and I will slice you in half!" he emphasizes each word. I didn't notice it before as he pulls a large hunting knife from his side and slowly drags the blade down the side of my face, over my neck and down to my chest. He slices open my t-shirt in one fluid motion, scraping my skin as well. He leans down and licks the blood from the small wound he has just created across my breastbone.

I struggle and squirm but it's no use. He is too strong for me and I am weakening. He is too heavy, too enraged. He lifts his hips briefly to rip down my pants leaving them around my ankles as makeshift shackles. In one swift moment, I hear the rip of my panties as they are pulled from my hips. This is not happening! Tears stream down my face. I want to die. Anything but this! I want to vomit, pass out, die! Anything. Quietly and painfully I squeak, "No, no, no please, no…" I feel his erection against my right thigh, and I hope at least it's fast. But it isn't. As he begins pulling his pants down, I scream again without even realizing it. He reaches for a pillow and slams it down onto my face. My pants are completely gone now. When did that happen? He has my knees pinned apart with his. It happens so fast and calculated I feel he is no stranger to this. And that thought sickens me even more.

Suddenly he rips into me with such force that I feel like I have been split in two. I scream again and again into the pillow. I cannot breathe, and I don't care, maybe I will succumb to the lack of air soon. I hope. I pray. He keeps going for what seems like hours and I know it has been only moments because I'm still conscious. He growls as he finishes mumbling something under his breath I can't hear exactly. Does it matter?

He removes the pillow and I try taking in a deep breath of air. I begin coughing, crying, sobbing. I still can't breathe. I'm gasping so hard that my throat is burning. He starts to laugh. LAUGH! A demonizing cruel laugh. "Oh, you are such the victim, aren't you?" he is millimeters from my lips as he speaks. Who is this man? This is certainly not the person I have known all of these years, or is it? Has he hurt other women? How long has he been thinking of doing this to me? Fuck, I know his parents. His eyes blaze at me. He looks like the devil, like the devil himself! And I, I am in Hell. He inhales and growls again "That was almost as good as I expected it to be. Shall we go again?"

What? No, God save me I just want him to go! He is a bigger monster than I could have ever imagined. What is worse than the devil himself? Him, yes Sam, he is.

This time is longer he has thrown me onto the floor now. Laying atop my clothes. Dirty and clean well, now all dirty. I hear him murmur how wonderful I smell. "Fuck you!" I snap. Oh, shit why did I say that? I need to just keep my mouth shut. "Fuck me? No, no fuck you!" he twists both of my wrists back behind my back, so I'm lying on top of them. I hear a snap.

"ARGH!" I cry out. My wrist, or arm I know it's broken. I can feel the slow throbbing intensify. I think I'm going to pass out, thank God. The pain is just too much. The pain from my head all the way down between my legs is excruciating. I start to fade… He swiftly smacks my face to bring me back to the here and now, but it's a lost effort and I am gone.

I fade back in for a moment and see he is grinning from ear to ear still on top of me but with both hands free as he whispers, "Oh good you're awake for this. I see the knife shine in front of my eyes then feel the cold steel travel down my face, neck and to my chest before I fade again.

I wake to the sunlight beaming through the window. I'm so cold. My head pounding, my arm throbbing and my …oh I remember he raped me; tortured me. Where is he? I think. I'm in a panic suddenly. I feel the dried blood on the back of my neck and on my shoulders. Between my legs, I still feel the warmth of fresh blood from his assault. I cannot move, I try but I can't. I try and shout for help, who would hear me? I scan the room for my cell phone, I can't remember where I put it. Is it even here? Did he take it? Where is he? If I just lay here will I bleed to death? Will someone find me? I can't

17

even lift my head let alone get out of this room. I'm trapped. Just then I hear a soft knock at the front door.

I begin to quiver with fear. Is it him? Oh God, help me please no!

"Nettie? It's Sara are you in there?"

"Sara!" I shout or try to anyway. Sara works with me at the same paper. She is also a photographer. That's right, we were supposed to meet this morning.

"Nettie? Is that you?"

I screech again as best I can in hopes she'll realize something is wrong. I whimper and my warm tears roll from the corners of my eyes into my blood-caked hair. I look over and see her through clouded eyes. She peers through my bedroom window and she screams, bringing her hand to her mouth in horror of what she sees. Well, I must look as bad as I feel. I see her take out her phone I assume calling for help. I sigh in relief as I am safe, for now. Thank you, Sara, thank you God! I close my eyes and drift again….

Chapter 3

Alive

I hear mumbling, low and faded in my head. Where am I? My eyes flutter as my mother and father come into focus. "Mom" I squeak. She turns to look at me and appears as pale as a ghost. It's apparent that she has been crying.

"Oh, God Antoinette! Oh, my beautiful baby girl!" She hugs me and I wince. She never uses my full name. My entire body aches.

"Sorry honey, I'm just so glad you are awake. The police want to speak to you as soon as possible so they can get this asshole!" I have never heard her so pissed.

"Do you know who did this to you?" My dad chimes in as he leans down and ever so gently places a kiss on my forehead. I flinch immediately, not in pain I just don't want to be touched.

"Sam" I whisper. Tears threaten to appear, and I push them down.

"Sam?" My father says in shock. "Sam your friend from high school? Sam Knox? That Sam?" I nod slowly. Ow, that hurts too. Oh, I forgot.... my hair. As I start to reach up to feel the bald spot, I notice that my right wrist is wrapped in a bulky splint. I look at my parents quizzically for a moment.

"A fracture to your right forearm. Clean though, the doctors said it should heal nicely." My mother gets the words out then begins to sob.

"What else?" I ask. May as well get it all out on the table now. My father steps forward and sits at the edge of my bed. My mother is too distraught to speak.

"Well," he croaks, and then clearing his throat begins again. "Do you remember anything?"

"Yes. I do, too well." I'm beginning to sound more assertive and less broken.

"Well, you have a cut down the middle of your chest, a few inches long. Not so deep that it needed stitches," he continues looking down and fidgeting with his gold wedding band. "He hit you across the right side of your face, punched actually. They thought he could've broken your eye socket, but he didn't. You have one hell of a shiner already though." Oh, God, I don't even want to see myself. He closes his eyes before this next part. It must be bad. "You were sexually assaulted and… are you sure you don't want me to have the doctor

20

speak with you about this?" he looks up at me this time. Oh, my poor daddy. I see the pain in his eyes. His big beautiful hazel eyes that match mine. They look golden today. I love my father. He is so handsome. He is the typical tall, dark and handsome man. Chocolate brown hair with not even the hint of gray in it. How? I don't know. He is a prince.

"No. Dad if you don't mind, I would rather hear it from you or Mom." I glance at my mother and she is not crying anymore but she looks horrified. She can't speak so I turn back to my father. I nod for him to finish.

"Well baby, when he…er…um…raped you" Oh shit that just made it all the more real. Someone saying that word raped, I was raped. "He was so rough that you tore, pretty badly." He pauses and I know this is incredibly uncomfortable for him to talk about, as it should. "You needed several stitches to repair the damage. He cut you on your chest, over your heart. four lines vertically, the same size. Those were deep enough for stitches. And you'll most certainly have a scar." Oh, I feel it now. My fingertips gently graze the wounds over my chest. He marked me. Gave me a constant visible reminder of him. Of this. Forever. Ha, scarred, I think. Not just on my body, but on my

21

soul as well. What a sick fuck! He cut me too? I mean he ripped me apart inside out for Christ's sake, and he had to cut me?! Sadistic mother fucker!

"Is that all dad?" I am brought back to this moment. He looks so broken. "Well, injury-wise, yes."

"Wow" is all I can think to say. He nods. I see his eyes glisten as they begin to fill with tears.

I have never in my life seen my father cry. My strong, supportive, amazing father. This is enough to throw me over the edge and I weep. I drop my head in my good hand and weep, heaving and crying so hard, that the sound that comes out is unrecognizable. Both of my parents come to either side of me and pull me into a protective cocoon with their arms. We are a ball of sobs. Desperate to comfort one another. I have never felt such pain. Such heartbreak. Not just for myself, but for them as well.

After what seems like forever our tears begin to subside, and we break from our embrace. All of us wiping tears from our eyes and snot from our noses. I giggle a small bit. "We look a mess!" they both smile in return. A sad and fake smile. My father stands.

"I need to go speak to the police and tell them it was Sam. I'll be right back. Do you need anything, my love?" He says gently to me.

"No Daddy" I shake my head. "I'm fine." I am not fine; I think to myself. Mom rises as well and presses the call button on the side of my bed.

"Yes?" the nurse comes through the intercom.

"She's awake," my mom croaks softly and with a slight grin.

As we wait for the nurse something occurs to me. "How did he get in?" I ask my mother.

"They don't know yet, dear. There was no sign of forced entry.

"Oh. I didn't hear him." I say. "I didn't even know he was there until he hit me." A lump begins to form in my throat again. But I have no tears left.

My mom speaks, "did you forget to lock a door or something?"

I shake my head no. "I know for a fact I checked the doors before I went to bed." Then I think…. was he already in my house? While I was in the shower maybe? Did he wait for me to fall asleep? Maybe he was watching me the whole time. The thought sickens me, but I choke back the sour bile at the back of my throat. No, he couldn't have been there. He had liquor on his breath when he was on top of me. A lot of it. He had to have left. Then how had he gotten in? It doesn't matter I suppose. He got in and there is nothing that will change that now.

The nurse comes into the room with a bright genuine smile on her face. She is wearing all white from her scrub top down to her K Swiss shoes. Her platinum blonde hair is neatly braided down her back and out of her face. She looks to be about my age. She is very comforting already. There is something very warm and genuine about her.

"Hello Nettie, my name is Claire I will be taking care of you today." I nod. "How is your pain level?" she asks.

"Ok I guess, could be better." She checks the IV in my arm and looks briefly at my swollen eye and scalp.

"On a scale of one to ten, one being no pain at all and ten being the worst imaginable, what would you say your pain level is?" Well, had I been asked this before yesterday I would have said a nine but after truly experiencing the worst pain imaginable, I settle on a four,

"A four, five maybe?" she glances at my chart.

"We can give you something more for pain. You're about due," she says politely. "The doctor will be in shortly. I paged him to let him know you were awake" she continues.

"Thank you, Claire," my mother finally speaks.

"Of course, Mrs. Madison." She looks to me now. "If there is anything, I can get you Nettie please don't hesitate to ask. There is water by the bed and the cafeteria menu if you feel up to it." I smile kindly at her. A real smile too. She is very sweet.

"Thanks." I murmur as she exits my room.

I certainly don't want food, but I'm parched. As I begin to reach for my water my mother beats me too it. "Thanks, Mom, just a little please," I'm afraid I may vomit if I drink too much. But I end up emptying the cup with just a few gulps. My thirst outweighs the pain in my throat. She refills it for me quickly and I drink down another cup. That's better. I sigh and lean my head back against the pillow behind me. Suddenly a panic sets in. "Mom! Get rid of the pillows, please!" She looks confused. The panic has escalated. "Mom, now please!" I begin to shake. My heart suddenly feels as though it's going to leap out of my chest. She moves in double time and takes the pillows from behind me and tosses them on the floor. She stares at me, her head cocked to one side waiting for an explanation. "He held a pillow over my face the first time he…. because I screamed." At this moment I think I can hear my mother's heart breaking. "I thought I was going to die." I continue "I would have rather died." A few tears stream down my face and I know I truly mean these words as I say them. He just ruined my life. He broke me. I will never be the same as I was…before.

Mom comes to my side yet again and very carefully and gently rubs her hand across my back. I don't want her touch on me, but I let her. She begins making small circles just as she did when I was a child. Slowly I do begin to relax. We stay like this for a few moments neither of us speaking. I lay back on the cool scratchy hospital sheets and thank her as I sigh. She takes her place back on the light blue faux leather chair at my bedside and I 'm suddenly exhausted.

Before I can think to even try, I'm asleep once again. I don't know how long it's been, but when I wake again in my hospital room. I am alone. I press the call button at my bedside and Claire's sweet voice radiates through the intercom.

"Yes, Miss Madison? Can I help you?"

26

"Um, yes." I stutter. "Are my parents still here?"

"Oh, I think they went to grab a bite to eat in the cafeteria. I'll find out for you." The intercom clicks.

"Thank you," I say. At this moment I'm feeling ok to be alone. In a way, I'm relieved by the seclusion. It doesn't last long because just as I have the thought, I hear footsteps approaching my room. I look up and it's a doctor, my doctor I would assume. Following not far behind him are one uniformed police officer and a woman dressed in a hideous navy-blue pantsuit. The officer is a man in his mid-fifties, maybe. He has a short buzz cut and a belly that hangs over his black leather belt.

How are cops overweight, don't they have to chase the bad guys? This guy couldn't catch a cold. I mean he even looks out of breath right now and he is just standing there. Next to him stands the woman looking awkward and mousy in appearance. Perhaps she works for the hospital or is an officer but just not dressed in uniform? I do notice she has quite a beautiful face. Not a stitch of make-up on and her hair is disheveled. She must be a new cop. What do they call them? Rookies? I don't know I think that's what they say on police

27

shows. Law and Order SVU is my favorite. How ironic, I could be on that show now. Fuck! I can't believe this is happening to me! ME!

As the doctor begins to speak my focus is back on him. "Hi, Miss Madison." He starts.

"Nettie please, you can call me Nettie."

"Yes, then Nettie. I know your father talked to you a bit about what happened do you have any questions for me?" I shake my head no. Not saying a word. I don't need or want to know any more. "Well, none of the damage done was too extensive. You will be in pain for a while and we have already started you on a round of antibiotics because of the lacerations you suffered." Suffered is right. You hit that dead-on Doc. "Also, I'm going to have the nurse bring you the plan B pill, the morning-after pill. Just in case." Oh, shit I hadn't thought of that. That bastard could have knocked me up. "A rape kit will be done as well if you consent?" he continues. I nod.

"Of course." He didn't use a condom. I shudder at the memory.

"Very well, our SANE nurse on call will be in soon to do that. That's someone who specializes in sexual assaults." He sounds so professional. Well, he is. I suppose I'm not the first rape victim he has

28

met. No, certainly not. Is that what I am now, a rape victim? A survivor? Oh, the good doc is still talking, I suppose I should listen. "Other than bruising and the stitches we need to keep an eye on, you should be able to go home tomorrow as long as we can manage your pain. All your scans came back clear. No internal damage or head trauma." Ha! I beg to differ. He looks briefly at my chart and scribbles a few things. He flips it shut. "Your arm should heal nicely. We'll keep it braced for now and hopefully won't need to cast it." He inhales sharply and continues, "Well then, if you have no questions for me the police would like to ask you a couple themselves." He smiles and turns to walk out nodding goodbye to the officer or officers, whatever. Back to them, I look. I can't help noticing that the older cop looks a bit nervous and the female stands looking very cool and calm. Dad bod speaks first.

"Hello Miss Madison, my name is Officer Hill, and this is Detective Montgomery." Wow! Detective? I didn't expect that.

"We have a few questions if you don't mind?" Detective Montgomery speaks up. She sounds more professional than she looks.

"Of course," I answer. Do I really have a choice?

"First of all, we want to know if you knew your attacker?"
Well, I thought I did.

"Yes, I told my father this already." They look at one another and the woman speaks again.

"I know, but we need to hear this straight from you." I adjust myself in the bed and sit up as best I can. This is not an easy task given the splint on one arm and IV in the other.

"Yes, he is a…well was a friend of mine. His name is Sam Knox." She looks at super cop and nods. He quickly scurries from the room. Just the detective and I now.

"We will put an APB out on him immediately. I'll send an officer to his residence as well as his place of employment." She takes out a small recording device from her inside blazer pocket. "I know this is going to be difficult Miss Madison, but I have to get in detail what you remember from last night. Are you ready?" Am I ready to relive the most horrific moment of my life? No, I'm not. I never will be. I really don't have a choice

"I'll do my best." I groan.

I go into the enormous detail of how we know each other and the walk home from work that day. I continue, about the pass he

30

made at me and the fact that it made me terribly uncomfortable. I don't feel as terrible as I thought I would, sharing this information. It almost feels as though I am telling some fictional story. That this story isn't in fact about me. When I get to the point where I fell asleep, I freeze. Detective Montgomery speaks first.

"Listen, Miss Madison if this is too difficult, we can take a little break." Her tone has changed. She is less professional and more sympathetic, trying to comfort me more than anything else.

"No, I want to get this over and done as fast as possible." She nods in acceptance. I take a huge intake of breath, close my eyes, and exhale. Here we go. "I was sleeping, as I said. I woke up when he slapped me, or punched me," I correct myself. "As fast as my eyes were opened, I was pinned to the bed." I can feel it all over me. The weight of his body on me, the smell of his cigarettes and the alcohol. I can feel his hands in my hair. "He was holding the sides of my head, by my hair." I lift my good hand to my head to demonstrate. I pause for a beat.

"Go on." She whispers.

"Um… well I tried to talk to him to maybe calm him, I don't know. He started going on about how I had embarrassed him or led him on in some way. I tried apologizing to diffuse the situation. It didn't work. As soon as I was sure he would rape me I struggled, and I screamed. God did I scream. That's when he ripped my hair out of my head." I take a small drink of my water in order to gather my wits. "After that is when I saw the knife. I didn't know he had a knife. He said if I screamed again, he would slice me in two. He was grinning. Like he wanted me to scream again." Ok now I feel like I need a break, but I don't say anything. I press on. "Next thing I know he sliced my shirt open and that's when he cut me the first time."

I run my hand gently over the bandage on my sternum. "He is sick, so sick." This I must have said aloud without realizing because I see the detective nodding in agreement. "I guess I screamed again because before I knew what was happening, he had a pillow pressed over my face." I take a sharp breath remembering the suffocation. Detective Montgomery speaks now.

"How long do you think dear? Did you pass out? Do you think he was trying to kill you?" I wrap my arms around my body tightly.

"No, as sick as it sounds, I think he just wanted to shut me up. I knew he wasn't planning on killing me, at least not right then. I know he wanted me to be aware, to feel everything." This is my undoing I can't think about him anymore. Tears stream down my bruised cheeks. The detective rises and in trying to comfort me places her hand on my knee. I jump in response, but she doesn't move her hand.

"I think that's enough for now. I will give you a break and we can continue later. I know how overwhelmed you must feel."

"Thank you," I whimper.

"No trouble at all. I will get in touch with you tomorrow. We have enough to go on for now. You rest now. Hopefully, we nail the bastard. I'm going to post a man at your door until we find him okay?" What? Would he come here? I mean he let me live the first time so why would he come here now? I wonder to myself why he did let me live. He had to have known he can't get away with this. I mean I know him for Christ's sake.

Before Detective Montgomery leaves, I ask her, "Why do you think he let me live?" She looks surprised by the question.

"Well, I don't know. Maybe he thought you would be too afraid to talk?" she shrugs her shoulders. "Whatever the reason you should consider yourself lucky. We'll get him, don't worry" Lucky?

Fuck you, lady! My life is ruined. What he did to me was worse than kill me. And damn well you better get him, or I'll get the fucker myself.

She senses my sudden coldness and excuses herself reaching forward to shake my hand. I extend my hand as well, with no enthusiasm at all. She thanks me and leaves me to myself. I'm tired and in need of some rest. My parents make a brief return and I tell them to go home to sleep. I'm exhausted and want so badly to escape this nightmare. Of course, before that can happen, I'm given my medication and a rape kit is done by the sexual assault nurse examiner, Stacey, I think her name was. I didn't listen much to anything she said. I was too out of it. I felt numb as she did a thorough exam and collected evidence. She assures me I'm finished being poked and prodded for now and without a word I roll onto my "good" side and sleep. I sleep clear through to the following morning. If anyone entered my room, I was oblivious to it.

The morning comes and I'm officially released to go home in the care of my parents, and I am ready. The police have contacted me letting me know that they picked up Sam first thing this morning. He had the nerve to show up to work as if nothing had happened. Of

34

course, his employer was aware of what he had done, and they called immediately to alert the police of his whereabouts. The police also informed me that they figured out how he had entered my home. When they searched him, they found my keys. He must have taken them before he left. This fact pisses me off more than anything. He knew when he was so pleasantly leaving my home that he would be back. He planned everything. Part of me had thought it was because he was so intoxicated but now, I know he had plans. Calculated plans. According to the police, he gave no reason to why he did it, but that part doesn't matter. I really don't care. He is fucked up! That's all there is to it. Just plain fucked up crazy!

It's about 11:30 a.m. when my parent's black escalade glides into the driveway. "Ah, we're home." My mother sighs and so do I.

Chapter 4

You Can go Home Again

I'm getting settled into my old room when I realize that nothing has been changed since I have moved out. Wow, this takes me back to high school in a flash. I gaze at the pictures on my bulletin board. Photos of my friends, and me at a track meet, graduation and prom. Oh, prom was the best. I went with my high school sweetheart Matthew. It was great, we took a limo with my best friend Jessie and her date Colton. They are still together in fact. Matt and I didn't last long after high school ended. I wanted to get serious and he wanted to well, sleep around. So, he did and when he decided he wanted more it was too late, I had moved on. He is a great guy though. We are still very close friends and I know he would do anything for me, and me for him.

My room is also filled with flowers and cards with get well wishes. I wondered why nobody had visited me in the hospital, but my mother informed me it was at her request. She didn't want me feeling overwhelmed with too much at once. I'm glad for that fact because I don't have the nerve to face anyone yet, I can't even face myself.

I've somehow managed to avoid seeing myself in the mirror up to this point. When I was getting ready to leave the hospital it almost happened, but I quickly covered my eyes. I had to use the bathroom on my own before I was able to be discharged. So, after the catheter was removed the nurse escorted me into the cold, too small bathroom. I got a glimpse of my mangled arm before covering my face with my good hand. I wasn't ready. Perhaps I am now? No. I brush the thought aside. I need to eat. I haven't had a real meal since before the attack, and this is the first time I have somewhat of an appetite.

I finish unpacking the few clothes my father has brought from my place and make my way downstairs. I smell that my mother is cooking something. Soup maybe? Not exactly a summer dish but I understand why. My stomach probably can't handle much more than that right now. The smell of the food is mixed with the smell of a baked apple pie candle. My favorite. Every time I smell that scent it reminds me of this home. My parents have lived here for their entire twenty-five years of marriage. I'm glad they didn't decide to move into a smaller place after I moved out. I love it here. As I make my way into the kitchen my mother is stirring whatever concoction she is making as steam rises from the pot. "Mmm. Smells good." My mother turns at my voice. She looks better today, rested. Her eyes still slightly puffy from the long last few days, but she looks more like herself now.

"Homemade chicken noodle," she replies. "I thought it would be a start. After you eat, maybe I can help you get into the shower." She says this delicately as if she is going to offend me.

"Mom it's fine I can manage."

"Ok, well if you change your mind, I would be happy to help. That's why you're here you know? So, Daddy and I can help in any way that we can."

"Speaking of Daddy, where is he?" I look quickly around and through the window, to see if maybe I missed him.

"He actually went over to your house, to get some more of your things. So, if there is anything you need, call his cell."

"Oh" I tense a bit before finishing. "Well, I would like my camera gear, and my purse, wallet, and cell."

"Don't worry he was going to get all that. He was getting a few more of your clothes and shoes as well." I nod.

"That's perfect. Thank you. I don't know what I would do without the two of you."

38

My mother sits a bowl of soup down in front of me and we both sit quietly. I really don't know what to talk about. I carefully sip the broth. I don't want too much. My stomach is in knots and I don't want to throw up. My face still hurts terribly. I carefully sip on one side of my mouth as the other is still incredibly swollen. Every time I blink, I feel as though I am being stung by a swarm of bees. After eating about half, I cannot stomach another bite. I decide a shower sounds great. I can take my brace off only to quickly shower and that's all. I excuse myself from the table and my mom clears our bowls.

"Remember hun if you need me just yell, ok?"

"Sure mom. I'll be fine though. I really just need to rinse these past few days away." She smiles purely out of pity.

I gather a pair of clean underwear and a comfy bra. I choose a shirt and sweatpants. Picking an outfit is the least of my worries. When I enter my childhood bathroom, I prepare myself to look in the mirror for the first time. I have imagined based on what I have been told of my injuries what I'm in for, but I don't think anything can truly prepare me for what comes next. My back is to the mirror and I take a few cleansing breaths. I need to do this. I can do this, I tell myself. "On the count of three. One, two....... three!" I turn and am horrified at what I see. Immediately the chicken soup starts to exit my body, thankfully I make it to the toilet. I am crying and vomiting at the same time. At this moment I'm wishing I accepted my mother's offer for help.

I finally compose myself after what seems like an eternity and will my quivering legs to stand and face myself again. My hair is matted to my head around the area that has recently been balded. The remainder of my dirty blonde hair is stained a pale shade of red. My eyes are incredibly swollen and bruised. My cheek is three times its normal size and looks as though I have a golf ball stuffed under my skin. Wow! My shiner is worse than I expected it to be. I look like Rocky. I close my eyes because I don't want to see myself anymore. I slowly strip down and examine my body. This I have seen already in the hospital. I have a lot of bruising and two small bandages covering the lacerations on my chest. I gently peel back the tape to expose my fresh wounds. I turn on the shower and after the water has heated to my liking, I carefully remove the splint from my forearm with a wince as the pain is still fresh.

Ahhh the water feels so amazing over my body. It's difficult to wash my crusted, blood-stained hair, but I manage. Washing my body,

I am careful of the stitches over my heart. I trace each wound gently with my finger. Perfectly straight lines up and down, precisely the same size. They remind me of tally marks. Why did he do this? I still don't get it. Did he just want to mutilate me more than he had? Make sure that even though I lived, I would think of him every time I looked in the mirror. I hope they fade.

The hardest part is the pain between my legs. It is so incredibly sensitive that just the water running over the area is difficult. I finish washing my body to the best of my abilities. It's good enough. I awkwardly step out of the shower and immediately dry my arm and hand, gently placing my brace back on. I continue to dry the rest of my body and dress in my most comfortable clothes.

When I head back downstairs my mother is on the phone. She smiles and holds up her finger informing me she will just be a moment. I walk onto the back deck of my parent's house and sit on the gliding love seat. It has a blue and white striped cushion that goes with the nautical décor outside. Their back yard is beautiful. There are flowers everywhere. My mother certainly has a green thumb. Unlike me, I kill everything I touch. Floating high above the green grass is my childhood treehouse. Surprisingly it still looks pretty good considering its age. It didn't really get that much use I suppose. I am an only child, so I rarely played in there unless I had a friend over. On my left at the far end of the fourteen-foot-wide deck is a hot tub that sits down into the deck. This my parents installed after my departure which I'm jealous about. It would've made some of those high school parties a little more interesting. I look around and breathe in the warm summer air. I feel so comfortable here, so safe and secure.

Behind me, I hear the sliding glass door and my mother slowly sinks into the spot next to me. She very gently places her hand on my knee. "How was your shower dear?" I can feel her gaze on me.

"It was fine. I was a bit shocked to see my face. I didn't realize how terrible I looked. I can't believe you and Dad have been looking at me like this." She shrugs.

"It really isn't that bad." Wow is she a liar! I don't call her on it, I just let it go. "Your dad is back. He put all of your things in your room. He said he was given a hard time because the police were still gathering more evidence."

"Why do they need any more evidence? They did the rape kit. Shouldn't that be enough? Not to mention that I was able to identify him. It's ridiculous. Should be open and shut." She enthusiastically nods in agreement.

Daddy joins us only a few minutes later. My mother makes me a chamomile tea to wind down for the evening and I use it to wash down my pain meds. For now, my stomach is finally feeling settled. I'm tempted to ask my father what the house looked like, but I really don't want to know. I will never step foot in there again. I already want to get all my things out and put it on the market. I mean how could I ever go in there again let alone sleep there. No way! I will sell it, start over. I have to.

We sit and make small talk for a while before I excuse myself to my room for the evening. I am exhausted. Before bed, I make it a point to speak to a few of my friends on the phone. Jessie and I talk for quite a while. She can always lighten my mood. She has the most infectious laugh I have ever heard, she sounds like a machine gun that won't stop firing. After we speak it's about eight-thirty p.m. and I'm completely wiped. I climb into bed and wrap myself into a cocoon of blankets and breathe deep the smell of fresh fabric. I have trouble settling my thoughts but eventually, exhaustion wins.

I don't know how long I am asleep before a horrific nightmare wakes me. I am back in that house in my bed, being broken all over again. I'm thrashing when I wake, and my entire body is pained all over again. Slowly coming back from a hellish sleep, I calm down, I breathe. Wow, that was so real. I feel as though I can still feel him holding me. I lie back on my bed, sans pillows and try my best to sleep again.

Chapter 5

My Savior

The next morning Sara calls and I invite her over for coffee. She has called me, but I haven't seen her since she found me lying helpless on my bedroom floor. She should be here any minute. I should put on some coffee. I feel terrible thinking of the way she must feel after such an ordeal. The police questioned her as well and from what I was told she was extremely distraught. She saved my life. I don't know what would have happened, had she not shown up. She is an angel in my eyes. I owe her everything.

I place two mugs on the table and a fresh carafe of coffee, ready for her arrival. My mom has left a plate of fresh cookies out for us as well. I find myself pacing anxiously waiting for Sara. I can't wait to see her but part of me is so nervous at the same time. I'm not sure what to even say.

The doorbell interrupts my subconscious rant. I rush to the door, overwhelmed, and excited to see Sara. I open the door and she looks as if she is on the brink of tears already. Before she can open her mouth to say hello, I throw my arms around her in an all-out embrace.

I immediately let the tears fly, as does she. We are sobbing together as one. Sharing an unspeakable bond. We hold our places until the tears subside on both our parts. I slowly break from her arms and take a moment to notice her beauty. She has a pale pink camisole tank on with lace along the neckline and she is wearing fitted denim capris and flip flops. Her long, shiny black hair cascades in soft waves down her back. She has the most piercing blue eyes I have ever seen. She is stunning. She should be in front of the camera, not behind it.

"Oh, Sara come in, come in." She enters the house with some hesitation. I understand her discomfort. She was the only one who saw me at my very worst. "Sara I'm sorry we are just getting to see one another. I have so much I want to say to you. Please come and sit I made coffee and there are snacks if you want."

"Coffee sounds great Nettie, thank you so much. You look well. Better I mean," she sounds surprised.

"Well, I don't feel as bad as I look. One day at a time ya know? If it weren't for you though Sara…" I pause and take a breath so that I don't start the waterworks again. "I ' sure I would have died.

Who knows? I may have suffered there for days." The thought sends a shiver down my spine.

"I knew something was wrong Nettie. As soon as I realized you weren't coming to the shoot…. I mean you are never late. I tried calling your cell and when you didn't answer, I went straight over. I thought maybe you were just sick or something. I never expected…." she pauses stifling tears. "I never imagined that is what I would find when I got to your house. It was the worst sight of my life." She is trembling and I find myself reaching over to comfort her.

"It's ok, I'm ok. Because of you and I will never forget that. I will be forever grateful, Sara."

"I'm just glad that you are okay." She looks as though she wants to say more but she doesn't go on.

"Alright well, enough depressing talk. How is work?" Finally, she seems to relax, and we talk for a while about how things have been at the office. She will be picking up the slack from my absence. I appreciate that. I don't think I'll be ready to go back for a long while. She tells me how excited she is that her favorite artist is coming to town to speak at a gallery opening and she'll get to be the photographer on the story. "How exciting!" I squeal.

"It's still four weeks away maybe you'll be ready to get back to work?"

"Maybe." I nod at her trying to convey enthusiasm.

Sara and I talk for about another hour before she has to get going. We share pleasantries once more and she leaves. As she pulls out of the driveway, we exchange a wave before I retreat into the house. I'm so exhausted. I decide to lie down on the couch for a quick cat nap. Ahhhh this feels nice. It is so quiet, and I have the rest of the afternoon all to myself. I get comfortable on our old couch and drift off.

The next week goes by quickly. It's a haze of doctors' appointments, interviews from the police detectives and time with my friends. I'm beginning to feel a little better, physically. My arm is still going to take some time to heal but I'm used to the unattractive brace. My face is beginning to take shape again, but the bruising is still prominent. The only thing I am most concerned about is the slicing and dicing that Sam subjected me to. That is still sore and a constant reminder of the incident. My mom has been hovering over me like crazy. Constantly asking me if I need anything. Peeking in my room at every turn. I know that she thinks I'm going to break. Well, I may have a breakdown but breathing down my neck is not going to prevent that from happening. It's so strange, sometimes I need that comfort and motherly affection but others I don't even want anyone to be in the same room with me, let alone speak. I'm an emotional nut case right now.

I have found a counselor that deals specifically with post-traumatic stress at the suggestion of my parents. I realize it's something that I need right now. I believe that therapy can really help people. I don't know if it will work for me, but it's worth a shot. I'm having nightmares on a nightly basis. So, if nothing else maybe she can help me to get my dreams back.

The phone rings and startles me a bit. I answer before the third ring. "Yes?" "Miss Madison?" its Detective Montgomery.

"Yes, Detective."

"I wanted to talk to you about some things we found in Mr. Knox's apartment. I'm not far, can I stop by?"

"Sure, no problem. I'll see you soon." I'm so nervous all of a sudden. What could it be? They searched his apartment soon after his arrest so why am I finding this out now? I'll get some answers soon. I decide to wait on the front porch for the great detective and she shows up not five minutes later. She jumps out of her black SUV quickly with an expression on her face that I have yet to see. Oh, this isn't good.

"Please sit, Miss Madison," oh shit, not good at all.

"What is it?" I cannot contain my lack of patience.

"These," She hands me a manila envelope and I open it pulling out the contents.

"Oh-my-god." My heart begins thumping in my ears, my breathing accelerates as I try and process what I'm seeing.

"I know this is disturbing," she whispers. I'm staring at myself, at least a hundred photos. Walking to work, with my family, in my home! My home! Some of these are from the winter. From months ago. He was following me?

Chapter 6

Peeping Sam

I am stunned and it takes me a moment to gather my wits. "How long has he been stalking me?" The detective shakes her head.

"We can't tell that for sure, but we looked through some of these and would assume at least four months or so."

"Wow," I say.

"Yeah wow. These are copies, you can keep them. I want you to go through each and every one carefully and let me know if there is anything unusual or anything at all that may stand out to you. Okay?" I don't understand.

"Wait, why? He is in jail now; it doesn't matter when or where or even why he took these photos." She pauses for a moment and then explains.

"No, see we don't believe that Sam was the only one who took photos of you. We think he hired a private investigator to follow you. Some of the pictures are really high-tech stuff, as you can see. Some were taken with night vision and others with a spy cam." Oh, so now they want to find out about this investigator. If he was hired to do this how much trouble could he really get into. Some of these pictures are pretty intimate. Many right in my house, so that would be illegal right? Imagining Sam and another pervert watching me. This just keeps getting better.

"So, what do we do now?" I huff.

"Well, *you* just need to look through the photos and tell me if you notice anything unusual or remember seeing anyone out of place at the times these pictures were taken. *I* will start to question any PI's in a twenty-mile radius and find out what prick would agree to do a job like this!" Oh my, I'm surprised by the take no bullshit attitude. She must be really disgusted by this creep. "Sorry, it just infuriates me what people will do for a buck." She sighs stuffing her hands in her pants pockets.

"It's fine detective, really. And thank you."

"Oh, and Miss Madison you can call me Leigh. Leigh Ann Montgomery. I think we know each other well enough to use first names," she holds out her hand to shake mine as if this is our first meeting. It seems a bit odd, but I oblige.

"Sure, Leigh." I repeat her name back. "and please call me Nettie."

52

"Very well Nettie, I will be on my way. I will keep you up to date as to what we find. Oh, and we hope to have that bastard on trial at the end of the month." She smirks and almost skips back to the car.

I head into the house and sit at the kitchen table with my coffee mug in hand. I take a stack of pictures and spread them across the table. Wow, there are a lot. Some are just me walking with my coffee and camera bag to work. Others at home, on my porch sipping wine, talking on the phone. But one group of pictures disturb me the most. They are all taken through my bathroom window. Some are far away but some are up close. Me looking in the mirror putting make-up on. One I'm brushing my teeth with a towel wrapped around my body. And another I'm in my bra and panties blow drying my hair. None, however, are with me completely nude. "Thank God!" It's some reprieve to know he didn't have naked pictures of me that he could ogle in the privacy of his home. Oh, gross! A wave of disgust runs through my body. I shuffle the pictures back into the envelope. I can't look at these anymore today.

I call my mother quickly to let her know what is going on and then decide to finally unpack the rest of the things my dad has brought from my place. I wonder what it looked like, the blood and

53

all. He never mentioned in detail anything he saw in that house. At least to me he never mentioned anything. Maybe he did to my mother. As I go through the bags I try and organize my clothes as best as I can, hanging some things in the closet and placing some in drawers. I check my camera bag and make sure everything is there and it's nothing seems to be missing or broken. The last thing I see is my cell phone. I remember not being able to find it that awful morning. I wonder where it was. I place it on the charger and once it's powered up I slide the lock off and flip through some missed calls from my friend, Matthew one from Jessie and another from Sara just an hour before she found me.

I check my email and see something that chills my blood. A message, that is sent from SMknox and time-stamped for four a.m. the day I was attacked. I click on the message with hesitation. I see that there is an attachment. When I open it, I'm horrified at what I'm looking at. It's a picture of me, after. I'm lying unconscious bloody and beaten. My clothes are torn off and I look like something from a gory horror flick. I'm unrecognizable to even myself. It looks like a crime scene photo. I guess I was wrong. He does have a naked photo of me. Sick mother fucker! Why? Why does he continue to shock me?

I mean when the cops picked him up, he had acted like he had done nothing wrong. He admitted everything, happily. He said I had given him signals all night that I wanted to sleep with him, so he gave me "what I wanted" The brutality of it was blown off. He acted as if it was a completely normal and natural act. I don't know what he is trying to pull. Maybe he is going to try and plead insanity? I don't even know if that is a real thing or they just do that in the movies. In any case, he *is* crazy.

I need to call Detective Montgomery and let her know what I found. I fish her card out of my bedside table and call her immediately. She doesn't answer so I leave her a short message making her aware of the email and photo. I don't know that it will make any difference in the case at all, but she needs to know.

The rest of the day goes fast. I keep busy doing my best to pick up after myself and make a nice dinner for my mother and father. They deserve it. They have been so good to me lately. I wonder when I will feel well enough to live on my own again. Maybe never. My cell buzzes and it scares the shit out of me. I pick it up but don't recognize the number. "Hello?"

"Nettie it's Detective Montgomery, er Leigh."

"Oh, hi Leigh. Did you get my message?"

"Yes, I did and I'm sorry you had to see that. We couldn't find your cell phone when we searched his apartment. We did, however, see the photo on his email. I just didn't mention it because I didn't want you to see it. I mean it wasn't necessary for you to see yourself in that… that state." I don't know how to respond.

"Well looks like that was a lot of work for nothing, huh?" she apologizes.

"No, no it's not your fault. I'll add it to my nightmare reel for this evening." I wish she would have told me sooner.

"Well Nettie, I will let you get back to your day. I'm here if you need anything. And remember please look through those photos if it's not too difficult. You think of anything you call me any time, day or night do you understand?" There is that authority back in her voice. I knew she hadn't been far.

"Of course detective, I will. No word on the private investigator?" I hear her sigh

"No, nothing yet but we'll get him. I promise."

When my parents arrive home, I fill them in on today's events, but explain to them I don't want to dwell on it. They oblige as we sit and have a delicious meal if I don't say so myself. They seem to enjoy it as well. This is the first night that things have felt somewhat normal. We talk and laugh enjoying one another's company. I think I can get through this. I really do. A shimmer of hope shines in my mind's eye.

Chapter 7

On the Mend

"Antoinette Madison?" A woman in purple scrubs dotted with small pink hearts says coolly. She has burnt red hair that reminds me of Ronald McDonald.

"Yes," I raise my hand shyly. "Nettie, please. Call me Nettie" I don't know why I am so annoyed today.

"Come on hun, you can follow me now." This is obviously not my first time at the OB/GYN, but it's the most anxiety I have had being here. I'm escorted into a tiny room with white walls and white cheaply tiled floors. This room that I have come to be familiar with still feels like I'm in a mental institution. They could have warmed this place up a bit. I mean most people who come here are happy right? Having babies, excited to be here. My thoughts are interrupted by Mrs. McDonald. What is her name again? Oh well, who cares? I won't have to speak to her much longer, there is no point in learning it now.

"You can undress and put on this gown. The doctor will see you shortly." I have never felt comfortable here. I don't like to be examined, well who does? Especially since that night, it feels as I'm being violated all over again with each visit. Just when I start feeling like myself, I'm knocked down a peg. As I wait the anxiousness builds. I can feel the small pricks down my arms and in my chest. I quickly undress and put the paper gown on myself as fast as possible before hopping up on the paper-covered table.

"Ah," that's cold. Man, I wish I peed first. Next to the examination table is a stack of cheesy tabloid magazine so I pick one up at random and flip through to get my mind off of the poking and prodding to come. I'm only about halfway through the drama of the latest "reality" show scandal when there is a brief knock on the door.

"Ready?" Dr. Graham says as the doors swing open. Well, you didn't wait for an answer, did you? I guess I am. "So, Nettie, how are you?" Dr. Graham is beautiful. She has dark curly hair that just brushes her shoulders and has very dark eyes to match. If I had to guess I would say she was close to forty. Young, she looks young. She really is sweet too, or at least seems to be. I like her. She makes me feel, well comfortable. As much as I can be in this situation.

"I'm fine, thanks." She looks at me skeptically knowing I'm lying through my teeth. I'm terribly uncomfortable can't we just get this over with?

She gestures to the stirrups on either side of the table and I know what to do. She is finally clearing me since "the incident". The last thing I want is my legs spread open... again. Yes, the incident, will it ever get better? It's only been 8 weeks; I don't expect it to soon. It was the worst night of my life. I hope to never feel that way again. So helpless, so weak, so.... God damn him for making me feel this way! I was strong, confident, and driven! He may not have killed me, but he certainly took a piece of me. I wouldn't wish this on my worst enemy. Although, *he* is now my worst enemy so maybe I would.

"This will be cold, Nettie." Dr. Graham brings me back to earth. She does her "normal" exam, checking that the stitches have healed and doing yet another swab to test for STD's. I'm used to the routine after being here for what, 3 times? Well, I know what will happen next, urine and blood to test for H.I.V and to be sure I'm not pregnant. I have had my period since so thankfully, the latter isn't true. Dr. Graham makes it quick as usual and I'm done before I can enter into a full-blown panic. "Good girl!" she says "You know the rest. Go on and get dressed and we'll do your labs, and you can be on your way." As I scoot up to the end of the table pulling the uncomfortable, scratchy white paper with me, I nod in recognition.

Before leaving the room, she looks at me with that look. The look I have been getting for weeks now. The 'you poor girl' look. The pity look. I HATE the pity look. "Everything looks good Nettie, but I want you to abstain from intercourse at least another month. Then you can resume normal activity, er um. Sorry. I...I mean you can physically. I mean, you know, you can if you want. Sorry dear, I didn't mean to ..." she almost looks as if she is going to cry. I interrupt her.

"I'm fine. Thank you, Dr. Graham. I understand what you meant." My voice is icy, and she gets the point. She pats me on the back and with a polite nod, she quickly exits the room. God, what is with her? She is normally so together. Maybe it's because it's our last visit. I take a deep breath and for the first time in a while, I sigh. I never have to step foot in here again. I have given my samples and I'm free to go.

"We'll call if there is anything to call about, Antoinette," the same fiery-haired, obnoxious nurse squeaks at me.

"Nettie," I say through gritted teeth. You would think my full name would be harder to remember. Get me out of this place. I have had enough stress for one morning.

Luckily, I don't have anywhere to be for the rest of the day, so I'm meeting my mother for lunch, not far from here. It's an old dive restaurant we have gone to since I was a child. We certainly don't go for the food, it's mediocre at best. We really go for the nostalgia of it now. As I pull into the greasy spoon called Mona's, I notice in the tiny dirt parking lot, that my mother's car is nowhere to be seen. I am a bit early but let's face it she is always late. I park at the right of the building and shut off the engine. It is a little busy for a Tuesday afternoon, but we never have to wait. I climb from my red four-door Honda and hear the beep, beep as I lock the doors.

When I enter the building, I notice Jen immediately. She is a waitress who has been here for as long as I can remember. She has salt and pepper beehive and is the epitome of the fifties waitress. Too much blush pushed across her swelled cheeks and baby blue eye shadow up to her pencil-thin eyebrows. A tiny beauty mark kisses her right upper lip. I have always wondered if this is real or if she has drawn it on like the rest of her face. She is a doll though, always has a smile on her face. Speaking of smile, she spots me and squeals as she makes her way through the small square tables in the middle of the restaurant.

"Nettie darlin' how are you?! Oh, it's been a while!" she stops for a moment and lowers her voice. "I haven't seen you since… um, well. How are you dear?" There it is again that look. I HATE that look.

"I'm doing well Jen thank you for asking," I say with a fake smile planted on my face.

"Really darling? Because you can talk to me anytime." Most people in this town don't really want to help they just want to gossip. I don't think Jen would be a gossip in this case but still, I remain tight-lipped.

"Yes, really I'm good. Much better." She nods not pushing the subject anymore.

I grab a small, quiet table in the rear that is right next to a window. The décor in this place has not changed much. The wall color maybe, but the pictures are all the same. The one with a small girl in pigtails leaning up against a wheelbarrow and holding a basket of red flowers is my favorite. I don't know why. I peek at the door every few moments to look for my mom but no sign of her yet. Jen comes to take my order and I just get an iced tea for now. I should wait for Mom before I order. I hope she hurries I'm famished.

Ten minutes later Jen is refilling my tea when my mother strolls through the door. She looks frazzled. She sees me and shuffles back to me dodging chairs and people as she does. Luckily, she makes it without a klutzy mom moment. She slides into the chair across from me and leans forward to kiss me on the cheek. "Hi baby," she puffs, out of breath. "Sorry I'm late; I went shopping and got stuck in line forever and then, of course, the traffic on the way here was atrocious. I hate going to the mall, you know? It's such a hassle. Not worth all the trouble. I mean really!" I try to stifle rolling my eyes at her. When she starts talking sometimes, well who am I kidding most times she just doesn't stop! I pull my annoyance into check and smile politely. Why am I being such a bitch today! It might be time to find my own place.

"Its fine Mom. Don't worry about it. I haven't been waiting long. Let's order, I'm starved." Before I can lift my arm to get her attention, Jen is there, cool and swift. She kisses my mother on the cheek and gives her a warm hello.

"Hi Jen," Mom says. "How are you, I feel like we haven't seen you for so long. God, I'm hungry, what do I want? What are you having, Nettie?" I mull over the menu once more and close it.

"I'm just going to have a chicken salad. Ranch dressing please Jen." I order and hand her my menu.

"Very well, hun, and you Mary?" My mom purses her lips and bobs her head back and forth trying to make a decision.

"I'll have the same I suppose," she says indifferently. "Since that is all you're having I guess I will skip the cheeseburger. I don't want to look like a pig."

"Mom, get what you want." I huff.

She is exhausting sometimes, but I love her I really do. She has been my rock my entire life and even more so lately. I feel like I had drifted back to infancy needing constant care and comfort. She was more than willing to be there for me, too. My father as well. He was taking care of Mom while she was taking care of me. And I appreciate that in them. I shouldn't be so short with her. She was damaged too. Maybe more so because she tried to hide her pain. I need to remember that. I'm not the only one who has suffered.

"So, I know you don't want to talk about it but how was your appointment. Everything ok?" here we go.

"Yes, Mom, it was fine. The same as last time. I'm fully healed and back to normal." I can visibly see her wince, but she tries to hide it. Normal I know she is thinking I will never be. "So anyway, they said they would call if anything comes up on my tests and otherwise, I can go on with my life. I don't need to go back. And I am not. When I need an annual, I'm going to a new doctor. I don't ever want to step foot in that office again." Mom gently places her hand on mine.

"I don't blame you. Discussion over. I won't press you any more. I just wanted to be sure the doctor gave you a clean bill of health."

Lunch seems to drag on forever and I have nothing else to do so why am I in such a hurry to leave. I think it's because lately, I'm much more comfortable by myself. The company of others has been more of a burden than a blessing. I just don't feel myself. I keep being assured by my counselor that it's completely normal to begin pulling away from loved ones. To me, it just seems pitiful and sad.

When we finish eating my mom insists on paying. Let's face it, I haven't worked in eight weeks so she kind of has to. I thank her and we make our way to the door. Jen shouts a goodbye from across the room and Mom and I both wave and smile in return.

Outside the restaurant, I walk my mom to her car. She gives me a big hug and then kisses me on the forehead. This is no small feat for her given she is a good foot shorter than me. We look so much alike, I'm told. This is a compliment to me. She is stunning. Her hair is the exact same color as mine although hers has a bit of a gray in it these days. It is cut into a short sleek angled bob. She always looks put poised and together. She has beautiful ivory skin and her makeup is always impeccable like she has none on at all. A natural beauty. I only hope I look that good when I'm her age. It's only twenty years away though. She had me young. I'm thankful for that. I think it's made us closer. We have had some great times together I hug her back gently. "I'll see you at home later, Mom. I'll make dinner if you'd like."

"No, no honey, Daddy and I are going to dinner with some business associates of his, so we won't be home. You should go out with some friends," she adds.

"Oh, sure no problem. I'll find something to do. I'll call you later then. Love you," I give her another swift kiss and turn to my car.

"Bye honey, drive safe!" she shouts across the lot.

I turn out of the parking lot and begin to merge onto Rt. 11. I'm stunned. "Oh shit, why did I go this way?" I haven't been this way for weeks. Habit, I guess. As I pass the exit for my old house the memories come slamming back to my brain and all too quickly tears swell in my eyes.

It was exactly eight weeks ago to the day, the last time I was in my house. Memories of that night flood my mind. Sam, the blood, the pain both physical and emotional …. The blare of a Semi-trucks horn knocks me back to the present. "Holy shit!" I was drifting from my lane. God, daydream much Nettie? Christ, you could have gotten yourself killed! Well, it wouldn't be the first time this year. I decide to get off the next exit and quickly turn back onto route 11 going the opposite direction. Fuck it! I have to face my demons. The house hasn't sold yet so technically it's mine. I need to get it out of my system. I head down two more miles and glide from the exit ramp. My home is not more than two or three miles from here and when I arrive, I sit staring, trying to get my bearings. After about thirty minutes and about six horrible pop songs later I make my way inside.

When I enter it's not as bad as what I had painted in my mind. It's completely empty except for the appliances. Even the patio

68

furniture is gone. Everything has been put in storage. Thanks to my father for taking care of all of that for me. I go to every room but *that* room. I want to save that for last. That room will be the most difficult. I'm there all in all about an hour and decide it's now or never. I enter my bedroom and look at the floor where my body laid just a few months ago. The carpet has been replaced to cover up the bloodstains. I feel numb, not sad or scared, or even angry. Just numb. I think I can still smell Sam.

My cell phone startles me. I check the caller ID and it's Jess. "Hi, Jessie what's up?"

"Nothing where are you? How did your appointment go today?"

I scramble outside so I don't feel as though I'm lying when I tell her, "I'm in my car going home. The appointment was fine"

"Well, I'm off tomorrow, Saturday and Sunday. What do you say to staying with me for the weekend and we can go out or stay in whatever you feel like?

"Yes!" I shout so quickly that she laughs her signature laugh.

"Ok then. Is your mom getting on your nerves a bit or what?"

"No, not exactly" I reply. "My parents just treat me as if I'm made of glass. I mean God as soon as the house sells, I'm ready to move out!" I really wish I could afford to now, but it just isn't feasible especially since I haven' t been back to work yet. I should call them and figure something out though. I can't sit around in limbo forever.

"So," Jess interrupts my thoughts. "Come over to my house after five and we will have dinner and drinks and go from there."

"That sounds amazing! I'll see you at five o' five." I giggle.

Our weekend goes by way too fast and it's Monday morning as I wake in my own bed. We went out one night and I could only manage dinner so the rest of the time we stayed in and just had a blast! We had some drinks, sang and danced our little hearts out. It was exactly what I needed to relax." The phone rings downstairs and I run to get it. By the time I get there, I'm out of breath.

"Yes?" I puff.

"Hi, may I speak with Antoinette Madison, please?" The woman on the other line sounds very official.

"Yes, this is she." I sound annoyed. Who the hell calls at eight o'clock in the morning?

"Sorry for calling so early, Miss Madison." Oh, shit I didn't say that aloud, did I?

"No, it's no problem. What can I do for you?"

"Oh, Nettie this is Dr. Graham." What does she want? I thought everything was healed fine. "I was calling to see if you might be able to come into the office to speak with me today?" I did have plans today I wanted to stop in and speak to my boss.

"I actually have a busy day today. What did you need?"

"Well, I need to discuss some of your test results from last week." Oh, shit. The blood drains from my face. What do I have? I feel sick. As if my life can't get any fucking worse that son of a bitch gave me something! I want to kill him. I'm feeling a bit faint as the letters H.I.V flash in my head.

"Just tell me please, Doctor Graham. I don't want to come in."

"Nettie, I would really like to talk about this in person."

"Doctor Graham!" I'm shouting now. "I am freaking out here and I'm not coming into that fucking office again so just spit it out or I guess I will never know!" She takes a long pause and I know she is hesitant but finally, she says the words.

"You're…pregnant." Everything goes black.

71

Chapter 8

Unexpected

When I come to, I'm on the kitchen floor. The phone is a few feet from me, and I hear her yelling at me. "Nettie, Nettie are you there? Can you hear me?" I slowly make my way to a sitting position and grab the receiver.

"Yes, I'm here. I....I don't think I heard you. Please tell me you did NOT just say that I'm pregnant." As I hear myself say the words I feel like I'm having an out of body experience, this can't be.

"Nettie, I know this is a huge shock. Can you come in and we can talk? We can do an ultrasound to see if it even a healthy pregnancy and discuss," her voice trails off and I already know what she is going to say before she says it. "your options." She finishes. "Can you see me in an hour, Nettie? I have an opening. Maybe you should bring someone with you."

Oh, this is going to kill both of my parents. I should try and call Jess first. She would be supportive without judgment. "I can't be pregnant they gave me that pill at the hospital that morning after pill or whatever. How is this possible? There must be some mistake!"

"I'm sorry dear, the Plan B pill is not one hundred percent effective. No birth control is. I will answer any questions when you get here okay?"

"Yeah, sure." I hang up before she can say another word. This is not real. This cannot be real. I touch my belly as I begin to weep. I feel sick. Sick that I have his demon seed inside of me. He has been attacking me since that night and he is behind bars. Fuck! I'm still sitting on the floor clutching the phone. I breathe in and out trying to calm myself before I call Jess.

She answers on the second ring. "Hey girlie, what's up?" I inhale and say it as fast as I can.

"I need you to come and get me. The doctor just called. I'm fucking pregnant!" Dead silence on the other end. Yeah, shocking isn't it. "You still there Jessica? JESS!" I shout.

"Ah, um yeah, I ….I'm just for lack of a better word SHOCKED. Completely and totally shocked! Um, I'll be right over. Are your parents there? What are you going to do? How did this happen?"

"Maybe one question at a time. I can't even remember my own name right now! Just get over here. The doctor wants me to come in and speak with her. Hurry please, I don't want to be alone."

"Yeah, I'll be there in ten minutes. Oh, Nettie I am so sorry. Love you."

"I love you too. Now hurry." I hang up and slowly peel myself from the cold ceramic tile floor. I make it to the kitchen table and sit with my head in my hands. Ouch, my head is sore. I must have hit it on the way down. My cheeks are still damp from my tears. Why did this happen to me? What did I do that was so horrible that I'm being punished like this? I sit dazed until there is a knock on the glass doors leading from the kitchen to the deck. I look up and it's Jess. She lets herself in.

"Why did you come to that door?" I wonder.

"I was knocking out front, but you must not have heard me," her voice is very soft and slow. She's treating me like a wounded animal that may run if she startles me. "Come on," she takes my hand. "Let's go to see the doctor. I have questions. Lots of questions."

Questions indeed.

75

When we arrive at Dr. Graham's office, I'm not sure of how long it's been since we spoke. I don't know if I'm early or late, but I don't care, and I'm sure she doesn't either. Jessica tells the receptionist we are there as I find us a seat in the corner away from everyone else. My mind is racing. Jess and I both stare straight ahead not saying a word. Occasionally she reaches over giving my hand a comforting squeeze. This is exactly why I called her. My mother would have been hysterical and spastic. I'm calm thanks to Jess.

The nurse calls my name and we both stand. Slowly following her into the exam room that I'm all too familiar with and we sit and wait. The silence is deafening and just as I think it Jessie speaks. "What do you think you are going to do?" I shake my head.

"I can't have this baby. I can't have a daily lifetime reminder of that man." I know this to be true. "I know the whole rape thing will never truly leave me, but I can at least move forward, right? Not if I have his…" I don't finish. I can't bring myself to think of this thing as anything more than it is. A horrible mistake. Jess nods in understanding. "I'll help in any way I can. Do whatever you need me to, okay?"

"I know, I know. That's why I called you. No judgment."

"No judgment," she mirrors. The doctor enters with her usual polite knock but doesn't wait for a response. She looks at me for a moment with sympathy, then speaks.

"I'm sure you have a ton of questions and concerns. So, fire away."

"Well for one the fucking no good morning after pill is at the top of my list!" I'm a little embarrassed at my outburst. She doesn't seem affected.

"As I said on the phone, that is not one hundred percent full proof. One out of every ten women may become pregnant. I'm sorry. What else?" she sounds like her professional self again.

"I had a period after the …." I pause searching for the right word, "attack." I settle on.

"Yes, I remember you saying that. Was it a normal period? Normal flow and duration for you? If not, then it could have just been spotting from implantation. Although some women do have bleeding when they're pregnant." I try and think.

"No, it was lighter than normal and lasted maybe three days, I don't remember. Oh, shit," I sigh.

"I know this is difficult for you but let's go do an ultrasound to see how the pregnancy is progressing. Okay?" I nod. We all stand, and Jess holds my hand as we walk down the narrow halls to the ultrasound room. With each step, it seems as though the hallway stretches longer and longer. When we finally arrive to the room there is another woman dressed in scrubs and the doctor introduces her as the ultrasound technician. "I will let her get you prepped and give you instructions and I'll be right back." Dr. Graham says as she exits the room. The ultrasound woman smiles a huge grin. She doesn't know my situation, or she wouldn't have that look on her face. I'd like to smack that smile right off her pretty little face.

"Ok hun, I'm going to leave the room and you can undress from the waist down and cover with the sheet okay?"

"Wait, wait, wait hold up a second. Why do I need my pants off for an ultrasound?" She looks at me as if I should know the answer to my own question.

"Oh, sorry since you aren't very far along this ultrasound needs to be internal." Internal! What the hell kind of twilight zone am I in right now! "It's completely painless." She adds. She continues holding up some device that looks like Bob Barker's microphone from

The Price is Right. She instructs me that it just barely goes inside me to give her an image and it won't take long.

"Fine," I huff. She leaves the room and Jessica begins to follow her. "Where the hell are you going?" I say exasperated. She looks like a child scolded.

"I thought you would want me to step out while you got undressed."

"No, don't leave me alone in here! You can just turn around until I'm decent." She nods and turns to face the wall. I quickly undress throwing my shorts and panties on the chair next to the exam table and jump on. Damn, I should have peed. Why do I keep doing that! I'm draped with the white paper and give Jessie the all-clear. She turns and stands next to me grasping my hand. Moments later the doc and ultrasound woman reappear. Dr. Graham turns off the lights and the tech takes her place on a stool in front of me.

"Go ahead and lie down and place your feet in the stirrups." She says. "It's not as uncomfortable as a pelvic exam." She informs me. I do as I'm told. I watch as the ultrasound tech glides what? A condom? Onto the wand, microphone whatever the hell that thing is. And puts some sort of gel on it, gross. This just keeps getting weirder and weirder. She inserts the mechanism and I jump from the cold. "Sorry." She says. All our eyes go straight to the monitor. She scans around for a few moments before settling on something that looks like a gummy bear, same size and everything. I see it before the doctor can point it out. Without so much as a sound, tears spill out of the corners of my eyes and down onto the table. Jess squeezes my hand tighter.

Dr. Graham finally speaks. "Yep there it is. It's official, Nettie. Right there in the middle?" she points at a tiny flash on the screen. "That's the heartbeat." She looks closely for a while as does the technician. She clicks a few buttons on the keyboard and moves the wand around some more. I hear strange noises coming from the machine and she rips off a piece of paper. She removes the wand and informs me we are all finished. I sit up quickly eager to get the hell out of here. She hands me something.

"For you! Your first picture of your baby." She grins.

"No. No. No," I snap and next thing I know I'm leaning forward and losing my breakfast on her crisp white sneakers. "Oops," I shrug. I look over at Jessie and she has her hand clasped over her mouth to avoid bursting with laughter. I smirk at her and roll my eyes.

"It's fine." The tech mumbles. "It happens more than you would think. Morning sickness." Jess snatches the pictures out of her hand and thanks her. The poor girl shuffles out of the room leaving a trail behind her. Dr. Graham instructs me to get dressed and says she'll meet us back in her office. She looks almost amused as well, almost. The second the door closes it's all over Jessica is doubled over in a laughing fit and I can't help but join.

"I guess you told that perky bitch!" she gasps through laughter.

"Ok, turn around," I instruct as our laughter fades.

When we get into the office with Dr. Graham, she explains that the pregnancy is progressing normally and that I have a decision to make. The mood has certainly shifted from five minutes ago. "If I want an abortion, how soon do I need to make that decision?"

"Soon. Like this week soon." I don't hesitate before speaking

"Schedule it." She looks surprised. How can she be surprised?

"You don't want to speak to your family first, think about it a little more? This is a big decision."

"No." I shake my head "This is my body, my life. He has already taken a piece of me and I will not give him anymore." I stand

81

with confidence and she nods. She had to have known this is the choice I would make. I mean who the hell would carry and raise the child of a person who brutally beat, raped and butchered them.

"I'll schedule you as soon as I can. I don't do that here, but I will refer you to a clinic that does. The staff there is wonderful. I'll give you a call as soon as I have something set up."

"Great. Fine. C'mon Jess." She follows without speaking and we leave hand in hand.

When we get into the car Jessica gives me a loving smile. "Home? Or you wanna grab a drink?"

"It's not even noon yet, Jess."

"So? I think with the day you've had so far, it's fine." I look at the clock, it's 11:45 a.m. She's right, I can do whatever the hell I want.

"Yeah, you know what? That sounds perfect." I'm suddenly conscious of the fact that I am pregnant. Well, I won't be for long. "You pick the place," Jess says as she pulls out of the parking lot. "Someplace we can get lunch too. Since I lost my breakfast, after all." As if on cue we both burst into a fit of giggles.

It's about two-thirty when we arrive back at my house and I ask Jess if she'll stay until my parents are home so I can tell them what's going on. I wish I didn't have to at all but, someone will have to take me. Jessica has already missed work today because of me I don't want to ask her to do it again. She agrees to stay with me, and I get us a beer from the fridge. We already started drinking, why not another. We sit on the back deck sipping our beers in silence. All I can hear are the birds and occasionally the faint sound of a train whistle. Finally, Jess breaks the silence. "Are you a hundred percent sure you don't want the baby?" My eyes dart to hers and she knows I'm pissed.

"How can you ask me that? Of course, I don't want this...this thing." I point to my belly.

"Baby," she corrects me.

"No! Thing!" I snap

"I'm sorry Nettie, I don't mean to upset you. I just don't want you making a snap decision that you may someday regret. I mean, believe me, I agree with your decision. I wouldn't want to do it either. I just want you to be ab-so-lutely one-hundred percent, without a doubt..."

"Well, I am!" I interrupt. With that, she places her hands in the air surrendering.

83

We talk for a long while about everything but the …thing and before I know it my mom and dad are home from work. "Here we go." I sigh, looking at Jess as I rise from the striped cushion. She grabs my hand and we walk inside. As my parents walk in, they give Jess a warm greeting but then notice we are holding hands. My mom's face looks still.

"What is it?" she asks.

"I think you both need to sit down," I nod at the dining table. They oblige and we join them side by side. Jessica is my crutch right now. I take an audible breath and begin. "Dr. Graham called today." My mother is holding her breath I can tell. Rip off the band-aid, just do it.

"I'm pregnant. I'm not keeping it. It will be gone soon. I don't want to talk about it. I just want it to be over. Please respect my decision," I state coldly. My mother releases her breath into loud wailing cries. My father looks stunned and he wraps an arm around her.

"Oh, Nettie I'm so sorry darling. I, I don't know what to say. I love you," my father's eyes look sad and hopeless. When I pictured telling my parents I was pregnant for the first time, this certainly wasn't it.

"I love you too Dad, I'll be fine." I don't even believe myself. "Mom please, stop. It will be alright as soon as it's done with." She tries her best to get it together but to no avail. I can't sit and listen to this. As I stand Jessie follows me to the hallway just outside the room.

"I'm going to go unless you want me to stay," she whispers.

"No, it's fine I should be alone with them now. Thank you for everything today." We hug each other tightly and when letting go I thank her again. I couldn't have done this without her.

"Here," she says stuffing the ultrasound photo into my pocket. She gives me a small smile and without another word heads out the front door. I close the door behind her and pause before returning to my poor, fractured parents.

My mother's sobs have slowed but my father is still at her side with his arm embracing her, kissing the top of her head. I'm the one to speak first. "Well, do you have anything to ask or say to me?"

"How are you feeling about all of this?" My mother's squeaks.

"I mean, I'm stunned, obviously, and devastated. Sickened, infuriated, the list goes on and on. But I do know what I want or don't want for that matter, and I hope you are okay with it."

"Of course, Nettie we completely understand." My dad states.

"Yes, it's your choice," my mom adds. Good, what a relief. I expected them to at least question my choice if not be against it entirely.

"Ok. I'm going to shower before dinner. I really am ok. I know this is tough for you too. But please, please try not to worry."

I head upstairs taking the longest shower of my life. Careful not to touch my belly. I don't even want to think about it. When I'm finished, I dress and by the time I'm back downstairs dinner is ready. We all sit and eat in silence, broken only by the occasional, "pass the salt." I hope things go back to normal someday. After helping my mother clean up dinner, I tell them I'm tired and go to my room. Which is a lie. I just want to crawl under my covers and pretend this day never happened. It's still light outside, but I don't care. I collapse on my bed, staring at my white ceiling fan and I begin to pray aloud.

"Please God help me. I know I'm not supposed to question you but I am. Why? Why would you do this to me? What have I done to be punished like this? I am a good person. I know I make mistakes, but I AM A GOOD PERSON!" I roll onto my side and pinch my eyes closed. A lone tear drops to my pillowcase.

When I wake in the morning, I'm surprised because I did not have even one nightmare, at least that I remember, the entire night. I gaze out the window and see it's still somewhat dark out. I sneak downstairs and both of my parents are up having their coffee. They go silent when I walk into the room and I briefly wonder if it's because they were talking about me. "Good morning," I say, my voice scratchy.

"Good Morning." They say in unison. It sounds rehearsed. I join them in sipping a cup of coffee before they go to work. My mother is an event planner and my father owns a local car dealership. He is not the typical salesman. He likes to hide out in his office as much as he can, is always incredibly kind, and would rather be out a few bucks then put someone in a car they don't need.

When they leave, I decide to sit down with the pictures that Detective Montgomery gave me again. I separate them as I go so that I know what I have examined and what I haven't. I'm meticulously going through every minute detail. My cell phone vibrates on the table

87

and I look at the caller ID. It's Dr. Graham's office. I answer and find I have an appointment made tomorrow morning. I quickly scribble down the address on the back of one of the photos. I'm given instructions to prep and told I need to bring someone to drive me home. Good. Tomorrow then. At least part of this will be over.

I spend the rest of my day cleaning and basically just trying to keep busy. I run a few errands, get some groceries, stop at the post office and the bank. My checking account is being sucked dry, and fast. I need to think about work. Shit, I need to call my boss! By the time evening rolls around I'm tired and so are my parents. We decide to order take out. I have explained to my mom that she needs to come with me in the morning and what time. "We need to be there at seven-thirty, so we can't leave any later than seven. O.K.?"

"Alright." She says defensively.

The morning comes all too soon, and we are in the car headed to the clinic. I'm driving because my mother well, terrifies the hell out of me with her driving. I don't know how she ever gets anywhere. We arrive just a few minutes shy of my appointment time and are taken into a separate waiting room. My mom tries to make small talk for a while, but after a few one-sided conversations, she understands that talking is the last thing I want to do. I can't focus on anything right now. My mind is racing, my knees are shaking, and I feel sick to my stomach. What the hell is taking so long? I glance up at the clock we have been here almost an hour now and I'm starting to get hungry. I place my hand on my belly and offer up a silent prayer. This time I'm more forgiving with God and simply asking him for strength. I think he owes me that. Just as I finish my name is called. I sigh and look over at my mother, offering a small assuring grin. Before I can stand without a word my mom wraps me in a quick, tight squeeze before I stand and follow behind the woman in blue.

When we arrive home, my father is at the door waiting for us. He has tears in his eyes as he puts his arms around me and my mother. Both of us with bloodshot eyes. We cried the entire way home.

"Oh, baby I am so sorry. You will get through this. All of this. It will all be okay. I promise you. How do you feel?"

"Sick" I manage. "Dad, I didn't do it. I'm having the baby." For the first time, I have said it out loud. A baby.

Chapter 9

The Choice

My dad looks completely and utterly shocked. "Are you sure? What made you decide this?" I try and keep my composure as I explain.

"Well, I've been praying a lot lately. I kept wondering why I was being punished. Why would God let something so horrific happen to me and on top of that, I'm pregnant!? I just didn't understand why. Why me? Then as I walked down that hallway at the clinic it hit me. Maybe this is God's way of giving me some light in the dark. Maybe this baby isn't a curse, but a blessing. If I can think of him or her as mine and not his then it's a gift from God. My gift. My child, "tears well up in my eyes. Somewhat happy tears. "This is what I make of it. I can let that man continue to destroy me or I can control my own life. So, that's what I'm going to do." My father looks relieved.

"I just want you to be sure this is what you want. There is no turning back."

"I know you do. And I think I'm making the right choice."

90

*

The next couple of weeks are a blur. I am so tired. I have never been so tired in my entire life. I've met with my boss at the paper and he assures me that Sara has done a fine job on her own. We agree that I will be back in one week. I have another appointment with Dr. Graham scheduled for myself and the baby. The baby, that still seems so strange. I never wanted to see Dr. Graham again but now I can't imagine having anyone else with me on this journey. I feel like I can be comfortable with her. My parents are even being supportive. My mom burst into tears the other morning and said how she cannot believe she is going to be a grandmother. Wow, a grandma, and I, a mother. I'm warming to the idea, I suppose. I have spoken with Leigh and informed her of my situation. She said that they haven't been able to find out which PI Sam used. Apparently, he left no paper trail and deleted any correspondence they may have had. He is smart, very smart. I need to figure out what the situation is with the baby. If he has any rights. I can't imagine he could, being in jail. What about when he gets out though? His trial should wrap early next week.

Thankfully I didn't have to testify. They had enough physical evidence. If they get a verdict early enough in the week, sentencing

91

will be shortly thereafter. He doesn't know I'm pregnant. I hope to go as long as possible without him knowing. He'll find out eventually, of course. This is a small town after all. I shake my head. He is not going to invade my thoughts. I try and gear my mind toward work. I'm going to take some test shots today to get back into the swing of things. It's been a while. I hope I've still got it.

I drive around for a while just trying to find something that pops out to me to photograph. Something to inspire me and make me passionate again. Before I know it, I'm at Millcreek rose gardens. It is so beautiful here. People come to take pictures for special occasions and they even have weddings here. When I get all my gear wrapped over my shoulder, I begin to casually stroll through keeping an eye out for something special. I look across the large lawn and spot a couple walking hand in hand. They can't be any older than teenagers, but they look so in love. I lift my lens and begin snapping candid shots of the two. I don't want to invade their privacy, but they are so adorable. They are giggling now and look so happy. The boy nuzzles the girl's neck and plants a quick peck on her cheek. Click, click, click. I got it. I move on to the gardens themselves. Beautiful red and pink roses line the lawn almost making it so that I'm fenced in. A gazebo sits at the south end surrounded by even more roses, this time yellow and white. This is where weddings happen. I have been to one or two here myself. It really is incredible. When I get married, I want it to be here. If I get married. I touch my tummy. Who will ever want to marry me? "Well, at least I'll have you," I talk to my tummy. Yes, at least I'll have you.

I snap a few more photos of the landscape and some passer byers. I think I should have enough so that I'm at least warmed up to go back to work. I'll have time later to look through them and edit what I need. I guess it's like riding a bike, you never really forget. I just hope I can keep up with this new life. This baby is making me so tired. And nauseated all the time. I have been reading *What to Expect When You're Expecting* and according to that, the sickness and fatigue shouldn't last too much longer: shouldn't, being the key word. I pack up my things and climb back into the car. I decide to call Jess and Matthew to see if they want to go to a movie or something. I'm in such a funk. I need to have a few laughs. Both are up for dinner and a movie. Jess has invited her boyfriend Colton, which is fine, I like Colton. It will be kinda strange though. High school all over again. We were a foursome, always hanging out together. This is exactly what I need.

We meet at a restaurant next to the movie theatre. It's a small little Italian place that I love. We opt for the latest "romcom". Obviously not the boy's first choice, but they know Jess and I will be happy, and we need a good laugh. Each of my friends enjoys a glass of wine and I'm so jealous. Wine would be great, but I have a little one to take care of.

I feel like the entire dinner we don't stop laughing. No one can make me laugh like Jessie. She is the funniest person I know. We finish our meals and head into the movie. God, I could fall asleep right now. I'm such a bore. "Nettie come on let's go pee before the movie. With me having some wine and you preggers I don't want to have to take a bathroom break," Jess says.

"I absolutely agree. And at the rate I have been going, it won't matter, I'll still need one!" we both giggle. This is so fun. I needed this!

The movie was great, and we all had a great laugh, even the boys got a kick out of it. I drop each one of them off because I, of course, am the default DD. I'm so thankful to have such great friends around me. None of them judge my decision. They are all supportive and treat me as if this pregnancy was wanted. Planned even. I'm not treated as a victim. I'm treated as an expectant mother. I like the way that feels. When I arrive home all the lights are out. I know my parents are home, but they must be in bed. I look at the red numbers on the dashboard, 11:52 p.m. I will not be far behind them. I haven't been up this late by choice in a long time.

After washing up and heading into bed I decide to flip through some more of the photos of me that the PI took. I get through a good amount of them before starting to doze off. I guess this means I'm done for the night. I have yet to find anything of significance in the pictures.

I only have one stack to go but I can't tonight. I'm too sleepy. Baby has won and he or she needs me to rest. So, this is what the next what twenty-some weeks will be like? I have no trouble falling asleep and wake to the smell of bacon and waffles. Mmmmm the best thing on the planet to wake up to, the smell of bacon. I'm famished. I hop out of bed like a kid on Christmas morning and make my way to the kitchen. My mom is dressed already and busy at the skillet.

"Hey, Mom." She jumps.

"Jeez, you startled me! I didn't hear you come in." she places her hand on her chest.

"Sorry, I smelled the food and rushed down. It smells so delicious. I am starving!" For some reason, I have a smile plastered on my face. I don't really know why but I'm in a good mood, a really, really good mood. For the first time in a long time, I'm starting to feel like me. A new me, but me. My mother and I sit at the table with our breakfast and I realize I haven't seen Dad yet.

"He's at work. Someone called in sick, so he didn't want the other guys to be shorthanded." Did she just read my mind? She surprises me from time to time.

"Oh, just the two of us then." I hold up my coffee and we clink mugs. She smiles a silly smile.

"You mean three." She winks and eyes my belly. "So, what are your plans for this beautiful Saturday morning?" I shrug.

"I don't know. You? Do you have an event tonight?"

"As a matter of fact, this is the only Saturday for the next two months I don't have anything to do. Do you want to have a mother-daughter day and we can go shopping?" That sounds great.

"Sure, I would love to."

96

"Well, let's finish up and get dressed. We can have the whole day." She is grinning from ear to ear. I haven't seen her this happy in a long while.

We have both showered and dressed and get in the car. Again, I'm the one driving. We head to the mall figuring we can just window shop a bit and see if anything catches our eye. My mom stops into a few stores. She gets some make-up and is generous enough to get some for me as well. It's always fun to get new make-up. It makes me feel girly. We are so enthralled in our day that soon it's lunchtime. We make a stop in the food court because I'm craving orange chicken and rice. I inhale my food and regret it immediately. I feel sick and too full. We walk off our lunch and find ourselves in front of a baby store. She nods at me to go in and I accept. When we are in the store my heart softens at the thought of a tiny little person fitting in these clothes. I can't believe it. I'm getting really excited. "Oh my!" I shout.

"What? What honey what's the matter?" Mom looks terrified.

"Oh, nothing I thought I just felt the baby move. I couldn't have though the book says not until 16 weeks. It must have just been gas." I flush scarlet in embarrassment. My mother giggles.

"Well, I remember feeling you early. You are so skinny you may have just felt the little bugger for the first time." She winks at me and I grin, once again placing my hand on my little bump. Maybe, I think. I can't believe I'm doing this.

Generously my mother buys me a ton of baby clothes, all neutral of course since we don't know the sex of the baby yet. She gets a few stuffed animals for the little one as well. We look at some baby furniture but can't buy anything yet. I don't even know where I will be living when the baby comes. My house has sold but I haven't found anything that I love yet. Of course, I want to wait until I'm back at work and can save some money. Plus, part of me isn't quite ready to move on.

We decide to end our day due to the fact that we cannot carry anymore in our hands. After packing the car, I glance at my mother and she looks confused. "Did we really buy all that?" The back of her SUV is completely packed with bags that we have trouble closing the hatch. I look back at her and laugh.

"No, you bought all of these, not me! Dad is gonna be maaaad." I sing as she bursts out laughing so hard, she is almost in tears. We get back in the car and head home. As I unpack the clothes,

I fantasize about what my baby will look like. I hope just like me. I don't think I can bear it if my baby looks like him....

Chapter 10

Mama Bear

The weeks turn into months and before I know it, I'm at my twenty-six-week check-up. There is no mistaking that I'm prego now. I love my belly. I rub my hand over the swell of my little woman or man. The ultrasound that was supposed to reveal the sex didn't go as planned. Baby was not being cooperative and had his or her legs crossed the entire time. Go figure. We get to have another ultrasound at thirty-two weeks so fingers crossed we will find out then. My mom has been to every appointment with me. You would think she was the one expecting. I guess this *is* her first grandchild. And I'm her only child.

Dr. Graham has measured my tummy and I am right on schedule. Baby is due on March 5th. It seems so far away but it's not. Christmas will be here before we know it. These appointments are so pointless to me if there is no ultrasound. Basically, it's "How are you feeling? Ok, see you in a month." I'm thinking my work is annoyed at me taking half days every month. And after my next appointment, I will be going every two weeks. Holy crap it's coming fast! I have been feeling the baby moving constantly and it's by far the most miraculous feeling in the world. I love it when I lay down at night and the little guy or girl starts doing summersaults. I will miss this the most after the birth, our time alone at night. Then again, we'll have plenty of nights like that.

I have been working a ton and doing a great job. Sara and I haven't even had many shoots together lately because we are so busy. The investigation is closed, and Sam was sentenced to five years. Five crummy fucking years, for screwing up my life. He has the possibility of parole sooner if he is good. So far, he has been "good". I don't even want to worry myself with the thought of him being out. I will do whatever I can to protect myself, and my child.

Luckily, I haven't had to see him in person since that night. Occasionally I would see him on the news or in the papers, but since the sentencing, he has become old news, as have I. Occasionally a letter arrives with the return address of the prison he is being held at and my blood runs cold. I don't bother opening them as I can see no good in doing so. No matter what he has to say, it will just get me upset and I need to take care of myself. I don't want to hear a word that sick bastard has to say. If he still thinks he has control over me, he is dead wrong.

I plop my now twenty pounds heavier ass on my ultra-plush mattress, sans pillows and get comfortable. When I do, I look at my nightstand and notice the manila envelope still sitting there. I haven't looked through these pictures for a long time. They still haven't found whoever took the other photos of me. Best they could guess is that Sam paid some low life PI some cash under the table and Sam isn't budging.

I decide to go through them again one by one. God, seeing the photos of me walking to work in what appears to be spring. Wow, he must have had me followed a lot longer than I even expected. The thought unnerves me. He always unnerves me. As I continue through the photos, I come to a few of me in my house. In my kitchen cooking, sitting in my living room watching television, and in the bathroom. The bathroom. This is the most disturbing. Someone watched me half-naked in my bathroom. Probably fully naked, but just didn't take any pictures. "Well, that was noble of him," I sneer. The one that is a close view of my face I gaze at. I look soft, natural, and most importantly happy. My head is wrapped in a towel and I'm fresh-faced. Just out of the shower.

I hope I can be normal again, in my own home someday with the baby. "We can be happy, can't we? Just the two of us." That song *Just the Two of Us* pops into my head and I begin humming. As I bop to the beat something catches my eye. Something in the picture I hadn't noticed before. In the mirror, you can almost make out a shadow. I stop what I'm doing and stare. I move over to the bedside lamp to get a closer look. Oh, fuck! The color drains from my face and I feel lightheaded. I'm focused on an eye one beautifully crystal blue eye. It's stunning. It's fucking Sara!

No, no, no, no! I try to deny what I'm seeing but I know. It is most certainly her. I have seen those eyes countless times and I have never seen any others like it. I fight through my shock and pick up my cell. I immediately call Detective Montgomery and tell her what I have found. She sounds surprised, not only to hear from me but at the possibility that my savior is also my stalker. She assures me that they will send someone to her apartment immediately to question her, while also making it perfectly clear I should not contact her myself. I begin pacing back and forth. I can't believe this. She is my friend! Why

103

would she help him why? She saved me. I don't understand. It just doesn't make any sense. How long has she known him? Before we even worked together? She seemed genuine when she came to see me after the attack. I don't know what to do at this point.

I decide I need to tell my mother. She is going to flip, everyone is going to flip. I hear her in her room and I softly knock on the oak door and it opens. "Hi honey, I thought you went to lie down?"

"Um, no I mean I was, but I started looking through the pictures again." She interrupts before I can finish.

"Oh, Nettie why would you do that. We had such a great day. Don't get yourself depressed again."

"Mom let me finish. I noticed something this time. Something I hadn't seen before. Something the police didn't see." I pause before I say the words. "It was Sara." She looks bewildered.

"What was Sara?"

"That was following me. She was taking the pictures."

"No," she shakes her head in disbelief. "are you sure?"

"Yeah, you can see part of her face. Her eye and part of her hair. I would recognize her anywhere Mom. It's her." She combs her fingers through her hair and slowly sits on the edge of her king-size bed. I join her. "I know its unbelievable mom. I don't get it myself. The police are going to speak to her now. Leigh said she will call me when she finds out any information. I'm going through a few more of these and see if I can't find something else that may help." She hugs me briefly and reminds me I'm not just me anymore. "Yes, yes I know."

At 11 am the following day, I finally hear from Leigh. She said they did speak briefly with Sara and she denied everything. They couldn't do much given that they can't positively ID her simply from that photo. How the hell am I going to go to work with her? I mean I haven't seen her much lately, but I do see her. What will that meeting be like? Fuck, how did I trust this woman? She is a psycho just like him. I understand he is messed up and was obsessed with me but what possible reason could she have had to help that man. I need to ask her. Maybe I should call. No, I don't even know what I would say.

I have some things to do today. I'm going to go look at a few places, a few houses I saw online. Hopefully, this will get my mind off that traitor Sara. Jess comes with me to look at three homes and there is just one I could picture myself living in, calling home. It's small but quaint. I don't need anything big. Just enough for me and the little

bambino. I smile. "I can see us here." I tell Jess.

"Yeah, I can see you here too."

"We can grill in the back yard and there looks like there is

room for a swing set." I pause. "The bedrooms are right across from

one another, so I won't have to go far in the middle of the night when

the baby wakes."

"I think it looks perfect for you Nettie. Both of you." Jess says

rubbing my baby bump.

It's a white brick ranch with mint green shutters, I can change

those. They are hideous. Inside is all brand new. Hardwood floors

throughout the entire house and the kitchen and bathroom have been

completely gutted. There is an incredible kitchen island with dark

granite countertops, with room for a few bar stools on one side. "I

love this kitchen." Trailing my fingers across the wall. "I think it's my

favorite room." We take one more look through and thank the realtor

as we leave. In the car, Jess asks if I really think I'm going to buy it. "I

don't know, it just depends how much money I can save over the next

few weeks. I have the money I made from the old place that I can use

as a down payment. So, we'll see if it's still available then. But yeah, I think it's perfect." Just then I get a very swift kick from my little one. "Ouch!" I grab my belly.

"What?" Jess looks concerned.

"Nothing, the baby just agrees. This should be our home." I can't control my face splitting grin.

We ride in silence for a bit. I haven't told Jess that Sara was the one following me yet. Knowing her she will track her down and kick her ass! Even though the thought brings a smile to my face, I know it's not the way to solve anything. Jess drops me off at home and both of my parents are there. I tell them all about the places we saw and the one that I hope will be my future home. I'm getting so incredibly excited to live on my own again. I have come such a long way since the night I was attacked. As awful as it was and as horrible as I felt, it changed me. It changed who I am. I feel empowered and strong. Like I can do anything. I will be a good mother. I will appreciate this little one and every moment of their precious life. My gift from heaven. The love of my life. Who would have thought? Something so incredible could come from something so dreadful, but it has and that's what I focus on every day.

I get dressed in preparation for a dinner date with my friend Matthew. I was sure to be clear with him that he is and will always remain in the friend zone. I'm pretty sure he thought I was nuts for telling him that, but after my history, can he blame me? I explained that I don't want to blur the lines between us because of our past. I think I loved him more than he loved me anyway. He was my first. I wasn't his of course but he said he wished I was. He was probably just saying that to get into my pants. Well, it worked. I laugh at myself. We are meeting at the restaurant about halfway between our two places and I am, as always, running a little bit late. He wants to talk about everything that's been going on with me, the pregnancy, the Sara revelation, and of course Sam. He has been pretty good at tiptoeing around the subject with me, as is everyone else, but he also wants me to "open up". I feel like I have healed enough that I can.

When I get to the restaurant, I don't see his car. He must be running late too. I decide I better use the restroom first before I get comfortable. I give my name to the hostess and head for the ladies' room. When I walk in, I'm relieved that I'm the only one there. I hate peeing when someone is listening. I walk to the very last stall because I like that there is so much more room. As I open the door, I feel the breath of someone on my neck. I scream in horror and a hand flies over my mouth to stifle the noise.

"SHHHHHHH be quiet!" Sara commands. Terrified at what she may do, I comply.

Chapter 11

All Eyes on Me

My heart is racing, and I instantly begin to sweat. All I can think is please, the baby. Please don't hurt the baby. I'm gazing at her, waiting for her to speak. And I can't control the tears welling up in my eyes. She looks as terrified as I am. Her pupils are dilated, and her breathing is rapid. She does not look her typical gorgeous self. Her hair is coarse, and her eyes look sunken and dark. Her face is pale where a rosy glow would normally be. She used to be so incredibly pretty. Maybe this is in my head. I used to think she was beautiful but now, I hate her. Now that I know she is ugly on the inside it shines through to the outside. The sight of her makes my fear turn to anger and fury. "What the fuck do you want?" I manage through clenched teeth. I feel my stance change. I will take her down if I have to. I will protect this baby. I didn't come this far just to cower in a corner.

"Oh God Nettie, I'm so sorry!" She begins weeping. What? I thought she was going to hurt me. Huge sobs, so uncontrollable that I'm taken back. I don't even know what to say. I feel like comforting her. *What? are you insane?* I think to myself. She betrayed me! She gave

110

that monster photos of me. She knew he was obsessed and didn't tell me. Fuck that! I am not going to feel bad for this bitch. She is the second most hated person in my world.

"I don't know what you are playing at with your sorry little tears, but I'm not buying it for a second. I have nothing good to say to you. So, stay the fuck away from me! I don't ever want to see your face again. Not only did you betray me and stalk me for HIM, that psycho, but you pretended to be my friend! My FRIEND! Then as if that isn't enough you are following me into bathrooms! Get a grip!" I'm screaming now. I hope no one else can hear me. "You have some nerve apologizing to me!" There is silence now for what seems like hours. I'm trying to regain some composure.

She takes in a deep breath and then speaks "Nettie," her voice calm and controlled. "I never meant to hurt you. You don't understand. He…. he *is* a monster. Please let me explain. Don't shut me out! I need you to know why…" she trails off. She still hasn't made eye contact with me.

"I don't owe you a damn thing!" I shout. I'm so angry I could spit. "Get out of my way and I better not see you ever again in my life! Whether you quit the paper, or I do is of no matter to me, but one of us won't be going back. Do you understand me? You know what you did. Even if you deny it to the police. You are a sorry excuse for a woman." She is still between me and the stall door, so I step forward challenging her. "Do not make me say it again." I'm calm and assertive. She steps to the side and I make my way past her opening the door. I let out a deep breath as I do. I don't know what if anything I was expecting her to do. Suddenly I'm startled by her soft words.

"He did it to me too." She whimpers.

"What?" I turn to face her, and I see it in her eyes. She is telling the truth. She looks so broken, like a child. "Tell me." I whisper. I'm trying not to frighten her. Wow, the power in the room has shifted since she stifled my screams.

She slowly undoes the top three buttons of her shirt and as she pulls it open and I see it. There over her heart, are three vertical lines. Perfectly matched, barely pink tally marks. Just. Like. Mine.

"Please, not here." She holds her hands up gesturing at the room. Oh, I forgot we were in a damn bathroom. It's very dimly lit and has red and gold striped walls, with cheap gold fixtures everywhere. She's right we need to have this conversation elsewhere,

112

especially if we don't want any interruptions. I'm not stupid though. I cannot be alone with her.

"Ok. My friend is meeting me. I'll go get him and we'll come to your house. I want him with me. I don't trust you, for obvious reasons. And I can't take any chances. You couldn't possibly blame me for that."

"Yeah, I understand. Thank you. Thank you. You have no idea how much this means to me just to explain," she is clasping her hands in front of her practically ready to kneel at my feet.

"Just go I'll meet you at your house." I roll my eyes as she rushes from the room. I text Matthew to see if he is here before I pee. God, I'm lucky I didn't piss myself.

My phone dings, good he's here. I wash my hands and rush out. I scan the room and see Matthew at the bar. I make a beeline to him and grab his hand dragging him out of the restaurant. He looks so confused. "What is it?" he gasps.

"It's Sara. She was here when I got to the restaurant. She wants to talk, and you are coming with me."

"What a minute. I don't think so! Are you fucking kidding me? You are insane!" He is genuinely mad at me. I haven't seen him like this in a really, really long time.

"Listen, Matthew, I don't have time for this ok? I would be calling the cops right now, but she said something." I pause. "She said he did it to her too."

"What do you mean? He attacked her? Followed her? What? I don't understand." He is so annoyed with me.

"I don't know just come on. I think she was raped too. She looked terrified. And … she showed me something. I don't know, I believed her, but I want you with me just in case." He shakes his head in disapproval but leads me to his car.

We take the 20-minute drive to Sara's home. I've only been here a couple of times, but I have no trouble finding it. It's a small two-story dark gray house and I remember there being beautiful landscaping. It's dusted with snow right now and the trees bare. It's still cute. When Matt pulls in the driveway, he looks at me and I know he thinks I'm making a mistake. I don't care. I need answers. "Wait here, please? I will have my cell phone in hand and your number ready to go in case I need you okay?" He nods. "I think she'll talk to me better alone than with you." I say. I know he is wondering why I don't want him to come in.

I approach the door and knock apprehensively. She answers immediately. She still has that sunken scared little child look on her face. "Let me start by telling you this," I say before she has a chance to speak. "That is my friend" I gesture to Matt. He is giving her the evil eye. "And he will be waiting for my call if anything, and I mean anything seems amiss. Got it?"

"Yes, I promise I just want to explain myself." We both enter her house and walk to the kitchen. She takes a seat at the table and waves for me to sit.

"I think I would prefer to stand. In case I need to make a quick getaway." I sneer at her.

She hesitates before finally speaking.

"He raped me too, before you." She adds. "And he cut me too. Just like you. Only three wounds, not four. You were the fourth." He has done this before. I wondered that. He seemed too comfortable with what he did to me. Why hasn't anyone else come forward? Maybe they didn't know him. My heart feels as though a million daggers are plunged in all at once. Those poor women.

"I don't understand. How do you know this? And how did this happen to you? Did you know him when we first started working together?" the thought sickens me. "Was our entire friendship a big elaborate hoax to get close to me? For him?"

"No, I didn't know him. He came into the office looking for you one day. He said he was in the neighborhood and wanted to take you to lunch. He was charming and sweet." Vile is the word that comes to mind for me. Disgusting. "You were out on a job, so he asked me to lunch. We had a really great time. He explained that you were old friends but maybe I shouldn't tell you because you used to have a thing for him. So, I just didn't mention it" Yeah, me interested in him, what a load of bullshit!

"So, what? You were dating? When did he hurt you?" I'm so confused.

"The first time I invited him into my place." She pauses closing her eyes. When she opens them again I can feel her pain. "Here." She looks around. "We had already gone out a handful of times and I thought it was going somewhere. I even had a conversation in my head on how to tell you." She shrugs and wipes away her tears. "I don't want to get into the details. You know them.

He raped me, cut me, and went on his way. He didn't beat me like he did you. Nothing on my face at all in fact. Although I didn't fight. I froze. Just froze. He told me if I told anyone, he would kill me." I'm glad she doesn't go into too much detail because I don't want a visual of him destroying her. Here. Right here in this home. She continues. "So, I didn't see him for weeks. And then suddenly, he showed up here again and hurt me again for the second time,"

"Jesus, Sara why didn't you go to the police?" I can't understand this. It doesn't make any sense to me if she knew who he was. She could have warned me. She could have prevented all of this. I stroke my belly.

"I was terrified. I don't have family here. I don't have anyone to comfort me, to help me. I wasn't even healed from the first time when he did it again." She begins to weep. I begin to weep. For the first time I feel sorry for her.

"So, where did I come into all of this?" I manage to get out.

"He said if I didn't follow you and take photos of you that he would continue… um… to hurt me." She can't say the word.

"Rape. Continue to rape you." She nods and I have my answer.

117

"You have to understand, I didn't want any harm to come to you. And I wish I would have been brave, oh God I wish I went to the police and put him in jail. I was just too terrified. He said he loved you. He said he would never harm you. And the night that you…. He told me not to follow you that night. I didn't know why. He was obsessed with you. I thought maybe he was going to pay me a visit, but he never did. Then the next morning the second you were late I knew. Oh, I knew, and I tried calling and you didn't answer so I went to you. I didn't expect to see you that…." She really is sorry. "that beat up. That horrific. I am so sorry, Nettie. Please forgive me." she is begging now.

Just then my phone buzzes. It's Matthew. I slide the lock to answer. "I'm fine Matthew. I'll be right out." I hang up on him. I look back at her. "I think you are reaching with that one Sara. Yes, I feel bad about what he did to you, believe me. I empathize. But you could have stopped it and you didn't. That's the bottom line. I meant what I said before. I never want to see you again. Do you understand?" I emphasize my question in hopes she gets the severity of my tone. "And I want you to go to the police. If there were more women, they need to know." I'm ready to get the hell out of here. But I need to know for sure. "Did he tell you there were others?"

"Yeah, sort of. He mentioned it one of the times. I don't even think he realized that he did. He called me number three. He never mentioned it again. And then after I heard about you about how many marks, he put on you, I knew you were number four." My heart is in my throat. He was branding us. This was his signature. Now the scars are not just scars, they are him. Like notches on a bedpost. He will permanently be on me. I feel like I want to scrub my entire body with steel wool to get him off of my skin. I get a pang of guilt for feeling this way, because of my baby. I'm supposed to look at the positive now. Supposed to. Easier said than done.

"So, you have no idea who the others are?" she shakes her head no. "Alright, I'm sick of giving him or you my time. I'm leaving. Do I need to miss any work to avoid you this week?" I cock my head to one side.

"No, I called and resigned as soon as I knew you figured it out. I'm moving. I don't know where yet, but I can't be here in this town. I will talk to the police as well. I promise." Ha! her make a

119

promise to me, that's rich. I turn to leave and after a few steps turn back to face her, this poor, would be beautiful girl who is ruined now.

"Goodbye, Sara." And I hope and pray this is the last I see of this woman.

I don't tell Matt much about what happened. I just want to go home. "Sorry about dinner. Raincheck?"

"Of course. Anything for you, Nettie. I'm just glad that psycho bitch didn't hurt you," he says raising his eyebrow in disapproval. "You're lucky she didn't. I should have called the cops. If anything would have happened to you because of my stupidity I wouldn't have forgiven myself." He looks over at me sincerely. "That girl is crazy."

"I think she is just wounded. She wasn't when I met her. She was stunning. He damaged her." Just like me, I think. Maybe I was too hard on her. I mean what would I have done in her position? I don't know. I could have been in that situation I suppose. I damn well know I would not want his hands on me again, but I would kill myself before subjecting another human being to his assaults. That's the difference between us. I would have tried. Tried for another resolution. Tried to help those other women before and the other women that were sure to follow. Maybe she is just weak. I feel so torn.

Part of me feels pain for her and the other part of me wants to hurt her myself.

I decide that if she goes to the police, I won't pursue any charges for the stalking, I will just let it go. I don't want to do anything else. I just want to put everything that has happened in the past just there. I want to protect myself and this child. I want all my focus on my future as a mother. Our future as a family. I smile to myself. "We are going to be a happy family," I say to my bump. "I promise."

Chapter 12

Moving On

The next day I have a photoshoot all day. I have no need to go to the office. Thank goodness, because I don't want any questions about Sara and her quick departure. I'm photographing a story about a murder trial. I hate court shoots the most. I feel like I shouldn't be there like it's a personal and intimate moment for those involved and I'm an invader. It's a mother accused of abusing her seven-month-old son, who as a result passed away. This is so sad. How can someone do that to a poor innocent child? There are a lot of sick people in the world. I know this all too well.

I take a few pictures of the woman on trial, the lawyers making their arguments and the judge. It should be enough for our editors to choose from. I'm just not feeling this today. I wish I was given a nice fluff piece instead. Why do they send the poor, damaged ones to do the sad stories? Oh, I'm the only one, they need to replace her.

I'm on my way home when I decide to call Detective Montgomery. I'm surprised when she answers. I expected to leave her a message. "Oh, hi Leigh. I don't mean to bother you, but I haven't heard any more about Sara and I wanted to see what the situation was."

"Oh," she sounds surprised. "Nothing since we last spoke. We are having someone try to enhance the photo to prove it's her. There isn't much we can do other than that." I'm so confused.

"No, I mean she was supposed to come in and speak with someone."

"I don't understand. You spoke to her? When?" She sounds upset. Maybe, because she had no clue.

"We spoke and she told me why she did it. Leigh, she's a victim too. Sam raped her the same way he did me. She said there were others too. "

"Wait, if he raped her why didn't she report it?" Now I'm confused.

"Leigh, you're telling me she didn't come in to speak with anyone about all this?"

"Well, certainly not with me. I will check into it and see if she filed a report, but I would have been notified. There is no way I wouldn't know."

123

"Oh, shit. She left." I can't imagine why she wouldn't want to tack on a few extra years on that assholes sentence. He can't hurt her now. Doesn't she understand that? I don't know whether to be furious or sad. I hope she changes her mind. If she would just go to the police, then maybe we could figure out who the other women are.

"Nettie?" Oh, I forgot Leigh.

"Oh God, Leigh, sorry. I drifted a little bit there. You were saying?"

"I just wanted you to tell me the whole story. Like, when did she get assaulted? How does she know there are others, and does she know who they are? I don't know if I would even consider her to be a reliable source after what she did to you." She likes me I can tell. She is acting like a big sister. Not that I would know what that feels like.

"Well, she said that the reason she followed me was that he had continued to rape her after the initial assault. He said he would continue to hurt her unless she helped him. He brainwashed her. She thought he would never hurt me. I guess I get it, she was terrified. He cut her as well, the first time he cut her three times. He also called her number three."

124

"So, the cutting is his way of marking his victim? Branding them so to speak." My stomach turns. "Oh, I'm sorry Nettie. That was insensitive of me. I'm just used to speaking to other cops."

"No, it's fine. It just seems so unbelievable to me. He is...just sick." For lack of a better word.

"Well he is gone now, and we will keep him there as long as we can. I'll work on these other girls and see if we can't find out who they are. We'll look into tracking Sara down as well. I need more details and I need them from her." She takes a deep breath. "So how are you feeling, physically I mean?" changing the subject.

"Not bad really. I'm not as tired as I was and no sickness. I'm just getting bigger and bigger by the second!" I let out a tiny girlish giggle.

"Good Nettie. I'm glad things are working out for you." I can hear the smile in her voice. "Well, I guess I have a lot of work to do dear. I'll talk to you very soon."

"Ok Leigh, thank you. Goodbye."

"Bye dear," she hangs up. I don't think my life could get any stranger. I pray that someday I can have a little normalcy. Maybe I will have a beautiful home someday and share it with the wonderful caring man and my son or daughter. I deserve a great life and that would be it. I truly believe I will someday. I suppose everyone has bumps in the road only mine are mountains. I still feel bitter at times wondering why me? But I need to get over that. It is what it is and all I can control is the here and now.

My cell rings and scares the shit out of me, "Yeah?"

"Hey, it's Jess. Matthew told me what the hell happened last night! What the fuck were you thinking going to that psycho's house?" uh oh, Jessica is mad. I'm in trouble.

"Will you relax? I'm fine and I had Matthew with me for protection." I roll my eyes.

"Ha! Like he could have done anything! He's a pussy!" Oh, there it is she is howling with laughter. I guess it's kinda funny. Matthew is not exactly the confrontational kind, to say the least.

"Alright, alright settle down. You're right. It was stupid but I had a momentary lapse in judgment. I don't regret going though. I found out a lot. Jess, he hurt her too. She's not quite the monster everyone believed her to be." Her laughs have died down and she is quiet.

"Yeah well, I feel bad for her being a victim, but had it not been for that bitch, you may not have been one of them. Don't forget that. She still did wrong in my book. I better not run into her scrawny little ass or I'll snap her in two!" God, she is so dramatic. It's not a big deal, now.

"Ok I'm driving; I'll call you later. Please, don't be mad," I pout.

"Sure whatever, call me later." I hear the click as she hangs up the phone.

I know everyone is simply trying to protect me and be helpful, but it's beginning to drive me insane! I think I'm going to make an offer on the house that Jess and I went and looked at. I need my space. I feel like I'm being smothered. Besides, I'm beginning to make progress. I'm excepting my new life. I mean the fact that the baby is coming distracts me in a way from all the bad stuff. I just hope it doesn't rear its ugly head after baby comes. If it does, I'll just have to deal with it then. One day at a time.

I decide right then to call the realtor and put an offer in on the house. Hopefully, I'm the only one. I really want my independence back. I should hear in a few days she informs me. This is so exciting!

I really hope that they accept my offer. Fingers crossed. I had a feeling about that one. It's going to be our home. I know it.

When I get home neither of my parents are home, so I decide to take a nice long bath and enjoy the quiet. As I slip into the lavender-scented bath, I realize how bad my body aches. My feet are starting to swell by the end of each day and right now I have cankles. I laugh out loud at myself. I can't believe how fast this pregnancy has gone so far. This is certainly not where I pictured myself this time last year, but my parents keep reminding me that everything happens for a reason. I stare at my belly as it wiggles and sways with baby's movement. "You like that warm water, do you? Me too." I find myself talking to the baby all the time. He or she is my new confidant. I wish I knew the sex so I can start to narrow down names. I have a few that are ok, but nothing that has really stuck yet. I should get a baby name book.

I soak until the water is tepid and my fingers are pruned. Climbing out I examine my changing body. My eyes can't help but go to the scars over my heart. They have healed as well as one can expect but they will never go away. I continue to follow the line of my nonexistent waist. Oh, shit what is that? Stretch marks! I didn't even notice those. Several horizontal lines on my right and left side, decorating my love handles. "Well, little one I guess you have made your mark." Geez, I haven't gained that much weight, have I? This girl better lay off the hostess cupcakes. Mmmm hostess cupcakes, the chocolate with the swirled white icing on top. Well, I can't deprive the baby if it's something it really wants, right? I quickly dress because now I'm on a mission, I'm like an addict wanting a fix. These pregnancy hormones are making me feel a little bit crazy. Oh, well I can be a little crazy if I want. I giggle out loud. Okay, I need a snack.

I don't even bother to get dressed since I'm alone. I wrap my red terrycloth robe around me and make my way to the pantry. "Yes!" we still have some of those delectable cakes. I grab a pack out of the box and fix myself a tall glass of ice-cold milk. I sit and look out the back windows. The snow is falling light and airy. Big huge snowflakes that look like fluffs of cotton. I hope my parents get home soon. I don't think we'll get much but you never know.

After the most wonderful, delicious sweets I have ever had I feel like something salty. God, how weird. I decide not to push it. I think of the stretch marks I have already attained.

Where are my parents anyway? I call my dad's cell and my mother picks up. Hey sweetie," it sounds loud where they are.

"Did you forget to check in with me? I was getting worried." I say in an overdramatic stern tone, purposely.

"Well aren't you the mother hen" she giggles "We are at dinner with the Altman's. I told you this morning, but you must not have been listening to me." Oh, I completely forgot. She did tell me. Well, the pregnancy dummies strike again.

"That's right you did tell me. I'm sorry. Are you having a good time?" I say changing the subject.

"Yes, we are just finishing our drinks and we'll be home. Will you be up?"

"No, I am so tired Mom. I'm gonna turn in soon. I'll see you in the morning okay?"

"Sure honey. Sleep tight. Daddy said goodnight too."

"Tell him goodnight. See you tomorrow."

We hang up and as I place the phone down, I notice the stack of mail that must have arrived today. As I sift through it, I see yet another letter from Sam. As separate it from the other mail to place it with the others, unopened, something compels me to open it. As I

130

gently peel open the adhesive, I can see it's written in red ink, making it all the more stalkerish. It simply reads.

Nettie

Take care of my baby. See you both soon.

Xoxo Sam

I can hear his voice speaking the words. The hairs on my neck stand on end. He can't possibly think he will be allowed anywhere near me or the baby. Well, it's official. He knows. Why in God's name would I do that to myself? I stuff the letter in with the others and decide I need to give these to Leigh. For the future, in case he gets out sooner than expected. I'm incredibly tired. I walk to my room and as I ascend the stairs, I realize how my body is beginning to feel the weight of my little one. I put on my most comfortable flannel pajama pants and a t-shirt and slide into bed. I toss and turn seeing the red words flash in my head. I'm so tired and just can't sleep. Baby starts to do the nightly ritual of kicks and flips and is that, what? The hiccups. The gentle rhythm eventually lulls me to sleep.

I wake screaming. Another nightmare. He was whispering in my ear. I feel like he is still in the room. "He's in jail, he's in jail." I calm myself. I haven't had a nightmare in a few weeks. I thought I was doing better. I look around the room just to be sure I'm alone. Just me. Maybe I should go see that counselor. I need the nightmares to stop, for good.

This is one thing that I can't deal with. It feels like he is violating me repeatedly. I don't want to live my life scared of him in any way. The letters pop into my head yet again. Every time I see that postmark and his handwriting on the envelope it rocks me. He is sick and twisted. I have complained numerous times to the prison about this and they assure me it will stop but soon there is another. I knew I shouldn't have opened it. Never again.

Chapter 13

Warrior

"Ouch!" God, a tremendous sharp pain tares through my stomach. I try and slow my breathing.

"Ow, fuck!" and soon another. This isn't right. "Mom! Mom!" I scream as loud as I can, hoping they are home by now. My mother and father both burst through my bedroom door. Their hair is a mess, faces drained and they look horrified as they notice me gripping my belly.

"What's wrong? Are you bleeding? Pain? What is it?" I don't know if I can speak.

"Pain." I manage to squeak out.

"I'll get the car. Mary, you call her doctor and tell her what's going on. We're going to the hospital." My father instructs and rushes out of my bedroom. My mother helps me get some socks and shoes on and quickly dresses herself before helping me to the front door. Just then my dad comes in and scoops me up with one swift motion, carrying me like a child. I notice he is still wearing his pajamas. He gently places me in the back seat and buckles my seatbelt.

Before I know it, we arrive at the emergency room. My mother is shouting for help and a nurse comes out with a wheelchair. Again, my father cradles me gently into his arms and nods at the nurse dismissing the chair. He wants to carry me. My protector. My daddy.

"Daddy, I can walk really. The pain isn't as bad as it was at home." I don't know if I'm telling the truth about this or not. I may just be getting used to the pain. Are these contractions? I don't think so because it's not constant. Oh, God I hope not, it's way too early. The baby has to be okay. It's a part of me, and I love him or her. My heart begins to ache, along with my belly.

The nurse assures us that Dr. Graham is on her way. She escorts us to a room on the maternity floor so that they can check me and baby to see what's going on. She helps me undress and put on a hospital gown. Not bothering to tie the back of it, she helps me into bed. Before I can even think it, my mother removes the pillows from the bed and gives me a reassuring smile. The nurse looks at her quizzically but says nothing. She attaches two belt type devices to my belly and informs me that one will measure to see if I'm having contractions and the other will monitor my baby's heartbeat.

"The heartbeat looks, great honey." She smiles. Thank God! But something is not right obviously. The tears begin to flow. And as fast as I can wipe them away, they reappear again. Just then Dr. Graham comes through the door looking fairly calm, but I can see she is concerned. She looks intently at the monitors I'm hooked to and tells the nurse to start an IV. I look at her and without even asking, she answers.

"You are having contractions. Pretty good ones too. Baby has a strong heartbeat, but I want to do an ultrasound to make sure everything is okay, and I need to check and see if you are dilated at all. She puts on blue hospital gloves and reaches under the blanket and sheet and tells me to relax. Yeah right, you are shoving your hand up my crotch! She is quick about it and informs me that I'm not dilated.

"That's good right?" I say with some hope.

"Yes, that's good but we need to stop the contractions before you *do* start to dilate. When this happens, in order to get it under control sometimes medication needs to be given. In your case it does." The nurse is by my side again and I see she is going to start an IV. I have never been one to fear needles. This doesn't bother me at all, in fact, it distracts me from the pain in my stomach for a brief moment. "She'll put the medicine straight into your IV and we'll have to wait and see if it works. You better get comfortable. Try and relax. Stress can make things worse." I'm so nervous. I offer a silent prayer. God, please let my little one be okay. This is the only thing keeping me together right now and I couldn't handle it if …. Just please God watch over my baby. Dr. Graham is back with the ultrasound machine and brings it to my side. She squirts the warm liquid on my belly and begins to move the wand around. She doesn't give anything away.

"May we come in?" My mother peeks her head around the curtain and I look at Dr. Graham. She nods. Both of my parents are at my side and we are all staring intently at the monitor. I can see and feel the baby move. That's a good sign, right?

The anticipation is maddening and finally, Dr. Graham sighs, "The baby looks fine." Oh, thank you, Lord, thank you! "There is one thing I see though." Oh no, what? What is wrong? "See right here on the screen?"

"Yes," I whimper.

"Do you want to know the sex?" My parents and I look at one another and our eyes light up.

"Yes, of course," I reply.

"Congratulations Nettie, you're having a boy." Oh, a boy. I'm weeping and laughing at the same time. My parents start whooping and hollering.

"A boy!" My dad shouts. "Finally, I'm not the only man! HAHA" He has his elbow bent with a fist and pulls it down to his hip. YES, he mouths.

"I guess it's time to start thinking of boy names Nettie," Dr. Graham says with a warm smile.

"I have been thinking of a few, and after tonight I think I may just have it."

"Oh?" My mom chimes in.

"Yes, Evan…. After the most wonderful man in the world. My daddy." My dad looks at me with the most love I have ever seen and his eyes well up with tears. "And ironically enough it means 'Little warrior'."

"Little warrior," he repeats "You have no idea how much that means to me, my darling Nettie."

Chapter 14

Family

I'm staring at the picture of my son. Oh, the feeling of him moving more and more is so comforting. I hear a muffled swooshing sound from the monitors as he changes position. My little boy. "I will love you with all my heart and soul," I say gently caressing my tummy between the wires and belly bands. "Just stay put until it's time will, ya? I don't need to start worrying about you already." I smirk at my parents. They are both overwhelmed you can tell. The tension in the room still palpable but the great Dr. Graham is very reassuring that they should be able to stop labor, for now. I may have to take it easy for a few days.

"Mom and Dad, why don't you go home and try and get some sleep?" I ask but already know the answer. I have scared the living daylights out of them yet again and I'm sure they won't leave my side.

"Absolutely not!" My mom scolds me. "We will stay right here with you and sleep on the floor if we have to." And she is serious about that too.

"She does need her rest though, I'm afraid," Dr. Graham addresses my parents. They both nod in agreement.

"Ok, we'll just be in the waiting room if you need us okay?" My father says still with a little gleam in his eye. I know he has secretly been hoping it was a boy.

"Sure Daddy. I'll be fine. I'm sleepy." And I am. All this stress and excitement, it just hit me like a ton of bricks. I can't wait for my normal, boring mommy mode life. They both kiss me and exit out into the hospital hallway.

Dr. Graham checks all the monitors again and tells me she'll be back in the morning unless there is any negative change. I should be able to go home early as long as the contractions have completely stopped. So far, the medicine is doing its job. I'm alone now and all I want to do is sleep. I lie back on the hospital bed and listen to the thump, thump, thump of Evans' heartbeat. The most miraculous sound in the world. My mind drifts and I imagine a blonde-haired boy with hazel eyes, running around the back yard of the white brick house I hope to call home. I can see a wooden swing set in the back and perhaps a dog. I realize I'm grinning from ear to ear. I hope he will love me as much as I love him. To think I haven't even met him yet and already he is the love of my life. "My little Evan. I love you, my whole heart." I whisper. The muffled thump, thump, thump gently fades into my dreams.

I wake to the lights being flipped on as a nurse enters. Jesus it's so bright I can't even open my eyes. "What time is it?" I croak.

"It's 4 a.m. Sorry hun, I just need to check your I.V." She walks around to the side of the bed and she types something into the computer and checks the monitors and my I.V. bags.

"Everything looks great. The contractions have stopped we just need to let the medicine run all the way through. As long as they don't come back you can probably get out of here in a few hours."

"Thanks." Now get the hell out and let me go back to sleep. She hits the lights off as she exits and now it's pitch black. My eyes adjust as I take a deep breath and it's not long before I drift once again.

I'm awakened by my parents whispering in the corner of my room. It's barely dawn. The room looks gray and dreary in the soft light. I sit up and notice that the thump, thump, thump is still going strong. I breathe a sigh of relief yet again.

"Close call." Both of my parents turn and smile with warmth.

140

"Yes, and Dr. Graham was in and said you can go home as soon as they get the paperwork done." Oh, I hadn't even heard her in here.

"Will I see her before I leave? I wanted to thank her," I frown.

"Yes dear, she is just outside signing a few things and she said she would speak to you about your instructions going home."

"Oh, good. Did she say if I can go back to work?" I hope so. I can't afford to buy the house if I can't depend on that paycheck. I hope I hear something soon about my offer.

"I think she wants you on bed rest for a few days." I was afraid of that. "Just as a precaution." She adds.

It's not long before the doctor is back, and she goes through a long list of instructions. I'm told that if I have any pain or bleeding, I need to call her immediately and report back to the hospital. I do have to be on bed rest but just for a few days, so that the contractions don't begin again. I'm allowed up only to shower and use the bathroom. I can handle that I guess. I just hope my boss isn't ready to fire my ass.

"Thank you, Doctor Graham. I really appreciate everything you have done for us, and I don't just mean today." To think that I couldn't stand to be in her office before. Now she is of great comfort to me.

"Of course, Nettie. I'm just doing my job." She gives me a wink and is off to save some other woman I imagine.

It isn't until two in the afternoon before we leave the hospital. It took forever for them to get my paperwork and instructions together. Then I had to wait for them to get the I.V. out of my hand. I have a nice little bruise where it was. We are all starving so we stop into the cafeteria for a quick bite before heading for home.

When we arrive, I'm surprised to see Jess and Colton standing on the porch wrapped in their winter coats and scarves. My parents must have called her. She meets me at the car and opens my door wrapping her arms around me tightly. I can tell she has been crying.

"Jessie, I am fine, really. It was just a false alarm. We are okay. He's okay." "HE?!" she is shocked. Oh, I thought my parents would have told her.

"Yeah, it's a boy! I thought mom would have blabbed already," I say unable to contain my laughter. I look at my mom and she shrugs, she gets it. "Sorry, Mom." Well, can you blame me? She can't keep a secret to save her life.

"Oh! I'm so happy for you Nettie! A little boy," she is grinning. I can tell she is trying to picture him as I have for the past 12 hours. It's hard not to. She shakes her head breaking from her thoughts. "Come on, bed rest I heard? Let's get inside. It's freezing out here." She's right about that it's much colder than it has been the past few days. It's so cold it takes my breath away.

I hate this about Ohio. I don't mind a little snow, but this cold. Arrgh, for lack of a better word, SUCKS!

We all peel away our layers of coats, scarves and other winter gear and soon I'm being escorted to my room. My mom, dad, and Colton leave Jess and me to ourselves for a bit. I lie down and Jess curls up right next to me. Just like a sister would do.

"So," she speaks first. "Were you scared? I mean did you think something was really wrong?" I nod and the tone in the room has changed. Tears well up in my eyes.

"Yeah, I thought I was going to lose him." I pause to compose myself. "I can't believe how my life has changed. I mean, when I found out I was pregnant it was one of the worst days of my life. Now I have fallen in love with this baby. With Evan, I can't imagine not having him now." She looks at me and grins.

143

"Evan? I like that. Your dad must be thrilled." I nod. I guess I can spend the next couple of days deciding on a middle name for Evan.

"So, have you decided on a place yet?" she says changing the subject.

"I actually put an offer on the one we saw the other day. I should hear back any day now." I cannot contain my excitement. "I hope they accept it. I can't afford to offer more than I did so keep your fingers crossed." I hold both hands up crossing my fingers and squeezing my eyes closed tightly. When I open them she is doing the same thing. We both burst out into a laughing jag that I have tears streaming down my face and my legs crossed so I don't wet myself. "Stop, Stop." I manage. I don't even know why we are laughing anymore. Oh, Jessie is my happy medicine. What would I do without her? Finally, our giggles subside, and she looks serious again.

"What is it?" I ask. She looks like she needs to say something but is hesitant.

"I have some news." She blurts out.

"Oh? What? Is everything ok?" I am dying here. What is going on?

"Colton proposed last night!" she holds up her hand and I'm nearly blinded by the rock on her ring finger. How did I not notice THAT!? "And I said yes of course! I'm getting married!" I'm so happy to hear some good news. I couldn't handle anything bad today.

"Jessie I'm so happy for the both of you!" I pull her toward me and give her a huge squeeze. It's about time, they have been together forever. When we release from our embrace, I grab her hand to take a closer look at this ring. "I can't believe I didn't notice it before. It is huge!" It's a beautiful solitaire emerald cut diamond. It must be a carat at least. Wow, I'm jealous. "It's incredible. He did a hell of a job! So how did he propose? Where were you? What did he say?"

"Actually, I always thought I would expect it when the time came, but I was completely shocked. We went to dinner and he was acting completely normal. Then he wanted to go for a ride. I thought that was a little strange because it was so cold, but it was a beautiful night and the snow looked so gorgeous falling. We stopped and when I looked up, we were in front of our old high school." She has a face splitting grin now. "Then he said, 'This is where I met you, fell in love with you, and this is where I wanted to ask you to be my wife. Jessica

145

make me the happiest man on earth. Marry me?' Then he opened the glove box and there was the black velvet box with a small red ribbon tied around it." A single tear rolls down her cheek. "And of course, I cried like a baby and just kept saying yes, yes, yes!"

"How romantic! Well, he gets points in my book for a great proposal and a great fucking ring!" Her machine gun laugh bursts out yet again. I give her another hug before she climbs out of my bed.

"I should go and let you rest. I'll stop by in the morning with lots of gossip mags for you and a few movies. I know it will be a little boring for you."

"Thank you so much! Tell Colton I said congratulations. I'm so happy for you really Jess. You deserve all the happiness in the world." I truly mean that. She is the kindest hearted person I have ever known. She is selfless and beautiful inside and out.

"Thanks, Nettie. Oh, and of course you will be my maid of honor?"

"I'm honored to have you as my best friend. And yes, I will be your maid of honor."

"Great! See you tomorrow. Love ya!" she blows me a kiss.

"I love you too." I blow a kiss back.

146

I'm so tired again already. I lay back on my bed and now realizing I will have to stay in bed for two days I'm rethinking the pillow situation. Maybe I can try them. I haven't been so panicky about it lately. I'm used to sleeping without them but maybe just to sit up in bed it wouldn't be a bad idea. When my mother comes back in, I'll ask her. It seems like a while before anyone comes in to check on me and I'm a little annoyed. Then I realize why. I can smell dinner. The aroma of grilled chicken is all I can make out. Shortly after my mother comes in with a tray and a meal. She is smiling a polite smile.

"I made a chicken salad for you. I thought it would be something light." She places it on the bedside table.

"Mom, I can't exactly sit up comfortably would you mind getting me a few pillows so I can be propped up?" She looks quizzically at me with her head tilted to one side.

"Are you sure? It's not going to bother you?"

"We won't know unless I try," I shrug. She disappears briefly to the hall closet and brings the two pillows that should normally be on my bed, and she motions for me to sit up. As I do, I feel the familiar prickle of tension climb up my arms. I take a slow deep breath releasing some tension and when the pillows are in place, I lean back into them.

"I did it!" I smile. I'm still a bit tense, but I did it. I can handle this. See I'm making progress without a damn counselor! One day at a time. One step at a time. "Can you stay with me while I eat though? I could use the company."

"Yes, of course. Then you should try to sleep. You need your rest. Oh, I almost forgot that realtor that showed you the houses the other day called and left a message for you." Oh shit, I haven't had a chance to tell Mom and Dad that I made an offer. I hope they aren't upset.

"What did she say?" Wow, I'm nervous, excited, and scared all at the same time. I want the place, but it seems so real all of a sudden. I will be all by myself until baby comes.

"Nothing, she just said to call her back when you get a chance." Good, I want to be the one to tell them.

"Mom, I did make an offer on one of the houses. She is probably calling to tell me if they accepted or not." She looks a little surprised, but I expected that. She is just used to me being here all the time.

"Well, good for you. I hope you get it. Although, I'm sure going to miss having my baby girl around." She strokes my cheek gently like she did when I was a child.

"I'll miss you and Daddy too Mom. Don't worry it's not far and I'm going to need help moving and unpacking after all." I look up at her batting my eyelashes as I do.

"Yeah, yeah I get it!" She giggles and so do I.

We sit and talk for a long while as I pick at my salad. I'm not all that hungry, but I eat a good amount of it. I'm occasionally aware of the pillows at my back and get a slight bubble of panic every now and again. For the most part, though I think I do well. When I finish my mother clears my tray and kisses me on the forehead.

"Get some sleep, darling. If you need anything, just holler okay?" I nod.

When she leaves the room, I decide to try and call the realtor before going to bed. I pick up my cell and dial her number. Why am I so nervous? It rings about four times and I just when I think her voicemail will pick up, she answers.

"Oh hi, Mrs. Hall, this is Nettie Madison. I was returning your call."

"Yes, Nettie, how are you?" I answer with a simple

"Uh, well I've been better." I don't want to get into my last days' events.

"Well maybe this will help. I have good news for you. The seller accepted your offer! Congratulations!"

I'm overwhelmed with feelings. I'm so excited. We have a home, Evan! Just you and me, kid. It must have been meant to be.

"Thank you so much! I'm so thrilled! So, when will it officially be mine?" I ask. I have no idea how this stuff works.

"We should be able to close by the end of the month. We just have to wait on a few things from the bank and you'll be moving in before you know it! I'll call when I have a date for you. Congratulations again, Nettie."

"Great and thanks again. I hope to hear from you soon." We hang up and I'm beaming with joy. This is turning out to be a great day! First Jessie's engagement and now the house.

"Things are looking up!" I say to baby. I decide I could turn in and sweep the pillows off the bed.

I think I did well. I don't want to wake however with one of them over my face. I inhale a deep breath assuring myself I have control.

I have wonderful dreams all night. Dreams of us in our new home. Beautiful green grass and flourishing flowers. Sitting out back in the summertime rocking on the swing with baby in my arms. We are happy. I'm happy. Finally, my mind is beginning to catch up with my body in the healing process. All thanks to my little warrior.

*

The next few days have gone by quickly. Jess has been over a few times and we spent almost an entire time looking through bridal magazines, for dresses and wedding ideas. She hasn't set a date yet, but they are thinking sometime next summer. I'm so happy for her and so excited to be a part of her special day. I will bend over backward to give her a perfect wedding. She has been a great distraction from the boredom of bed rest.

No more contractions, baby is moving like crazy and I'm feeling great. I have to go and visit Dr. Graham today to officially get cleared to go back to work. I'm lucky that my job doesn't entail anything strenuous or I probably wouldn't be allowed back quite yet.

My boss was very understanding, but I don't want to push my luck. There has still been no word on where Sara has disappeared to, but I'm not surprised. I don't expect to ever see her again. She is a coward. Since she flaked on telling the cops about her attack and what she heard about there being other girls. I don't feel so bad for her. She made the decision to let that asshole stay on the streets and now he may be out in five years because of her. I hope I never see her again. She is a horrible excuse for a woman.

"Knock, knock!" My mother sings. I guess that means it's time to go see the great Doc.

"Hey, Mom. I'll be down in a second, okay. I just need to brush my teeth real quick." I hold up my toothbrush.

"No problem, I'm going to go warm up the car. I'll meet you downstairs?" I nod and she leaves me be. I head into the bathroom and brush my teeth and run a comb through my hair one last time. God, I need a haircut. I still have an uneven spot where that bastard ripped a chunk from my skull. Maybe I should just get it all cut off. That wouldn't be a bad idea. I'll think about it. I remember to pee this time. I don't know if she'd want to do a down there exam today or what but just in case, I'm prepared.

The drive to the OBGYN office is fairly normal. My mother and I make small talk and she tiptoes around asking me for the millionth time how I'm feeling. I can't wait to get into my own place. Oh, shit I forgot to tell my parents that I officially got the place.

"Um Mom, I meant to tell you. I called the realtor back and they accepted my offer on the house." I try and sound excited so that she is excited as well. She plasters a huge fake grin on her face and offers up a generic congratulations. That's it? I know it will be hard for them I mean I have been living with them now for six months, but she couldn't have thought I would be there forever. "Mom I know you like me being at your place and so do I, but you should be excited that I'm ready to move on. It's not far and you can help me decorate and come visit all the time." Well, not all the time I think to myself.

"No, I know. I just worry about you living alone that's all. You know me I always worry about my baby."

"But Mom, I won't be alone." I say caressing my bump. She smiles and nods.

"You're absolutely right. You will never be alone again." Now she looks accepting. What a relief.

When we arrive at the office we don't have to wait very long. In fact, the office seems a bit deserted today. We meet with Dr. Graham and it turns out she does need to examine me just to be sure that I haven't dilated. It's a quick and painless exam. Thankfully, there is no action yet. I realize I was holding my breath and audibly exhale.

"That's good news. What about work then, can I go back?"

"Sure, Nettie just no heavy lifting for the next week and just try not to be on your feet all day. Take it easy okay?" Dr. Graham instructs, giving me a teacher to student look.

"Yes, I will take it easy, I promise," I place my hand over my heart reflecting my sincerity.

"Alright well, with the holidays coming up we can make you an appointment say, in four weeks. You know the drill. The girls out front can make your appointment. Give them this." She hands me a piece of paper with the instructions that I'm to be seen in four weeks and I relay it to the secretary at the front office. She hands me a card with my appointment time and date on it. I will be 32 weeks. Holy crap that is insane! This pregnancy has flown by. After that appointment, I will go every two weeks and then every week until

154

baby comes. I can't believe it. I better get the house ready fast. I hope we can close soon.

"What's the matter, you look nervous?" my mother asks.

"Oh, I was just thinking how fast this pregnancy has gone and how much stuff we still need to do. I hope I can get into the new place soon. Since we know it's a boy now maybe we should start shopping for nursery décor. I emphasize WE so she knows I need help affording all the furniture and things.

"You're right he'll be here before you know it," she pauses, thinking for a moment. "I'll tell you what. Why don't you and I go shopping this weekend and just pick out a few things and then as soon as you get into the house, Daddy and I can buy them. Maybe make a baby registry." Ew, I cringe at the idea. A baby registry for the rape victim who got knocked up. My friends will like that.

"No Mom, I don't want a registry or anything like that. I think it's kinda creepy." She looks at me as if she is appalled.

"I said nothing about a shower! It will just be for me and Dad. I won't even tell anyone. It will just be, so we get exactly the things you wanted. You know me, I won't remember what you picked out before we even leave the store." She sure has a point there. I'm surprised she doesn't forget her own name sometimes. I giggle to myself and I know she notices. She has a shy grin on her face as well.

"Alright, I'm sorry for getting defensive. It's just this isn't a normal pregnancy and I don't want to glorify my situation. Not that I'm not happy about it…now. I just don't want people to pity me or think I'm a weirdo." She frowns at me taking my hand.

"No one thinks that." There is that fucking pity look. Oh, and a head tilt no less. So, she even still has pity for me. "Let's get going," she continues. I grab the keys from her giving her the biggest all teeth smile that I have. There is no way she is driving me around anymore. I'm surprised we haven't been killed yet.

When we arrive at home, Mom grabs the mail out of the wooden mailbox, and we head inside. She plops all the mail on the table and begins to flip through it when she suddenly stops. I know it's from him. I hold my hand out to her and she hesitantly gives me the letter. When I read the return label it isn't from the prison, it's from county family services. Family services? What in the hell? I'm nervous to open it, but I rationalize that there is no way it could possibly be what I am thinking in my twisted brain. They can't let him have any rights to the baby, that would be madness. I will leave the country before I let that happen. I open it neatly and gently remove the folded yellow papers. I begin to read:

Dear Ms. Madison,

The enclosed documents are to inform you that the following Samuel M. Knox is contesting that visitation be granted to him as the biological father of your child while incarcerated and physical parental rights after his release. A preliminary hearing is scheduled to be held on January 12th at 10 a.m. You must attend if you wish to have your statement taken into consideration for the judge to make a ruling. Thank you for your time.

Sincerely,

Hank P. Tollidge, Mahoning County Family Court

"Piece of SHIT!" I rip it in two and throw it on the table.

"What is it?" My mom looks so terrified.

"Oh, nothing I just have to go to court because that asshole, piece of shit wants visitation that's all! There is no way, right? RIGHT?" She shrugs her shoulders. I know she wants to be supportive, but the truth is we just assumed he couldn't see the baby, but I guess we never knew for certain. I need to call a lawyer. FUCK!

This is all I need right now, to be stressed out more than I already am. Part of me wants to go see him and tell him what a prick he is but I have a feeling that's what he wants. "Do you know any good lawyers Mom?"

"Uh, yeah I do actually. Someone I went to high school with is a lawyer. I'm not sure exactly what kind though. I'll give him a call okay?" I nod. I can feel my face twisted up in confusion, sadness and pure rage.

"Yeah, call now!" I snap. I realize I'm panting. I have never hated someone more in my life and if I could kill him I would. I don't care what the consequences would be.

"Alright, why don't you go lie down or something? I don't want you working yourself up too much, especially after our little scare. Now go!" she commands. I follow her advice and turn to go to my room. I'm seething. I sit at the end of my bed and take a deep breath. Ok, let's think about this.

First of all, he has to prove he is the father, right? So first we would need a DNA test. He will have to jump through a few hoops himself. And how in the fuck is he paying for this shit anyway? Then it occurs to me. He wasn't rich, but his parents are. No, his parents

158

wouldn't possibly help him after knowing what he has done. In that moment, I need to know. I pick up my cell phone and click on the yellow pages app. And type in Knox, Samuel. Yes, Sam is a Jr. This is going to be fucked up, but the adrenaline is coursing through my veins and I need to do something. I don't even notice that the phone is ringing already. Shit! What do I say? Eh, I'll just go with the flow.

"Dr. Knox speaking" Shit a part of me hoped he wouldn't answer.

"Yes, Dr. Knox this is Nettie, Antoinette Madison." There is an audible quiver in my voice, but I continue. "I want to know why the fuck you are helping your demented rapist son try and get visitation of MY child?" There is a long pause. I don't know if he is still there, maybe he hung up.

"Um, Miss Madison. I don't think it's a good idea that we speak." He sounds cold. He sounds like Sam. I feel my blood boiling.

"Yeah, well I don't think I should have been brutally raped and carved, but I was! So, you can talk to me on the phone or I will show up at your doorstep! Which would you prefer, SIR!" Yeah, that was good, Nettie. You are in control, not him.

"Ok, Miss Madison. I'm not helping my son, exactly. I don't agree with his choice to want anything to do with that…child. But if he wants to, I will provide the financial means for him to do so. He is the father after all, as you claim." I claim! Fuck you, you, sick son of a bitch!

"Well first of all Dr. Knox, your son raped me, and this baby wouldn't even exist had I not decided to give him a chance. I decided it's not his fault that his father is a sadistic prick. It was not his choice how he was conceived but now it's my choice how he lives. And so help me God, I will do anything in my power to keep your son from mine. ANYTHING! I just wanted you to know that it's a waste of your money and time to try and pursue this. No one in their right mind would allow that monster around a child. And you sir, are just as bad as your son for helping. Does your wife know what you are doing? From what I remember she actually seemed to be a nice person although I thought you were too." I'm out of breath. God my mind is racing a mile a minute. This man is lucky he is not standing in front of me or I would pummel his ass.

"Son? You are having a boy?" Shit, why did I say that? I can hear the grin in his voice. Did he not hear what I just said? Oh, what

160

have I done? He is going to tell Sam. I wanted him to know as little of this pregnancy as possible. He continues, "and as far as my wife is concerned, not that it's any of your business, but she and I aren't together anymore. Ever since Sam was arrested. We have very different views on what is right and wrong for our son." He barely pauses and I'm shocked at his next statement. "So, what have you decided to name him?"

"That is none of your fucking business! Don't think you will ever see him either. Now I know where Sam gets it from. You are delusional! Drop the shit because you will not win! No, you know what? Spend all the money you want. Spend every dime you have. I'm not worried. Not at all."

"Then why are you calling me Nettie?" His voice pierces the deepest part of my soul. I feel just as scared as I was that night.

"FUCK YOU!" and I hang up. Why? Why did I call him? I guess I expected what? Some sympathy? Yeah right! Same blood, same man. I touch my stomach. The same blood as my little man. Do I really believe that? No. my son will be nothing like them. Nothing! I look up and my mother is standing in the doorway with her hand over her mouth and tears running down her cheeks. I didn't even realize she was standing there. I begin sobbing as well.

"Why won't they just leave me alone? Leave us alone." Too much damage has already been done. I feel like I have been violated all over again. They cannot see him. Ever. Never ever. I won't let it happen. I need to be strong.

My mother is by my side, kneeling in front of me. She places her hand over my belly and begins to pray. I close my eyes. "Dear Lord, please bless this beautiful child who has miraculously come into our lives. I know he is a blessing from you, Lord Jesus, and we ask for your love to fill our hearts at this difficult time. We give ourselves to you and know whatever happens is your will. Please Lord give us patience and grace to handle anything that may come our way. Give us strength please Lord and strength to this helpless baby, Amen."

I'm weeping through my closed eyes and I believe that the words my mother is saying have truly reached the heavens. She is right. My son is here for a reason and there is a plan for our family. For my little warrior and for me. I will be strong enough for both of us. "Thank you, Mom, I needed that. You have no idea. I will fight tooth and nail for my child, and I will win!"

162

Chapter 15

Change

I have a meeting with my mother's friend, the lawyer, at the end of the week. We need to have a game plan. Until then, I'm going back to work. I need to keep myself busy, as do my parents. After my dad found out about the preliminary court hearing and my very unpleasant telephone conversation, I had to talk him out of going to track down Dr. Knox and doing what we all want to do to him. I feel like my entire family is suffering along with me, which is infuriating. None of us deserve this. I mean, how much longer can we hold it together? It's like the moment we get somewhat happy we get a huge slap in the face. Distraction is good. I need to go to work.

I end up working twelve hours my first day back, which I know is completely ridiculous, but the day flew by. I tried my best to focus on work and not let the drama seep in, but of course it did every now and again. Okay, more like every other minute. I'm trying so hard to keep it together but there is only so much I can take. When I arrive at my parents, I get a call from the realtor and we get to close on my house on Tuesday of next week. Yay! At least a little good news and moving will be a great way for us to try and forget, even if for a moment about our troubles.

I call Jessica first to tell her the good news. Of course, she answers after just one ring. "Hey, where have you been all day? I have been calling you." Geez, worry much.

"Sorry, mom! I had to work." I can barely contain my smirk.

"Ha-ha, very funny. Seriously with all the worry you put me through this year you damn well better call me every, I don't know, two hours at least!" I laugh out loud. How ridiculous. She has got to be kidding. "I mean it Nettie. I'm scared when I don't hear from you. I feel like I'm constantly on edge." Wow, I didn't realize that all of this is affecting more than just my parents and me.

"Sorry, Jessie. I guess I have been a little insensitive to my friends. I won't make you worry again. In fact, I called to tell you that I will be getting the keys to my new place next week and although it sucks being winter and all, I was hoping you would help me move." I say this in the sweetest, please don't hate me tone and she sighs in defeat.

"Yes, of course, anything for you. I'm sick of moving you though, you know. So, could you please stick around this place a while, eh?"

"Sure thing. I promise. Evan and I won't be leaving there for a very long time." We hang up and I decide I better start packing. I find a few boxes around the house and start to pack up just some of my clothes that I cannot fit into anymore. Almost everything I have is in storage, so I don't have to do much. I gently fold my most comfortable jeans and pack them away. I hope I can fit in them next year. The thought makes me sad. I have never had to work very hard at being fit but I can see the effects of baby on my ass and thighs. I thought girls gave you big asses. That must be an old wives' tale because I have certainly proved that theory wrong.

Next, I decide to pack a few of my books and photos. I come across some old CDs tucked away. Why I still have some of these is beyond me. Who even listens to CDs anymore? Most of these are from high school. As I flip through, I'm reminded of parties, proms and wonderful memories with my friends. Oh, to go back to that time just one night. Now I'm strolling around my room singing along to my party anthems from years ago. I'm such a loser!

165

I decide I have done well enough for today and stack the lighter boxes in the corner. When I turn around my dad is in the doorway holding in his laughter. "Jesus, Dad you scared the crap out of me!" I put my hand on my chest trying to contain my heart. "Did you enjoy the show? I know I'm a little rusty, but I think I can still get the crowd going." I smirk at him.

"Very entertaining. I had no idea you could sing so, um, well." I roll my eyes at him with my hands on my now very wide hips. "What exactly are you doing in here anyway?" he says gesturing to the boxes.

"Well, I close on the new house next week and I thought I would just get a few of the easy things out of the way to make less work for you, Dad," I give him my best I'm the greatest daughter in the world grin.

"Oh," he is frowning now. I figured they would be a little disappointed, but we all knew this day would come eventually. "I was just kind of hoping you would at least stay until the baby was born. I mean what happens if you go into labor and you're by yourself?" I tilt my head at him. He looks like the child, not the parent. His beautiful eyes green today. He looks pitiful.

166

"Daddy" I walk over, reaching up and putting my arm around him. "You know I will call the second I'm in labor and expect you and Mom to be there at a moment's notice. Don't worry we'll be fine, really." I stroke my little warrior and my dad visibly relaxes.

"I know babe. I just worry about my little girl and my soon to be namesake," he pats my belly and offers up a weak smile. "Come on, let's go get some dinner," he grabs my hand and pulls me into a quick hug.

My mother has made yet again, a fantastic meal of stuffed sweet peppers and mashed potatoes. Mmmm, I'm going to miss this so much when I'm living alone. Maybe she will make me a few things so that I can stock my freezer. Good idea Nettie, she can't say no to her prego daughter.

*

Finally, the day has arrived to meet with my lawyer, and I can hardly wait. I just need some reassurance that I have nothing to worry about. I need someone who knows what they are talking about to say it out loud that my child cannot and will not be taken by that monster.

We arrive at a cozy office in the downtown area, surrounded by corporate offices. It's a small brick building with a sign that reads

167

Lewis Law Offices. A bit of a tongue twister. I have spoken to Mr.

Lewis on the phone and he seems nice enough. I felt very

comfortable talking to him because he seems fond of my mother.

Very fond in fact. I wonder if they ever dated. I'll have to ask her

sometime. Not now. When we enter, a young man sits at a small desk

in the waiting area and we approach. He looks up and pauses eyeing

me. What, do I have something on my face? He stands to extend a

hand.

"Ms. Madison. Hello, Mr. Lewis will be available in a few

moments. He is just on a call right now." Huh, who is this guy? "I'm

sorry, do we know one another?" His face flushes in embarrassment.

"Oh, no I just recognize you. I mean from the papers and TV.

Um, from last summer," he explains. Yeah, I get it. I know what

you're referring to, you idiot.

I don't acknowledge him any longer and grab a seat in the

corner. About ten minutes go by then Mr. Lewis enters. He is a very

handsome older man with silver hair, but the sexy kind like George

Clooney sexy. Of course, he's not as handsome as my dad, but in my

eyes no one is.

"Mary Madison? Wow, it's been a while, huh?" Yeah, they certainly dated. He has that look in his eye. He is gazing at her, practically drooling at the mouth. Hello? I'm here too!

"Christopher, it's great to see you. You look…well wonderful." Ok Mom, a little obvious. What the hell is going on here?

"Hi Mr. Lewis, my name is Nettie. Mary's daughter, we spoke on the phone." I'm all too happy to interrupt their little reunion. Don't get any ideas buddy!

"Yes, Ms. Madison it's a pleasure. You look just like your mother. Please, both of you come in." He escorts us into his all too small office. Against the back wall is a beautiful maple desk with a few photos taking residence. I can't see them as they are facing his chair, but I assume they are of his family. The desk looks too expensive for such a mediocre office. Damn, I hope he is good.

"Please ladies, have a seat. We have a lot to discuss." He motions to the two chairs seated directly across from him and he sits. Opening a manila folder in front of him he takes out a stack of papers and neatly flips through until he seems to find what he is looking for. He finally speaks again. "Okay ladies, here is what we are looking at. Mr. Knox as you know wants some sort of visitation with the child while he is incarcerated. However, in order to do this, he would have to obviously prove that he is, in fact, the father. That means a DNA test, which I will make sure doesn't happen until the baby is born. We don't want to put the baby or you under any undue stress especially after preterm labor." He pauses taking a deep breath and then continues. "So, here is my plan. We go to the preliminary hearing and propose this to the judge. If Mr. Knox wishes to continue pursuing this matter, which he will, then at least it won't be done until after the baby is born."

"You don't think he could actually get some sort of custody, do you?" I interrupt him.

"Well, I believe that when the judge hears what he has done to you and the fact that the baby was conceived due to a sexual crime, it will be damn hard for him to, but..." What the fuck does he mean but? There is no way that is possible. What the hell am I going to do if that happens? It can't that's all, it just can't. "The laws for those convicted of a felony in Ohio are this: he wouldn't be able to have custody at all if he had committed a sexual or abusive act against a child. Since the crime was against you it's a bit of a technicality now. I don't want to scare you I just want you aware that there is a chance. Believe me

170

though Nettie, I will do everything in my power to make sure that doesn't happen." Alright well, now I'm freaking out! I thought I would feel better after meeting with him, but now I'm just plain scared. I was hoping to hear there was no chance at all. My mother sensing my anxiety grips onto my hand.

"Don't worry. He won't get anywhere near either one of you." She says trying to comfort me.

"There is some bad news," Mr. Lewis continues. "You do have to appear at the preliminary hearing, and he will be there too. There is no way for me to get around that. I have put in an order that he have no contact whatsoever with you and that has been granted. There is no need for either one of you to say a word. Myself and his attorney are the only ones who need to speak. Got it?" I nod. I don't even know what to say. I can't face him. And he'll see me pregnant. Oh, the thought makes my stomach turn. Maybe this was his intention the whole time. Maybe he doesn't expect to even get any sort of custody of the baby. Maybe he just wants to see me. I squirm, again.

"Well, if I have to, I have to. Do we need to discuss anything else today?" He shakes his head no.

171

"No, your mother has paid my retainer and I will meet you at the hearing. Be there a little early so we can go in together, okay?"

"Sure." I extend my hand to him and he shakes first mine and then my mothers. Lingering a bit longer than I like on her handshake.

My mother and I don't speak the entire way home. I think she is doing the same as I'm and running each and every scenario in her head. Maybe nothing will happen or maybe he'll have the right to see my son. I can't even believe this. There are no words. My head is spinning. No, no, a man who rapes and tortures a woman and just so happens to knock her up is not a fucking father. Anyone in their right mind will see that. I don't need to worry. I need to focus on Evan and only Evan. So, what if I have to see Sam, right? I can just walk in with my head down and don't look at his ugly, satanic face. Oh, shit now all I can picture is his face.

Stop tormenting me! How does he continue to have control over me? "I'm totally fucked up!" There I finally say it out loud. "He has totally fucked me up. I need to get control of my life and I just don't know how to do it!"

"Nettie, I don't know how I can help. You are doing amazing in spite of what has happened. You will be okay. Someday you will look back on this and see it as just another one of life's struggles that you got through. And believe me, honey you will get through it!" My mom always knows how to make me feel better. I swear she could write one of those soup for the soul books. Ok, I guess we're in for a bit of a fight. And I will make sure I am more than ready.

*

Finally, the day of my house closing arrives, and I'm handed my keys. My keys! My family and friends have agreed to come over this evening and help me clean before the official move-in. We are surely at a disadvantage moving in the winter it flat out sucks. Although I have to admit it's kind of funny. Everyone is cleaning in their winter coats. I decide to find my camera to take some photos. Where did I put it? After looking in every box that we brought over I find it in a box marked, "Kitchen". Yeah, of course, why wouldn't I think of that? I roll my eyes.

I decide to start with my mom, she is an easy target. I sneak into the bathroom and she is scrunched over the toilet scrubbing the floor around it. She is wearing her red bomber jacket and looks hysterical. Click, click, click. She looks up and glares at me. "If you take one more unflattering picture of your mother, I will break that thing." I tiptoe gently backward out of the room.

When I make my way into the kitchen, I see my dad and Jess. Dad is cleaning the refrigerator with a long wool trench coat on and black leather gloves. Again click, click, click. I startle him so much so, that he bumps his head on the top of the freezer. "Oh shit, Dad sorry!" Jess and I both look at each other and burst out with laughter.

We work our butts off until about 11 pm and when we arrive home, we are all so exhausted. I'm thankful for all the help from everyone. Christmas is in a few days and our house looks beautiful. My mother always loves to decorate. There are pine and white lights draped up the banister and ceramic snowmen on the mantle. I love Christmas time in my mom's house. The smell of pine and cranberry fill the air.

We all go to our respective beds and turn in for the night. I'm out in an instant, but all too soon I'm awakened by yet another nightmare. This time I'm walking hand in hand with my son in, I don't know, it looks like a park. I look up and see him, Sam, his eyes are glowing red and he is scowling at us. As if in slow motion I reach down and scoop up Evan. Before I know it Sam is running at an accelerated speed and rips the baby from my arms. I'm trying to chase them, but I cannot move. My attempts to scream are fruitless and I wake. I have a huge lump in my throat and my cheeks are damp. I hug my belly and try to calm myself. "Oh, baby when will this stop?"

I lie back and look at the bedside clock, 2:15 a.m. I close my eyes and drift into sleep yet again. Thankfully this time it's dreamless.

Moving day goes incredibly smooth and my house looks like a home. I can't wait to stay here. After Christmas I will officially stay by myself. My parents have been so generous in their gifts to me. They have done far too much. They bought me some furniture for the new place including a crib and a few things for the baby. Those things will be delivered this week.

*

Christmas and New Year's fly by, and before I know it I'm at my 32 week check-up with Dr.Graham. When I enter the institution like room this time, I'm comforted. The white walls and floors now make me smile. My how things have changed since my first visit here. It's turned into a happy place for me. I'm draped in my paper skirt sitting on the edge of the bed buried in my thoughts when Dr. Graham makes her normal entrance. We go through the routine but this time she informs me that I'm 1cm dilated. Suddenly, worry comes over me.

"It's fine. You could be only 1cm dilated for two months. Everything looks perfect. He is measuring right on schedule and his heartbeat is normal. So just relax and enjoy the rest of your pregnancy." I can't control my very loud sigh. I can't believe I only have eight weeks. Unfortunately, in just four days this week will be tainted, when I have to go to that fucking hearing. I shake the thought from my head. Today is the good day of this week. I thank Dr.Graham, and she reminds me I will be back in two weeks this time instead of a month.

"Great, I will see you in two weeks then." I cannot control my excitement.

When I get into the car, I call everyone and let them know how my appointment went and I'm headed back to work. I have settled into my new place and so far, I'm adjusting just fine to being alone. Of course, the nightmares are there, but I feel like I'm used to them. They are nothing compared to the nightmare I will have to endure seeing that asshole on Friday.

My lawyer has assured me, yet again that he can read my written statement and I don't even need to look at Sam. I hope not. I will do my best to avoid him. I'm just upset he will see me pregnant, with his child. I shiver at the thought of his eyes on me. His eyes on Evan. I will have to mentally prepare for all of that. I can do this. I'm strong. I will show him he has no impact on my life anymore. He will not have control over me in that courtroom. I will never give him that satisfaction.

Chapter 16

This Means War

I wake early on D day. Our preliminary custody hearing. I cannot sleep. I still have a few hours before we need to leave. I get into the shower and soak under the hot spray. I'm trying to wash away the day that hasn't even happened yet. I have to see him for the first time since his brutal attacks. Tears begin to mix with the warm water and spread down my cheeks. How on earth am I going to be in the same room with him again? I want to kill him. All I can hope is that things go quickly, and I can avoid his gaze. I'm afraid of what I might do or how I may act in his presence.

I let the water rush over me for a while longer, as I gently massage my tummy, having a special moment with Evan. I softly pray. "Dear Lord, protect us today. We need you now more than ever." I know he is always with me deep down, but it isn't hard to doubt him given the last year of my life. I need to be strong now.

At 9 o'clock my parents arrive to drive me to court. I'm wearing a gray sweater dress with black tights and black casual boots. My belly looks bigger than ever and I don a long coat to hide my pregnancy as best I can. I don't want him to see my stomach. My mother and father are both dressed to the nines. They look very professional and in control. We all pile in the escalade and are on our way. It's deafening in the car. No one says a word the entire way. And I know they are just as angry and terrified as I am.

After we arrive and are greeted by Mr. Lewis, he escorts us into the courtroom. We are the only ones there so far, aside from the bailiff at the front of the courtroom. There is also a stenographer or whatever they are called, sitting to the left of where the judge will reside. I follow my lawyer to the front of the courtroom where there are two tables opposite one another. It looks similar to a TV courtroom, just much smaller. We sit on the right side facing the judge's bench and my parents sit directly behind me. Mr. Lewis gives me a brief synopsis of how the day *should* play out.

"He will be escorted in with his lawyer…" I immediately tense. "He will be handcuffed and a uniformed police officer beside him at all times." He reassures me sensing my fear. "You don't even need to look at him if you don't want to. Okay?" I nod. I can't speak my stomach is in my throat. I feel a little dizzy. He continues. "The judge will come in and we will rise. When we sit back down, she will

179

explain why we are here and ask for both parties' statements. I will contest custody based on the paternity testing that we discussed and then we will go from there okay? This should at least postpone things until after the baby is born."

"Alright, I just want to get this over with." I sound like a child now. God, I feel like I have regressed back to the beginning right after this all happened. I hate not being in control.

"Okay Nettie, just be strong," he surprises me by hugging me tightly. How nice of him. He seems truly emotionally invested. I quickly think again that maybe it's because he has feelings for my mom. He does have very kind eyes. "Showtime!" he says startling me.

Before I can even stop myself, my eyes are blazing at the heavy wooden door as it opens. First enters a skeevy looking lawyer, with slicked-back hair and pinstriped suit. Just then it happens, I see him. His hair is a little disheveled and his hands cuffed together in front of him. As I make my way to his eyes, I notice his cheeks flushed crimson. When I get to the window of his soulless shell, they are not red like they are in my dreams, but they are dark, striking, terrifying. I'm back in my bedroom for a moment with his eyes just inches from mine. I can feel his breath in my face and smell the booze and cigarettes. He is staring right at me. I'm frozen, locked in his gaze.

I'm petrified. His eyes never leave mine and it's as if in slow motion he moves across the room to his place at the table. I see the corner of his lips curl up into a smirk. What a sick son of a bitch. He looks happy. Happy for Christ's sake. I can feel the tears well up and I do my best to force them back down. I cannot stop myself from looking at him. He breaks eye contact for just a moment, and I see he is looking at my stomach. I place my hands over it in protection. Once again, his eyes meet mine and he winks. WINKS! Like he is flirting with me! He mouths something too, but my eyes are still locked on his and I don't make it out.

My vision begins to blur, and I feel as if I'm going to pass out. Just then my mother physically grabs my face and turns it toward hers, bringing me out of his spell. "Nettie, don't look at him! Don't give him the satisfaction, do you understand me?!" I nod trying to catch my breath. Thank God she brought me back to earth.

We sit for what seems like forever and I keep my head down looking at the table in front of me. I can feel his eyes burning into me. I hear him whisper from time to time and shutter as his voice pierces the deepest part of my soul. I feel the baby moving and I wish I could get him out of here. I don't want him this close to that evil, that monster, his father.

"All rise!" The bailiff seems to shout breaking the tension in the room. We all do as we are told, and I continue to keep my eyes focused in front of me. I feel as though I'm in some sort of daze. All I hear is the muffling of voices. His lawyer, my lawyer and before long the smack of the gavel and I look up at Mr. Lewis.

"What just happened?" I ask. I hadn't heard a word. I try to gauge his expression, but he gives nothing away.
"You didn't pay any attention? It's fine, like I said no ruling on the visitation. After the baby is born a DNA test will be issued and then another court date will be set from there. Don't worry. You are rid of him for at least another few months. The judge we got is good too. She seems disgusted with him. Things are looking great." He smiles. Oh, thank God!

Just then I look up at Sam again. WHY? Why the hell did I do that? He is walking out of the room, but his head is cocked back looking at me. I don't think he has taken his eyes off of me the entire time. Then he mouths something again, but this time I catch what he says. "See you soon."

"FUCK YOU!" I shout at the top of my lungs. My mom grabs my arm to keep me from lunging toward him.

He smirks again and says aloud this time, "Been there, done that," and he seductively nips at his lower lip. Then turns out the door. My blood is boiling. I'm seeing double. I want to burst through that door and rip him apart limb from limb! Suddenly my knees fall weak and I'm on the floor. I cannot catch my breath I'm sobbing and gasping for air. My mother and father are at my side, trying to comfort me. I hear a whaling sound like an animal wounded, and I realize the sound is coming from me.

Finally, after what seems like forever, I come back to reality. I'm still slumped on the floor and my father scoops me into his arms without a word. I lay my head against his chest and feel his heart beating. A rapid angry pace. I briefly wonder how he could possibly carry me and my extra weight, but he manages. When he places me in the car my mother crawls in the back beside me and I place my head in her lap. She gently strokes my hair again and again in a comforting

183

rhythm. Tears again begin to roll down my face and I don't bother to wipe them away. It won't keep them from coming.

We arrive at my parents and I don't question why. I'm in no condition to be alone right now. My father opens my door and reaches his hand out to help me into the house. We walk in silence and he walks me to the couch. I lie down as my mother places a blanket over my legs. I notice my coat is still on, but I don't care. I'm shivering. Daddy lights the fire and they both sit close to me on the couch. We sit in silence.

I must have fallen asleep because the next thing I know, I open my eyes and my parents are nowhere to be seen and I scream for them in fear. "Mom...Dad!" they both come running in.

"Yes dear we are here, right here," my mom is at my side. "Are you okay? We were just in the kitchen. I want you to stay here tonight. I'll make us a nice dinner and if you want you can invite Jess over." I shake my head. Oh, shit I didn't call Jess she is gonna kill me.

"I need to call her and tell her what happened. She must be furious!" I jump to my feet to make the call.

My mom interrupts. "No, she called here looking for you and we explained everything. She was going to call your other friends and let them know too. She said to call her when you were up to it. I really

want you to stay tonight honey. It's been a stressful day."

"No, actually Mom I want to stay at my place." She looks

upset. Her eyebrows furrowed. "I'll see if Jess will stay with me there.

Okay? I just feel comfortable in that house. Nothing against you or

Dad."

"Alright but I want you here if Jessie can't stay. Deal?"

"Deal," I mirror.

I'm back at my house and Jessica is going to stay with me

tonight. She has brought over a few of our favorite movies and some

snacks. I told her that I'm not in the mood to eat but she doesn't

listen. She also brings a bottle of red wine for herself and I do indulge

in one very small glass. I'm sure it's fine. I need it after today. Maybe it

will help me to sleep. After hours of talking, and Jess trying to distract

me with wedding planning, the day seems to catch up to me.

I blink my eyes and it's pitch black. I'm on the couch and look

down on the floor and Jess is next to me, fast asleep. Wow, I guess the

wine did the trick. I don't even know how long I've been asleep. I

gently step over Jess and make my way down the hall to use the

restroom. When I finish, I decide to continue sleeping on the couch. I need someone close to me right now. Plus, I don't want her waking up with me gone.

I try to sleep but no luck. I lie there until the sun comes up. I think of him and his eyes the whole time. I think of the wink. I think of his words. *See you soon. Been there done that.* I squeeze my eyes shut tightly in hopes it goes away, but it doesn't. Forget it I need to get up. Again, I carefully tiptoe over Jess and waddle into the kitchen. My feet are freezing. I make a cup of tea for myself and touch brew on the coffee pot for Jessica. As quietly as I can I sit at the kitchen island looking out at the snow-covered yard. Soon after, I hear a faint groan and before I know it Jess is sitting next to me. "Sorry, I tried to be quiet," I whisper.

"No, you weren't loud. I smelled the coffee. It's awfully early. How long have you been up?" she asks rubbing her eyes.

"I don't know. I woke up in the middle of the night sometime and couldn't fall back to sleep." She nods in understanding and pats my back as she rises to get herself a cup of coffee. We sit for a while and make small talk. But when we run out of topics, tears spring to my eyes thinking of the day before. She immediately pulls me into her arms. I can feel her chest heaving as well, as she cries right along with me. I'm so glad she stayed the night. I couldn't bear to wake up here alone. Not after yesterday. Finally, we peel ourselves away from one another and she wipes her eyes.

"You will never be alone Nettie. Do you know that? She places her hand on my belly. I will help with Evan as much as you need, and I will stay with you as many nights as you want. You mean the world to me and now so does he."

"Thank you, Jess, I know you will be here. You always are."

She changes the subject. "You are due in, what? Seven or eight weeks? Let's get that baby's room ready. What do you say?" A smile spreads over my face.

"Perfect idea. Let's focus on the good things."

Chapter 17

Rock A Bye Baby

I have already decided to decorate Evans room in an underwater ocean theme. The baby bedding and paint are here, and the furniture should be delivered today. We start by, of course, putting on some working music so we can dance and sing at the same time. Jess and I make a great team. I tape off the baseboards as she follows doing the edging. We haven't stopped dancing the entire time, although I'm very out of breath. I have picked a beautiful pale blue for the walls and a light green to accent. By the time I'm done taping, I start rolling and before we know it, we are done. We high five one another in victory, before deciding to get some lunch.

We order pizza and sit on the baby's floor and eat. It looks beautiful already. I can't wait until it's finished. We get one more coat of paint on before the delivery men are here with all the nursery furniture. They put it together and place it in the middle of the room, as not to disrupt the freshly painted walls. My parents have graciously bought me an elegant crib with a dark wood finish, a matching 6 drawer tall dresser and a changing table to boot. Jess and I open the baby bedding that is donned with every sea creature you can imagine; there are sea turtles, tropical fish, seashells and an octopus. I throw the linens into the washing machine down the hall. I give a quick sniff of the baby laundry soap before putting the cap back on. Mmmmm, I love that smell.

Once the paint has dried, we carefully move the furniture to its intended place. Of course, I change my mind about five times and finally she says. "Tough! It stays here I'm sick of moving it!"

"Okay, okay, it can stay there." It looks perfect. It feels perfect. I begin hanging photos of underwater scenes that I have had framed. I place those on the wall over the changing table and a few more over the dresser. I decide not to hang anything over the crib. I wouldn't want anything falling on the baby. A pang of anxiety suddenly shoots through me. I'm going to be a mom. I'm going to be responsible for another human life. The thought is unnerving. Can I handle this? I guess I have no choice now. As I look around his beautiful room, I hear the laundry buzz. Jess goes to retrieve the bed linens and I get out the stuffed animals that my parents also bought for the baby. I'm one lucky girl and I know it. I look around the room and I smile at Jess with pride. It's perfect. From the walls to the pictures to the stuffed animals all the way down to the little mobile with starfish and seashells hanging from it.

"Good job!" I hold up my hand and get a high five in return.

"Yeah, we're awesome," Jess smirks. "And to think we did this all in one day. Do you feel a little better now?"

"I do. It was a good day. Thanks for helping me. Thanks for distracting me. I can't wait to have him here." I really mean that. I am so ready to meet my son. I look at the empty crib and start the count down. Less than two months until my due date.

My mom and dad stop over later that night to see the nursery and they bring take out. Chinese, yum. They are amazed at how fast we put things together and I'm damn proud myself.

"It looks so perfect, Nettie. I think you girls may have missed your calling!" she giggles.

She hands me a huge bag and when I open it, I give her a cockeyed look. "Mom more stuff! You and Daddy have gotten too much already!"

She shakes her head. "Oh, no. those are from some of my friends and coworkers, they just wanted to get you a few things honey that's all."

"Oh, well that was nice of them." As I begin to unpack the bag, I find diapers, wipes, clothes, and burp cloths. Wow, really nice! My mother helps me put things away and as I look around, I can't think of anything else that I'm going to need. I'm planning on breastfeeding, so I don't need formula or bottles. Though I suppose I should get a few just in case. I'll worry about that later. I still have time.

My parents and I have a very nice dinner together and no one mentions the court fiasco from yesterday. We relish in the fact that there will soon be a little addition to our family and that it will certainly be the light in such a dark year. They stay until about ten o'clock and then excuse themselves. They both need to go to work tomorrow and I may do some exploring and photographing myself, just to keep busy.

I decide I'm not quite ready to settle into bed. Instead, I get my camera and go into Evans room. I snap a few photos of the nursery and I catch a glimpse of myself in the mirror on the back of the bathroom door. I realize I don't have any pictures of myself pregnant. Not one. I turn and begin to take a few of myself in the mirror. My hair is still damp from my earlier shower and I'm wearing a

191

pair of snug-fitting gray yoga pants with a pink short sleeve V-neck t-shirt. I lift my shirt over my belly briefly to get a full belly shot. My belly button is almost completely disappeared at this point. I giggle to myself. I look cute but oh so funny. I look down and see the baby pushing to one side, so my stomach is lopsided. I get a few photos of that from my view as well. "Something special for your baby book my little one. I love you, my whole heart."

I make my way to the kitchen placing my camera gently on the counter. I'll have to get those printed sooner than later. I make myself a cup of green tea and nestle up on the couch. The room illuminated only by the lamp next to me. I decide to read from one of my baby books for a bit before bed. I imagine what Evan might look like. I see beautiful golden hazel eyes. I hope he has my eyes.

*

Two weeks later, I'm again at the doctor's office for my appointment. Nothing new this time. She doesn't check to see if I'm dilated because I haven't had any contractions. We make another appointment for two weeks and I'm off again. My mother and I meet at our restaurant, Mona's. We haven't been here since before I found out I was pregnant. Jen is there, as usual, and I'm bombarded with questions. She cannot take her hand off my belly. Geez, I think. I know her and all, but how about some personal space. This is still my body you are touching, lady. The baby isn't out yet.

"Oh, honey you look fantastic. You are glowing," she squeals with delight. "And it's a bouncing baby boy I heard!" Of course, you heard everyone in this town knows my business. I smile trying to be enthusiastic, but the normally lovely Jen is on my last nerve already. My mother and I sit and have a nice long lunch together and talk about everything from baby to work and back to baby again. She reminds me I should make a list of things to pack for the hospital. I'm after all getting to the gray area when I could go into labor soon. I will do that tonight. It will give me something to do. Jess has been busy making some wedding plans. They've decided to get married in August of this year, which gives me enough time to lose my baby weight, I hope.

I snap back from my daydreaming and my mom and I are soon on our way. We drove separate since I was at the doctor's already. When I arrive back home, I decide I should pack my bag now, before I forget. I dig out a cute little duffel bag from my closet. It's black with small pink flowers all over it. After packing myself the necessities such as comfy clothes, bras, underwear, and toiletries. I then head into the baby's room and get out my new diaper bag.

This I bought myself. It's adorable, a little expensive, but I couldn't resist. It matches the blue and green of his room and I had his name embroidered on it as well. I grab the outfit that I have decided to bring him home in and place it in first. I throw in a few diapers, wipes and burp rags. I know the hospital will have all this stuff, but I would rather be overly prepared. I put both of our bags into the hallway closet for easy reach. If my parents are the ones who will have to find them. I want it to be in an easy place.

I plop down on the couch and look around my home. "I need to clean too before you come." I say aloud. This place is a mess. As I sit there trying to relax, I can't stand it anymore and I begin to clean. The floors are steamed, the kitchen disinfected, and the entire house dusted. I open the fridge to reward myself with a root beer. "Ew. Yuck." I start cleaning the fridge out too. God, I'm like a cleaning maniac, and I hate to clean. Ok, now I'm totally exhausted.

I call and check in with Jess and we have a good long talk. When we hang up, I decide to give my mom a call before I turn in.

"Hey, mom, what's up?" I say excitedly.

"You sound good dear. Nothing is 'up' here. What are you doing?" I can hear the grin in her voice.

"Not much. I cleaned today and got our hospital bags packed up. I'm getting tired now but at least I got a lot accomplished today." I hear her hum

"Oh, so you had a burst of energy, did you?" What does she mean by that?

"Yeah, I guess so. Why?" I'm totally boggled by her sometimes.

"They say that when you nest the baby is coming soon." Nest? Huh?

"What do you mean, nest? And of course, the baby is coming soon we know that." Always believing all the old wives' tales, my mom.

"Nesting is just when you have the urge to get everything ready for baby and yes, I know you are due soon, but it means like soon, soon." That's a bunch of crap but I don't say that to her. I don't want to hurt her feelings.

"Okay, mom. That sounds interesting." She doesn't believe me. I don't believe me. "Anyway, I'm going to head to bed I'll talk to you in the morning. Love ya!"

"I love you too honey." And we hang up.

I decide on a bath tonight to relax. My body is sore and tired from all the work today. I decide on a lavender bubble bath and sink into it slowly. The smells and the feeling of the soft water on my body feels amazing. I stroke my belly which is almost entirely out of the water. Evan begins kicking and wiggling like crazy. I start laughing out loud. I place the shampoo bottle gently on my belly and it begins tipping and bouncing all over the place. I'm laughing so hard now that tears are falling from my eyes. Oh man, I'm going to miss being pregnant, but I can't wait to see this little guy. He is entertaining already!

I soak for a few more minutes and then get out and towel dry. A wrap my terrycloth robe around my more than swelled tummy and head to bed. I'm too tired to even get PJs on, so I just climb under my down comforter and snuggle in.

When I wake the next morning, I stretch out and look through the window. By the way the light is coming in I must have gotten a good night's sleep. I swing my legs to the end of the bed and as gracefully as I can, push myself up onto my feet. When I do, I feel warm liquid trickle down my legs. Oh shit, I just pissed myself. I waddle my way gently to the bathroom with my robe tucked between my thighs. When I reach the bathroom, it happens again. That is when I realize that my water just broke.

I immediately grab my purse and fish out Dr. Graham's phone number. I leave a brief message and then call my mother. I try not to panic but I can't help the shakiness in my voice. As soon as the answers I cut her off.

"Mom my water broke can you come over?"

She hesitates. "Are you sure honey? I mean when I was pregnant with you, I would cough and leak a little if you know what I mean. I'm sure your water didn't break, it's too early." She sounds so light and confident.

"Well, I get a little trickle every few minutes or so mom. Is that pee or is that my water breaking, because I think it's the latter!" I'm just plain rude right now.

"Sorry, of course, I will be right there. Did you call the doctor?" what a dumb question.

"Yes, I called the doctor, just get over her now I'm freaking out!" I hang up on her. Okay, well so far, I'm having no contractions. Then I guess it's possible it's not labor right? No, who am I kidding I'm leaking like a broken faucet. Oh, shit! I'm pacing now. Well, I guess I could get dressed. I throw on a comfortable skirt and sweater and put a towel between my legs.

God, this is ridiculous. I can't put pants on I'll be soaking wet by the time we get to the hospital. Oh, shit this is not happening, it's too early, right? Shit, shit, shit! Ok, now I'm beginning to panic. This can't be good for the baby. Breathe Nettie just breathe. "We have come this far my little man, we will get through it, right?" Right. It will be fine. "Everything is going to be perfect," I reassure myself.

My mom comes crashing through the door with my father in tow. Geez, that was fast. They both rush to my side. Dad speaks first.

"Are you okay? Any contractions yet?" I shake my head no. "Did the doctor call you back yet?" Again, I shake my head no.

We all pile in the car and about halfway to the hospital the good Dr. Graham finally calls me back.

"Hi Nettie dear, how are you?" she sounds so calm and collected.

"Not good!" I shout at her. What do you think lady? I dislike her again at this moment.

"Honey, don't get all worked up. I want you to calm down. I told the hospital you were on your way and if your water did in fact break, I will meet you soon okay?" What does she mean? IF. Why doesn't anyone believe me? I'm not continuously pissing myself for Christ's sake! "Nettie can you hear me?"

"Yeah!" I snap at her too.

"Alright. Don't panic. If it's time for baby to come, we will deal with that okay?" I hang up on her. I don't want to listen to the comforting, talk to me like I'm a damn child act right now.

When we arrive at the hospital emergency room there is a nurse waiting at the doors with a wheelchair for me. "I can walk," I say to her.

"Sorry, but it's protocol honey." I plop down into the chair in a pout. I'm taken up to labor and delivery where they do the exact same thing they did to me last time I was here. I'm hooked up to monitors but no IV yet. The nurse checks the fluid I'm leaking with a little dipstick and does, in fact, confirm that it's not pee. See, I'm not an idiot people! I am having contractions but so small that I cannot even feel them. The nurse calls Dr. Graham and informs her of my situation. When she reenters the room, she lets me know she is going to check and see if I'm dilated. Before she does my dad exits the room without being told. Of course, he doesn't want to see me like that.

The nurse grins at me and says, "Let's get you comfortable honey, you're going to have a baby today. 4cm already." Oh-my-god! I'm not ready for this. The baby is not ready for this. It's too soon. Is he going to be okay?

My mother looks at me and smiles the most artificial smile I have ever seen. She is as terrified as I am. My dad returns just a few moments later and we tell him. He doesn't even try to hide his concern. He puts his head in his hands and sighs.

"It will be okay you guys. We've come this far. Everything will be fine." Am I trying to convince myself or them now?

It seems like no time at all before Dr. Graham gets there. The nurses have put in my IV and are giving me fluids so that I can have an epidural. I'm looking forward to it as the contractions have started to get painful. Not unbearable by any means, but just uncomfortable. Dr. Graham informs me that I will be given something called

Surfactant which apparently will help the baby's lungs if they are not fully developed.

"This is my biggest concern with the baby being as early as he is, but I don't want you to freak out Nettie. I have delivered plenty of babies at this stage that have been one hundred percent healthy.

"Any that haven't been?" she looks at the floor before she answers.

"Yes. Some that haven't been as well." Yeah, I thought so. She shouldn't be so confident.

It's another hour before the anesthesiologist comes to give me my epidural and by that time, I'm very much feeling the pain. My mother and father are told to leave the room for this, and I don't question why. I'm sitting on the edge of the bed with my gown wide open in the back. The nurse hands me a pillow to hold onto, which I try and refuse but she persists. I'm hugging a pillow and my head is resting on the nurse's shoulder. I can smell her perfume. Something fruity with a hint of vanilla. It smells heavenly, it's a nice distraction from the horribly uncomfortable pain of the needle being put into my spine. It's over before I know it and I am resting comfortably back on the bed. Wow, this stuff is good!

My parents come back in and take their place at my bedside. "How are you feeling baby?" my dad asks.

"Good actually. I don't feel a thing. This is amazing!" I'm nice and relaxed now and begin to realize how tired I am.

"Good." He says with relief. The nurse enters again to check my progress. I'm now 8cm dilated. Wow, this is going fast. It has been only 4 hours since I woke this morning. She tells me I should try and sleep while I'm comfortable so that I will have plenty of energy when it's time to push. I agree.

My mother closes the curtains and kisses me gently on the cheek. I roll slightly on my side but with all these wires and belts I don't want to move too much. Like the first time I was here the thump, thump, thump helps me to fall into a daze, not so much sleep but at least I rest for a brief time before suddenly feeling a tremendous amount of pressure in my pelvis. I grab the call button and buzz the nurse. "Yes dear," her voice echoes through the intercom.

"Um, yeah I think I need to push. I mean I don't know. I just feel something strange." The nurse comes in followed by my mother and father. She checks me before my dad has a chance to leave. At this point I don't give a shit who sees what. I feel a rush of adrenaline.

"Yep, ten centimeters and you are one-hundred percent effaced. It's time to meet your baby. I'll page the doctor." My dad gives me a kiss on the forehead and wishes me luck before exiting the room. My mother is at my side and she is holding my hand. I begin pushing holding my breath for ten seconds and I relax. The nurse alerts me when the next contraction is coming, and we begin the process again and again. I'm getting exhausted.

Dr. Graham is here, and she looks at the clock. "An hour and a half of pushing, Nettie we are going to have to do better than that. You aren't making much progress." Screw you, lady, I'm doing the best that I can! She messes with something on my IV and soon my contractions intensify. What the hell did she do?

"I turned down your epidural so you can feel the pressure. It will help move things along, trust me. I need you to push with all your might, okay?" She sounds like one of my high school coaches. A little too peppy for my taste. I do as I'm instructed though and really feel it this time. "Good, good!" she shouts. "That a girl. Now we're talking." She begins getting her gloves and gown on and pulls a stool up, so she is directly in front of my crotch. This is so weird. It's time to push all too soon and I'm so tired, but I do my best. "Yes, Nettie come on!"

"I can see his head Nettie!" My mom shouts now. This gives me the motivation I need, and I push again with every ounce of strength that I have.

"Okay stop, stop!" Dr. Graham instructs me, and I do as I'm told. Oh God hurry, this is a horrible feeling. Then once again she shouts for me to push and I do. I feel a sudden ripping pain and then pure relief. As I look down, the last several hours just disappear. I see a tiny little man with a heck of a lot of hair and I exhale letting my head plop back on the bed. They take him away far too quickly and I'm giggling.

Then I look up at my mother and she is silent. In fact, now I notice the silence. He hasn't cried yet. Dr. Graham is still between my legs taking care of me and there are people in the corner attending to Evan. I can't see him I only see the backs of three or four people scurrying about. I feel like an eternity passes and I realize I'm holding my breath. I look up at my mom and she is crying. She squeezes my hand tightly and I close my eyes. Please God. Please God. Please God. I repeat this mantra for what seems like forever and then there it is, a wail of a cry! A glorious scream over, and over again. It is the most wonderful sound I have ever heard. Finally, my son is here, and he is crying. I'm sobbing with joy. I look at Dr. Graham through my clouded vision and she is smiling from ear to ear. She has tears in her eyes as well. She nods at me. When the nurses are finished checking him over, they wrap him up tightly and bring him to me.

I'm overwhelmed as I look into the eyes of my beautiful baby boy. He is perfect. He is still crying but now it sounds more like a cat purring or something. I giggle. "Well hello, my little man. You *are* quite the warrior, aren't you?" As I speak, he quiets immediately, and his eyes widen. He recognizes my voice. I stare into those big beautiful gray eyes I kiss him gently on the forehead and hold my lips there for a moment. He feels warm and soft against my lips. I nuzzle his nose with mine and he blinks. He is the most perfect sight I have ever seen.

"You are my greatest accomplishment, Evan. I will protect you with everything that I have. I love you, my whole heart." And I know according to the baby books he can't smile yet, but I swear he does.

Chapter 18

Just the Two of Us

I'm staring at the most perfect man I have ever met. For the first time in a long time, I'm happy, blissfully happy. I have never felt like this before. It's amazing. I look up at my mother and she is in awe of him as well.

"May I hold him?" I think this is what she says. It's hard to tell through her sobs.

"Of course, Grandma." I gently pass him to her, and she takes him with care into her arms. He looks like a little porcelain doll in her embrace. "He is magnificent, isn't he?" she nods but doesn't speak. Her chin is quivering still. She doesn't hold him long before passing him back to me.

"I need to go get your dad! He is probably freaking out." She rushes out of the room and it's just me and my little man for a few precious moments. I gently stroke his forehead and his eyelids gently fall closed. I put my face against his and smell his sweet baby smell. I can feel his breath rhythmically in and out. He fits perfectly into my arms. As if he is where he was meant to be. At this moment I don't doubt that this is God's plan for me. I was meant to be his mother and he was meant to be my son. I'm truly blessed.

There is a soft knock at the door and my father pokes his head in. He smiles and tiptoes over to us. I don't think I have stopped smiling. Daddy places his hand on the baby's head and lets out a sigh.

"Wow, he is perfect. Just handsome." Just like you Dad.

"Here, you can hold him. He just fell asleep. You should see his eyes. He has my eyes," thank God.

"He looks like you when you were born." He holds Evan in his arms and gently kisses him on the tip of his nose. He lifts the cap gently from his head just enough to see the mess of dark hair on his head. He looks at me wide-eyed and mouths. "Wow." He is in love too. How can you not be with such a perfect little innocent being? "I can't believe I'm a grandfather. I must be getting old, huh kid?" He says to the baby. Well, the circumstances are not what any of us had planned. I hoped to have a hell of a career going right about now and fall in love and then have babies. But it's okay. God had a different plan for me.

"Do you want to stay awhile? I wouldn't mind closing my eyes for just a bit. I'm so tired." I can hardly keep my eyes open. Who knew this whole process could be so exhausting?

"Sure honey. We'll just sit right here next to the bed and rest too. How about that little guy? Sound good to you?" I guess now I'm chopped liver since the cute baby has arrived. I grin and close my eyes.

I wake to the baby crying and my eyes fly open. My mom is now holding Evan and she is rocking him and shushing trying to calm him. She looks over and sees that I'm awake.

"Sorry Nettie, I wanted to try and let you sleep but I think the poor guy is hungry. The nurses gave him a quick bath and just brought him back." I smile and reach my arms out to take him. Here goes nothing. I have read all the baby books on breastfeeding but I'm a little nervous about the whole thing. I get comfortable and I'm surprised when he latches on immediately. Phew.

"This isn't so bad," I say to my mother. "It's kind of comforting actually." My mother lets out a soft giggle. "What?"

"Wait a couple of days until your nipples are raw and he chomps right on one!" Ew, Mom way to ruin a bonding moment. "I'm just saying it gets uncomfortable for a bit and then you get used

208

to it." She pauses and gathers her purse. "Daddy is in the cafeteria. I'm going to go get a bite to eat with him okay? We'll be back soon. Can I get you anything before I go? How are you feeling?"

"Okay, I'm sore and still tired but fine."

"Good, then we'll see you in a bit." She kisses me on the forehead and then Evan. She completely ignores the fact that he is nursing right now. I lean my head back and begin to hum to him. I'm soaking in every moment with my little warrior. I can't wait until we can get home.

Just then the bedside phone rings. Holy shit! The baby and I both jump and he begins to cry. I hold him up at my shoulder and begin patting his back to soothe him. With my other hand, I reach around and grab the phone.

"Hello?" I can barely hear anything because Evan is still whining in my other ear. He is nuzzling my neck looking for food. "Hello? You'll have to speak up the baby is crying."

"He sounds perfect," he hisses. It's him, it's Sam. How in the fuck is he able to call me? And how did he know I had the baby already?

"Leave us alone!" I slam the receiver down startling the baby again. "Oh, Mommy is sorry baby, don't cry." I kiss his head and pat his back gently again and he begins to calm. I try and feed him again from the other side this time, but he doesn't seem interested. I settle on cuddling him instead. Just then the phone rings for a second time. I snatch it up quick and scream "Leave me the fuck alone asshole!!"

"Whoa, you got your panties in a twist or what?" Oh, thank goodness, it's Jess.

"Sorry, Jessie he just…Sam just called here." When I say it out loud, I get a chill that flows all the way up my spine to the base of my neck.

"Oh, shit. How did he even know you had the baby already? And how in the world does the prison not know he is calling his victim? You need to talk to your lawyer about that. They need to put a stop to that. As if the letters weren't bad enough." She's right. The letters I could just throw away, but is he going to start calling me now? Sick fuck!

"Yeah you're right, I will get it taken care of." I trail off. "Sooooo are you coming by to see your nephew or what?" I change the subject hoping she follows suit.

"Yes, I'm on my way I just wanted to make sure you were feeling up to a visitor."

"Always for you Aunt Jessie!" I can hear the smile in her voice when she answers.

"I'll be there in ten minutes! I can't wait!"
After about an hour Jess finally graces us with her presence. She looks frazzled.

"Where the hell have you been? You said ten minutes. It's been a flipping hour!" she looks out of breath.

"I know, I know I got a damn flat tire and had to call Colton to come change it for me and then traffic was terrible." She breaks mid-sentence as she notices we are not alone. She gazes at Evan and puts both hands up to her face in awe. She begins the machine gun but this time she is crying not laughing.

"Can I hold him?" I nod and hand him over. He is awake now, but his eyes still look sleepy. She has her nose buried in his neck and inhales deeply. She looks up and me and finally speaks. "I want one." We both giggle. "Wow, he is just so perfect. Aren't you little one? You look like your mama huh? You have her eyes." She turns to me once more. "So how was it? The labor? Awful? Painful? Scary?

Tell me. No, don't tell me. I don't want to be scared." I interrupt her rant.

"It was not the most comfortable experience, to say the least…But, totally worth it." I'm beaming as I say the words. I would do it a thousand times over to have this sweet little boy.

"Well, I'm so proud of you. He is amazing and he really does make me want to have one. All in good time, I guess. I'll bring that up to Colton on our wedding night!" She laughs out loud. I can just hear her telling him right after they say I do. 'Oh, and by the way let's get pregnant' he'll die! I mean it took him how many damn years to propose in the first place? I keep my mouth shut though. I want her to have a baby. How great would it be to have our kids close in age? What if she had a girl and they got married? Awe how sweet would that be?

"What is with the huge grin?"

"Oh, nothing. I was just fantasizing how great it would be if we had kids the same age. We could do sports together and dances and all kinds of fun stuff!" I can feel myself getting excited. I'm such a dork.

"Slow down you're putting the poor kid in high school already and he's only a few hours old!" She is right but I just can't help but think of him when he is a toddler, in his quirky teen years and when he is grown up. I hope I can make him happy. And I hope he always loves me too even when he is a moody teen. I want to raise him to be respectful and kind. I can tell by looking into his eyes that he will be nothing less.

"Yeah, I need to enjoy day by day. He is pretty great, isn't he?"

"Yeah, I would say more than just pretty great." We are both beaming with joy staring at Evan. I could do this for hours.

*

The time in the hospital comes and goes. When we leave Evan weighs in at six pounds. He has only lost a few ounces since his birth. The doctor gives both the baby and me a clean bill of health, which means we get to go home. My mother wanted me to stay with her for a few days so she could help, but I declined her offer. I want to be in our home from the start. She is, however, going to stay tonight in case I need help. I'm still really sore so I will need someone around I suppose. Plus, most women have their significant other to help out once they get home. See, this is why I should get a husband, for help! I laugh in my own head. Nah! I can do it myself.

When we arrive home my kitchen island is filled with flowers and balloons. I look quickly through the cards. They are from Jess and Colton, Matthew, my work friends, and one more. I hesitate to look at the card expecting to be from…. him and as I open it, I'm relieved to see it's from Detective Montgomery. I should call her. That is so sweet of her. We haven't spoken for a while. They must not have heard any more from Sara. Oh, well. Better off I guess, she's gone.

My parents help to get me settled and watch the baby while I shower. We enjoy a nice home-cooked meal that my mother made and after dinner, I'm completely exhausted. It's only eight o'clock but I don't care, I'm going to bed. I sit and feed the baby before handing him off to my mother. We have decided that she will stay up with him until he is ready to eat again and then bring him to me and he can spend the rest of the night in the bassinet in my room. This should at least give me a few hours of uninterrupted sleep. I have never been so tired in my life and I swear I'm asleep before my head hits the bed.

The first night home is a long one. I feel like Evan is up constantly. Who knew I would miss the hospital nurses so much? He squeaks constantly while he sleeps which then makes me think he is awake when he isn't. By the time I finish feeding him, it seems like he is ready to eat again in an hour. My mother reminds me that my milk hasn't come in yet and he will sleep longer then. I hope so. I can't handle this no sleep thing.

*

By about our third or fourth day home we have gotten into our routine. My milk has come in, so he is sleeping better. Instead of taking an hour to feed him we have cut it down to about half that. We are like a well-oiled machine. The last few nights have just been the two of us and I think we're managing well. He is such a good baby. He only cries when he is hungry. When he wakes in the middle of the night he simply eats and gets his diaper changed then is back in his slumber. I am very lucky, I can tell already. We make a fantastic team. I'm dealing well with the lack of sleep I think, for now anyway.

My mother has been making fun of me that I'm going to blind the child taking so many pictures. I can't help it, that is what I do for a living. What does she expect from me? I love putting him in all the different outfits he has and with these cute little man hats that are just too adorable not to take pictures of. I'm going to document every moment of his life. He is so cute.

I can't miss a thing. He has brightened my world more than he will even know. He has brought me back to life and I'm so grateful for him. I feel like my heart could burst I'm so in love. We are one tiny, happy family.

*

Evan is one-week-old today and I can't believe it. My wonderful friends have offered to bring over pizza and beer to give me a little adult time. I told them that's fine as long as they don't stay late. I already sound like a mom. It has been so cold out lately that we haven't gone anywhere except for his one doctor's appointment. He is back to his birth weight already. He will be a little chunk here before I know it, the way he eats.

Everyone should be here soon, so I pick up as best I can and put Evan in his most adorable little blue fuzzy sleeper. I comb his thick dark hair and giggle as I do. "You look like you are wearing a rug, silly boy." I swear he grins at me again. I stroke the sides of his face and kiss his little lips. He purses them together as I do, and I can

216

tell he is sucking on his tongue. He looks handsome. "You are dressed to impress, little man," I say in my most annoying baby voice.

I hear the doorbell ring and I'm suddenly so excited! I can't wait to just sit and relax and talk with some adults, other than my parents. I'm holding Evan and we open the door to cheers. Jessie, Colton, and Matt. They must have all drove together. Jess is the first to snatch Evan out of my arms and cuddle him. She holds him in one arm as she wiggles out of her coat. The rest of us take the pizza and beer out to the kitchen. All of us load up our plates with pizza and the boys grab themselves a drink. We make our way back to sit with Jess.

I look over at Colton and nod my head toward Jessie. "You are seeing this aren't you?" He looks at her and then back to me confused.

"What?"

"Ha, look at her, she has got it and you better watch out?" He still doesn't know what I'm saying. He can be so dense sometimes. "Baby fever Colton, she has baby fever!"

"What? No, you don't. Do you Jess?" He looks at her wide-eyed.

217

"Hell yeah, I do! I would steal this little guy if I could. Save me the trouble of being pregnant and in labor. Just get the cute kid and all." We all laugh but the funny thing is, we all know she means it.

"God, I have missed you guys so much! I feel like I have been speaking baby talk for the last week and not just to Evan, but to my parents too." They giggle at me and it's a sound I have so dearly missed.

"So," Matt begins. "How is motherhood treating you? You look great!" Yuck, I feel disgusting. I barely have time to wash my hair I know I haven't had a stitch of make-up on in the last week at least and my sweats are still my best friend.

"Thanks, Matt, but you are lying through your teeth. I will say my boobs look awesome though." A roar of laughter erupts through the room and soon I'm getting tears I'm laughing so hard.

What a great night. When I'm done eating, I take the baby back from Jess so she can eat. I excuse myself and take him to feed him and put him to bed. He goes down like a little angel and I'm grateful. I kiss his little head and wish him goodnight and sweet dreams. "I love you, my whole heart, baby."

Back out in the living room, the boys are having some deep discussion about football or hockey or something. I don't know, I don't follow that stuff. Jess and I go to the kitchen. I pour us each a glass of Merlot and we sit at the island and talk.

"So, how are you feeling?"

"Pretty great actually. I'm tired all the time of course but I'm used to it." She frowns.

"I mean emotionally, how are you feeling?" Oh, I haven't really had time to think about anything but Evan.

"I don't know, good, I guess. I have just been focused on the baby and haven't really thought much about Sam. I mean I still have nightmares but now he doesn't attack me. I have dreams that he takes the baby. I panic when I wake up from those. I mean, I know it can't happen. I just worry. He is so precious to me. I can't imagine ever letting Sam even see him, let alone touch him." She looks at me with that pity look I hate.

"Someday you will stop thinking about him. Your life will be yours and Evan's and it will be perfect." She is sincere. And I almost believe her.

"I know we are getting there, slowly but surely we'll get there." Suddenly the boys join us in the kitchen with a look like they are offended.

"What? You don't want to hang out with us?" Matt says with his lip out giving his best fake pout.

"Oh sorry, you poor babies need attention too," Jess mocks them.

We all sit in the kitchen for another few hours and when the baby wakes again to eat, they excuse themselves to leave. It's getting late anyway. Well, for me it is. I appreciate them. But they are now wearing out their welcome. Every second of sleep is precious with a newborn.

When they leave, I feed Evan sitting in the glider in my room and he falls immediately back to sleep. I rock him for a while more before putting him in his bassinet. I love staring at him. He is just perfect. There is not another baby on this planet that is this cute. I mean there can't be, right? Sure, every mom says that, but I mean it. He really is the cutest. I kiss his chubby little cheek and smell his lavender baby lotion. That smell is the most special scent. I kiss him once more and slowly lay him down to sleep. I myself snuggle under

my covers and I'm gone too.

Chapter 19

Growing

Evan is four weeks old today already. I cannot believe how fast this past month has gone and we are not even to where my due date was. It's nearing the end of February and it's still snowy and cold, of course, but we have managed to do a little bit outside the house. We have ventured to my parents for visits and spent one day at a baby store spending gift certificates I received after he was born. Even though he has only been here for a month I feel like he has always been a part of my life. He is filling out and developing his own little look now. Already he seems like his eyes are darkening from that baby blue. His mop of hair continues to thicken on his tiny little head.

I'm taking him into my office today so he can meet everyone. I have been pestered like crazy by the girls I work with to see him. Afterward, we have his four-week checkup. I'm anxious to see how much he weighs. I really like his pediatrician so far. He is a younger guy, pretty cute too. I made it a point to fix my hair and put on some makeup today because I knew I was going to see him. I'm such a dork. Like anyone would be interested in dating a woman with a newborn.

What the hell? I'm nowhere near ready to date anyway. I snap myself back out of my irrational daydream.

When we arrive at work, I'm bombarded by every female that works in the building. I take Evan out of his carrier and let them pass him around. He is actually pretty great with letting people hold him. He is not strange about that yet. I mean, I know he prefers his mama to hold him, but I like that he doesn't mind others. He is still awfully young to know any different though. He sleeps more than he is awake. Watching these women ohhh and ahhh over him makes me feel so blessed that he is mine and I get to spend every waking minute with him.

We spend only about an hour there and I need to be on my way. As we walk out the door everyone is stuck in baby talk, waving and smiling at us. I look at my phone and we are running a bit late for our doctor's appointment.

We arrive at the pediatrician's office just in time. I greet the front desk secretary with a smile. She is on the phone, so she points at the clipboard in front of her for us to sign in. I sign, Evan Tate Madison and we have a seat. Evan is fast asleep, but I know he will want to eat soon. Maybe I should duck into the bathroom and feed him really quick? I decide I should and pick his carrier up and just as I'm about to inform the secretary when Evan's name is called. We follow her back to one of the many exam rooms and have a seat.

"Um, how long do you think the doctor will be? The baby is going to want to eat soon and I'm breastfeeding." I give her a look of embarrassment and she tells me I will have time.

"First just let me weigh and measure him. I'll be quick." As she does, I'm surprised to find that he has doubled his birth weight and has already grown an inch. Holy crap that is insane! In just four weeks? When she is finished, I change Evans diaper, so he is a little more awake to eat. I adjust myself as to feed him and drape a receiving blanket over his head and my exposed breast. We settle into our feeding ritual and as I look around the office, I see his diplomas on the walls and notice one is from Ohio State. Why would he want to work here? I wonder why he didn't stay down there, hmm. Then about 10 minutes later there is a knock at the door and in walks the most beautiful man I have ever seen in person. I feel my face flush crimson immediately. How mortifying. Oh, I forgot how gorgeous he is.

224

His face flushes too as he greets me. He can't be too much older than me. His hair is dark with a slight wave to it. His eyes a deep chestnut brown and he has a five o'clock shadow going on. I find myself wondering what his body looks like under his white lab coat. Oh my God, snap out of it and put your boob away! I turn and get myself together before greeting him.

"Hi, Nettie, how are you? You look well. Motherhood agrees with you." Oh, yes, the first time I saw him I was in the hospital and totally embarrassed. Dr. Graham was the one who recommended him, Dr. Lincoln Conner. You would think she would have warned me that he was handsome and young. No, I expected some old geezer with white hair and a bow tie. And I, of course, looked hideous. My hair greasy and a mess and my eyes puffy and tired.

"Hi, Dr. Connor. Sorry about that I thought I had some time before you came in." I shake my head trying to forget my embarrassment.

"No, it's fine, it actually happens all the time." His voice is so sweet. He is very charming. I'll bet he is married and as I wonder I look at his finger. Hmmm, no ring but that doesn't mean he isn't in a relationship. I mean how could he not be.

225

"So, what exactly do we need to do?" I look down at sleeping, Evan.

"If you want to undress him, I will be quick to examine him and then he will have to have a few vaccines and that's all for today." He smiles and I catch a glimpse of his perfectly white teeth. I'm staring now, at his mouth and realize I'm smiling. I quickly undress the baby and lay him on the exam table. He starts to get a little pissed. It's probably because he is cold. He was all bundled in a warm sleeper sack and now his little naked body is exposed.

The exam is done quickly, and I bundle my little man up, but he is still exposed from the waist down. Dr. Connor gives him two fast shots in each thigh and he only cries for a second and is soon sleeping again. I finish getting him dressed and place him gently back into the car seat.

"So, the nurses out front can make your next appointment and he looks perfect. I would keep Tylenol in him for the next 24 hours just to avoid pain or a fever. A slight fever is normal but anything high you can call me, alright?" I nod.

"Do you have kids?" Oh, shit I can't believe I said that aloud. He smiles but has a very uncomfortable look on his face.

"I do, um did. A girl. Very long story," he totally shuts down. Why didn't I just mind my own business? Maybe he is divorced, and the mom has custody of the kid or maybe the kid is older and wants nothing to do with him. Either way, I shouldn't have asked.

"Sorry, I didn't mean to be too personal." He smiles appearing to be a little more comfortable.

"No, it's fine. Not too personal. Well, you two have a great day and I will see you soon." God, he has a great smile.

"Thank you, Dr. Connor," I reach out my hand to shake his.

"Lincoln, please," he softly shakes my hand back. "My friends call me Linc. Pleasure to see you again, Nettie." I get butterflies in my stomach at the sound of my name from his lips. I have to practically pry my hand from his because I don't want to let go.

"Very well, Linc. We'll see you soon," I have got to get outta here I can tell I'm flushed again.

When we get to the car, I stare at myself in the rearview mirror. God, what am I thinking? He is my son's doctor and I want to ask him out. It has been so long since I have gone on a date with anyone. Then after Sam, I can't imagine someone having their hands

227

on me. But it's nice to know I still have that feeling left somewhere deep down. Deep, deep down. I suppose I could have a relationship, someday.

"Right now, though, it's just me and you kid, and I like it that way." I can hear him squeak and assume he is agreeing with his very wise mother.

When we get home, it's lunchtime, so I grab myself a quick bite and as soon as I finish my growing little man is up and ready for lunch himself. After feeding him I lay him on the floor on a blanket and let him wiggle around. I'm laying on my right side with my head propped up just staring into his beautiful eyes. He is just kicking his little bird legs. I laugh out loud. Damn, is he a cutie. He starts to get a little fussy and when I pick him up, he does my favorite little baby thing, he scrunches his little face and tucks his knees up to his belly pushing his tiny little baby butt out while arching his back. I need to take some pictures of him. I swaddle him tight and place him in his crib for his nap. I go to fetch my camera and when I come back, he is fast asleep. I snap a few photos and he wiggles, hearing the clicking of the camera, but it doesn't disturb him too much. I gently stroke his hair; I could sit and watch him like this for hours.

I peel myself away from him so that I can get some laundry and cleaning done. While I do, I decide to call my mother and let her know how things went. I fail to mention the cute Dr. Lincoln Connor. I love his name, Linc. She tells me how busy she has been at work but assures me that when I'm ready to go back to work. She will be available at least two days a week to watch the baby. Oh, man I don't want to go back to work. I want to hit the lottery so I can afford to stay home with the baby forever. Wouldn't that be great? I'm lost in my own thoughts and my mother has obviously noticed.

"Hello, earth to Antoinette?!" she sounds annoyed.

"Sorry, my mind wandered a bit. What did you say?" I do this a lot when I talk to her. I can't help it she rambles at times.

"I asked if you wanted to come for dinner on Saturday for your birthday. Or if you want, we can go out somewhere?" Oh yes, my birthday. Not really looking forward to it. I think I would rather just stay home altogether.

"Dinner at your place sounds good. Can I invite Jess?" Maybe she can leave the old ball and chain at home, so we can have some girl time.

"Of course! She is always welcome. I'll call you later with some ideas for dinner and you can choose from there, alright?"

"Sounds perfect Mom. I'll talk to you later. Love ya."

"Love you too, sweetie." As I hang up the phone, I realize how close the anniversary of the attack is. The day that my life forever changed. I haven't received any more calls from Sam, but that doesn't mean he hasn't tried. My lawyer tells me that the DNA test needs to be done soon. I should just call him to get it over with. I decide it's now or never.

I will have to take the baby to a clinic where mine and Sam's lawyer will both be present to ensure that the test is done properly. It will be a simple swab of the inside of Evan's mouth. Totally painless, I'm told. I don't even know why they are doing this. I know Sam is the father. Anything to bide some time I suppose. So, we schedule it for one week from today. Good, I will be glad to get that done and we imagine it will be another good month before Sam can get another court date. Enough worry for today. I need to get this place in order.

*

I wake up Saturday morning and it's my twenty-ninth birthday. I feel about ten years older than I did last year. It's almost depressing how I feel today, but I try and think of the good things. At least it's not the big 3-0. I wouldn't trade being a mother for the world. I have a great family and wonderful friends who love me to death. I'm looking forward to tonight, Jess is coming to my parents for dinner and the baby and I are going to spend the night. Mom has volunteered to get up with Evan so that I can have a drink. Which reminds me, I need to make sure I pump today so have milk stored for his night feeding. He is like clockwork now. He eats at about 11 pm and then is up at 5 and back to sleep until usually 8 or so. I can deal with that. I have been staying up to feed him his late bottle so, getting up only once during the night is pretty great.

When we arrive at my parents, I take the baby in before making two more trips to and from the car. Geez, we are only staying one night, but he needs a lot of stuff. The house is decorated with balloons and streamers making me feel like I'm a child again. My mother, the party planner that she is, always makes a big deal of decorations. There is a gorgeous centerpiece of flowers and candles on the table as well. Now, this arrangement is not childish. It is very elegant and donned with my favorites; lilies and roses. They are real too, I can smell them from here. She has really outdone herself. We are a little early, so Jessica isn't here yet. My mother fixes me a glass of wine and I sip incredibly slowly on it. I know I will get a buzz for sure if I'm too quick to drink it.

Finally, after an hour Jess arrives. She looks adorable in a pair of dark jeans and a coral colored sweater that hangs down past her butt. She gives me a huge hug and kiss and of course makes a beeline for the baby who is sleeping in my father's arms. She so has baby fever.

"Happy birthday, Nettie. Get in my purse I have your present in there." She nods over to her bag.

"You didn't have to get me anything!" I can't believe she would do that we're too old to exchange gifts.

"It's just something small, don't worry." She smiles and gives me a wink. I wonder what it is. I reach into her bag and pull out a CD with a red bow on it. I open it and it's a mix CD that simply reads, Birthday Mix, in black marker. "Get ready to dance baby! That's the mix I made you for your 21st birthday. And I brought a cd player," she giggles. She is the best. What a great idea. We are gonna have fun.

"I can't wait to hear it!" I'm gleaming. Something so small and it's incredibly thoughtful. We haven't had a girl's night in forever.

After yet another fantastic meal from my mother, we all enjoy a cup of coffee and make small talk. Before long, my mother offers to take the baby upstairs so we can get on with our girls' night. My parents have a finished basement with a small bar and television room, so we grab our wine glasses and make our way down.

Jess pops in the CD and we both take a seat at the bar. I'm anxious to hear what the first song is. As it begins to play, I smile immediately, it's Sublime. Not exactly dancing music but certainly party music. I have a buzz already. This can't be good. I still have a kid to take care of tomorrow. The next song up is a little old school JT. And that's when we both get up and start dancing.

"Great idea on the music," I say, already out of breath. I'm bopping around with my wine still in hand and I know I look ridiculous. Oh, well I'm letting loose and I don't really care. We can't stop laughing at each other because we think we are good dancers, but the truth is, we're not. We ARE however, masters at lip-syncing. We both are demonstrating by singing into our merlot glasses.

Once we begin to wear out, we take a seat on the carpeted floor of the basement and slow down the music. Then we do what we

233

do best, talk. She tells me about her wedding ideas, and I give my input. I'm so glad I will be able to fit into a bridesmaid's dress.

"So, did you pick anything out yet, for us?" I ask.

"No, I want you to come with me. Maybe next week if you have time? I have it narrowed down to a few I found in magazines, but I haven't seen them in person. I also think I found *my* dress and I need you to come give some input on that as well. They are at the same bridal shop." She just has a sparkle in her eye.

"I am so happy for you Jess, really. You are going to be such a beautiful bride. Any dress you try on will be stunning. I can't wait for your wedding, it's going to be a blast!" I love going to weddings and this one, for obvious reasons will be extra special. "I'm just glad I know and like your fiancé. I couldn't imagine if I didn't."

"Don't worry. If you didn't, I wouldn't be getting married," she snorts as she begins to giggle. I join right along with her. The funny thing is she is serious. "Well, really you're like my sister and I have to have you around forever. I can't have some man scaring you off." We *are* like sisters. Both of us are only children and that made us bond even more than we would have otherwise. I would be the same way. If she didn't like someone I dated, it would be the end of that.

It's probably unhealthy if you think about it, the codependence, but I don't care. She is that important to me.

I wake up the next morning with a slight headache. Nothing I can't handle but I hope it's not one of those progressive hangovers. I didn't really drink that much but, being that I haven't been drunk for so long, it didn't take much. Jess is already gone. I don't know if she snuck out last night or this morning. I hope she wouldn't have driven drunk.

When I get upstairs my mom and Evan are up and he is enjoying his breakfast. I look at the clock in the kitchen and it's 8:30 am. Wow, that is sleeping in for me.

"How was your night dear?" She looks super tired. I wonder if he was up all night.

"Great! We had a lot of fun. Thanks for getting up with him," I lean over with a kiss for him and my mom.

"He did pretty great for the most part, but man does he squeak during the night. I barely slept, thinking he was going to wake up every five minutes."

235

"It was a great birthday Mom, thank you." I take a quick shower and Evan and I go home to spend a lazy Sunday together watching movies. Yes, that sounds like a perfect day to me.

Chapter 20

The Nightmare

Today is Tuesday and it's the day of the DNA test. I don't know why I'm so nervous about it. I know there isn't anything to it. I just hate thinking about Sam or anything to do with him. I want to enjoy my life with Evan, and not think of all this custody shit. When we arrive at the clinic, Mr. Lewis is already sitting in the waiting room. He stands to greet me and looks at the baby with curiosity.

"Congratulations. He's a cutie," he has a genuine smile on his face. My, what babies do to people. It is so stinking cute.

"Thank you, I think so too." He gestures his hand for me to sit and I comply. We don't have to wait long before Sam's lawyer shows. He acknowledges Mr. Lewis and tries to speak to me, but I pretend as though he isn't there. I turn away to hide Evan's face. I don't want him telling Sam what my son looks like.

A very official man comes out and calls us into the back. He puts a pair of latex gloves on and informs us all how the process works. The baby is sleeping thankfully so it's not hard for the man to take a swab from the inside of his cheek. Evans face purses up as he

237

does, but he never wakes. When we are finished, I say goodbye to Mr. Lewis, and he tells me it will take at least a few days for the results but he'll call me as soon as he has them. Big fucking deal, I think. I already know the results. Isn't this just a formality?

I walk directly past the other asshole lawyer and head straight to my red Honda. I need to wash this thing it's filthy from all the salt and snow. I have been thinking of maybe getting something bigger. I always have so much stuff to lug around with the baby. Oh well, one thing at a time, I guess. I can't really afford anything right now anyway.

When we get home, we go about the rest of our normal day. I can't wait for it to get nice outside, so we can go to the park and takes walks. I feel like we are trapped in this house. As much as I adore Evan, I'm just getting a little bored being cooped up like this. I try and call a few people, but no one answers. Oh yeah, everyone works. I decide now would be a good time for an impromptu photoshoot of little man. I pick out a few outfits and make a drop cloth with a white sheet I find. I use pillows and things to prop him up and take about a thousand pictures. One I have him with his head resting on a teddy bear in only his diaper. Another, I have a fedora hat that I found at the baby store and a black Windsor tie. I place him in his car seat for this one and he looks like a little gangster. I can't help but laugh.

I need to get these printed today. At least some for myself. When we are finished, I get him back into some snuggly clothes and put him down for his nap. I sit with the computer for about two hours editing and cropping the photos. I email a few to my mother and print some small ones for myself. I put them into multi-sized photo frames, putting a few in the living room and my favorite with the hat on right beside my bed. He is too stinking cute. "I'm one lucky lady," I whisper to myself.

I'm feeling a little lonely lately, though. Everyone is so busy with their lives and I feel like it's just me and Evan. Not that it's a bad thing, I just wish I had someone to talk to, an adult, I mean. All in good time. I will have a life again. Until then, I will cherish these nights when my son has no choice but to stay in with his mother.

I make dinner for myself and sit at the kitchen island. I was starving and I eat everything on my plate. Today has been a long day and I'm looking forward to sleep. I begin our nightly ritual and give Evan a bath with the sleepy time lavender baby bath and put him in comfy jammies. I don't know if the baby bath really works, but I like to think so. I enjoy our play and cuddles until his eleven o'clock feeding and we both turn in. I have been putting him in his crib at night to get him used to it and he is doing well, better than I expected. How did I get so lucky with this kid?

The first night was a bit of a challenge but he seems to like the little mobile above his head. I tuck him in and kiss him gently on the forehead smelling that soft lavender smell. "I love you, baby boy. I love you, my whole heart. See you for our five AM date," I kiss him again and nuzzle his nose. I wind up his mobile and leave the room as rock a bye baby rings in the background. I crawl into bed myself and turn the monitor up so I can hear everything. The music relaxes me and soon I'm asleep.

My sleep is disturbed with nightmares yet again. This time I'm outside working in the garden on a summer day and I hear a car door. When I walk around to see who it is, I don't recognize the car and quickly remember that Evan is in the pack and play out back. I try and run as fast as I can, but it's as though I'm trudging through mud. When the back yard is in eyesight, I find Sam smirking at me with the baby in his arms. He turns around and runs off with him. He is lightning fast and as I try to chase after him my feet move slower and slower until I'm paralyzed. I'm wailing and screaming but he is soon out of sight.

I bolt upright in my bed panting and sweating. It was just a dream. A nightmare. God, when will they stop? I can't handle these much longer emotionally, or physically. I lie back in bed and take a deep relaxing breath to regain my composure. I turn and look out the window the sun is up. The sun is up? "It's light outside?" I mutter quizzically. "Why didn't Evan wake up?" I look at the bedside clock and it's 7:30 am. The monitor is silent. Why isn't he up? Oh, God, my worst fears have come true.

I bolt into his room as fast as I can, almost tripping in the hallway. When I burst through his doorway and get closer to the crib, I see he is there. I breathe a sigh of relief. Oh God, he must have just slept in. His sleeping just keeps getting better and better. I move closer to him. Reaching into the crib I pick him up and notice that he is limp. Oh, fuck, he is limp. I now notice his little lips are slightly blue and his face pale. Suddenly, panic consumes me. I'm floating on the ceiling watching myself holding my infant son in my hands. I watch myself fall to the floor and hold my ear to his mouth. He is not breathing.

241

I try to get back in my body and when I do, I begin CPR, I don't even know if I'm doing it right. I tilt his tiny head back and place my mouth over his as well as his nose. I give a gentle breath and see his chest rise. I then place two fingers on his chest and pump three times. Oh, God am I doing this right? I realize that I somehow need to get help. I'm breathing so rapidly that I'm beginning to get lightheaded. I'm screaming and crying choking on my own breath.

I carry him to the living room and place him on the floor. I dial 911 as fast as possible and continue what I'm doing. I don't hear a word the woman is saying I simply give her my address and tell her to hurry. I'm hysterical. I don't even recognize myself. I'm screaming for him to wake up, screaming for him to breathe. "Please baby, wake up! Oh God baby, don't leave me. I can't lose you. Don't leave me. Be strong my little warrior, be strong Evan!" Please, God let this be another nightmare please, please. I squeeze my eyes as tight as I can and open them again.

Through my clouded eyes, he is still there in front of me and now it isn't just his lips but his whole face that is blue. I scoop him up in my arms and hold him weeping cursing screaming. NO, NO, NO please NO! Just then the paramedics arrive, and I'm still clenching onto Evan. They pry him from my arms, as I collapse like a rag doll on the floor screaming at God, cursing him, and praying at the same time. Pleading to save my son.

I feel someone wrap their arms around me and when I look up, it's my mother. When did she get here oh, maybe I'm dreaming? I wrap both arms tight around her and she comforts me.

"Come honey, they are taking him by ambulance let's go now so we can follow him," she is stern and grabs me and pulls me to my feet.

"Mom what are you doing here?" She looks confused.

"You called me, Nettie! I couldn't understand a word you said so I just came over and the paramedics were here. You don't remember?" No, I don't remember. Is this really happening?

"Mom, am I having a nightmare?" She shakes her head no.

"No baby, I'm afraid not. I wish you were." She is sobbing now too. "C'mon I'll call Daddy to meet us at the hospital. When we get in the car my head is spinning. I am so confused.

"Mom, where are we going? This isn't happening. I have a lot of nightmares like this. I'll wake up. It's fine. He's fine. I think I better get on some sort of medication for this though. This is by far the most vivid. Can you wake me up now please?" My mother just looks at me in awe and shakes her head. She says nothing.

When we arrive at the hospital, I'm almost robotic, and she leads me into a room, where my Dad is already waiting. He rushes to my side and wraps his arms around me. He too is sobbing at this point, but I, however, am not.

"Daddy, it's okay, I'm just dreaming that's all. I'll wake up soon and it will all be over," I give him a reassuring smile. He shakes his head and squeezes me tighter. "It's real isn't it?" I whisper.

My mother goes to the front desk and speaks to a nurse who leads us back into another room. We sit there for what seems like hours when a man, a doctor immerges in a white lab coat. I jump up first.

"How is he? Can I see him now? I really should get him home and he is probably ready to eat I'm sure." The doctor looks at me and frowns.

"Dear, I'm so sorry but your son. He didn't make it." *I? He what?* I turn to my parents and they both begin to wail.

"I don't understand." I stare into his eyes waiting for him to give a different reply.

"I'm so sorry dear." He places his hand on my shoulder and I'm once again transported to the ceiling. She is crumpled in a ball rocking back and forth screaming. God, that screaming. Tell her to stop, it's hurting my ears. It is absolutely piercing. When I finally manage to realize, I am the one making all the noise. I drift back down to my body. I look up at my mom and I see two of her.

"I want to hold him," I whimper. "I want to hold my baby."

A nurse is there and as gently as possible, tells us we can see him. I follow her down a long cold white hallway and feel like I'm walking to my execution. When we arrive, it's not what I expect. They put me in a regular hospital room, and he is lying in a clear plastic hospital bassinet swaddled in a blanket. His dark beautiful hair is disheveled. I pick him up and kiss him on his forehead. I sit in a rocking chair nearby and begin to rock him gently. Smoothing his hair down with the tips of my fingers I begin to sing him a lullaby. I choose 'Twinkle Twinkle Little Star'. When the song ends, I kiss each of his eyelids and say a prayer that he is in heaven with God. As I do, I don't know if I truly believe he exists. I curse him in my head for taking the one bit of light I have in my life, my precious baby from me. My little warrior has been taken from me. The nurse comes in and tells me it's time. I say one last goodbye to Evan.

"Evan Tate Madison, I love you my whole heart and I always will. You don't know the joy you have brought to my life. I will never forgive myself for not protecting you. It was my job and I failed. I love you, I love you".

*

I don't even know how I end up home, but my parents are trying to comfort me. I don't hear a word they say. I go to the kitchen and fish out a bottle of wine taking a huge swig and break the bottle in the sink. My mother tries to put her arm around me, and I push her away.

I march into Evan's room and slam the door, locking it behind me. I slip off my shoes and pick up the blanket that he had been swaddled in, just hours before. I bring it to my nose and inhale deeply. I can't help but begin weeping. My whole body heaving in emotion. I can smell him. I lift my leg up over the side of the crib and climb in. I place the blanket over my face and curl up into fetal position. All I can smell is lavender and baby. I shake in a rhythmic motion picturing his perfect little face in my mind. My baby. My Evan. My warrior. Why would God do this to me why? "WHY!?!" I scream. I lay there in his crib and cry until my head is throbbing and somehow or another I sleep.

Chapter 21

Aftermath

When I wake, I rub my palms harshly over my face, hoping to wash away the image of my poor baby. I'm still in the crib. His scent lingers over me. I haven't been dreaming. It wasn't a nightmare. It was real. My baby is gone. My heart is broken, shattered into a thousand pieces. I want to die.

My head is pounding and there is a lump in my throat that won't go away. I have no idea what time it is, whether it's the same day or not. I don't care I want to go with him. I want to be with my son. I close my eyes again and begin to sob. What have I done in my life that is so terrible that I deserve this!

There is a faint knock on the door. "Go away!" I scream at the top of my lungs.

"Nettie, please let me in. Please baby." It's my father. His voice desperate. No, I don't want to talk to anyone.

"NO, go away. Leave my house! Let me be!" I want to sleep. I want to die. This can't be happening. I want to rewind and be back to putting him to bed that night. I want things to start all over. I want to wake up and start our normal routine. I want us to go about our normal day and I want him to be fine. Please let me start again. I don't want to leave this spot. I reach over my head and pull on the mobile and a soft song starts to play, and I close my eyes, tears streaming down my face again. I don't know how much time has passed but eventually, the tears slow, until I feel as though I have not one left to shed. A giant lump remains in my throat and I can't swallow it. I decide to try and peel myself out of the crib, still gripping his blanket in my hand. I shuffle into the kitchen and my parents are still there. They look broken and exhausted.

My mother meets my eyes with relief. Maybe because I'm not huddled in his crib anymore. "Honey, I hate to say this, but you need to think of arrangements." This isn't happening. How can I bury my son? A child I didn't even want to have but now has completely transformed my life. My father then speaks.

"A grief counselor called from the hospital and left her number. She also gave some information about a local support group for parents who have lost children to SIDS," he can barely get the words out.

"So, it was SIDS, officially?" I ask. I thought I did everything right. No loose blankets. I took all his stuffed animals out of his crib before I put him to bed. I just don't understand.

"Yes, there is nothing that could have been done, baby. I'm so sorry. God, am I sorry." He squeezes my hand and presses it to his face. I can feel his tears on the back of my hand. I feel so numb. Like the life has been sucked out of me.

"I don't want to make the arrangements. Can't you guys just do that?" they look at each other and then back to me.

"Don't worry about the expense, we'll take care of it. But I think you need to make the decisions. It's your child and I don't want you regretting that you had no part in how he was laid to rest." The cost, Jesus that's the last thing on my mind.

"Mom, I don't know, really. You do it. I don't want anyone there just you two and I guess Jessica. I don't want a whole service. I just want to pray for him and let him be with God." I don't know if I believe there is a God anymore. If there is, this wouldn't be happening right? I hope that I'm wrong because I need Evan to be in a good place, a peaceful place. Among angels.

*

The funeral is on a Saturday, one week after my birthday. I'm standing in front of a tiny gray marble coffin with delicate silver trim. It's draped with beautiful yellow roses. This is one thing I wanted a say in. Yellow roses usually make me smile. The casket will stay closed. I don't want anyone to see him. *I* can't even bear to see him. I said my goodbyes in the hospital.

The Priest is speaking, but all I hear are low mumbles. I can't focus on anything but those roses. When he is finished, I feel my father's hand on my back and he nudges me forward. This is it. The last time I will be in my son's physical presence. I approach him and gently place both hands on the cold surface of his casket. I bend down and kiss it gently and say my last words to him. "I love you, my whole heart, Evan. My little warrior. You have changed my life more than you will ever know." As I walk away, I gently run my fingertips over the soft yellow roses and pluck one from its place. I bring it to my nose and inhale deeply. I look over to my parents and Jess, their eyes stained with tears and without a word I walk to the car.

As I'm getting into the back of my parent's car, a shadow in the distance of the cemetery catches my eye. I hadn't noticed before, but I see a car parked off to the side. Without thinking, I march over to where the person is standing. I can't believe someone would come to gawk at a funeral service for my child. When I get closer, I see it's a woman, it's Sara. What? This bitch still following me.

The closer I get the faster and angrier I become. When I'm close enough, she speaks first.

"Nettie, I'm sorry. I just wanted to pay my respects. I know I'm the last person that should be here." I don't know what to say. She looks awful. Not like I remember her. She looks so sad.

"What in the hell? Have you been watching us this whole time? WHY?" I don't really give a shit at this point. She is crazy.

"No, I heard about... the baby and I just,. I'm so sorry Nettie, it's so sad. I know you may not believe this, but I really felt like we were good friends. I do care about you and I'm sorry about your loss. That's all I wanted to come here and say."

I want to ask her why she didn't go to the police, but none of that matters now, does it? I can't force her and frankly, I have better things to worry about. Without another word I leave. I don't owe her a thing and I'm exhausted. I want to go home and sleep, forever. I don't offer my family any explanation as to the encounter with Sara and they don't pry. No one says a word when we arrive back at my house. We walk in together and my mom prepares some of the food that has been sent by friends and family. I always wondered why people feel the need to send food when there is a death. I suppose it's to make things more convenient, but when you're depressed the last thing you want to do is eat.

I go to my room to change my clothes. I slip into my all too familiar sweats and vintage t-shirt and climb into bed. Today was the first day I had showered and gotten dressed this week. And it's only because my mother physically shoved me into the shower. She has been staying with me, although I have repeatedly told her to go. I want to be alone. I want to cry, I want to sleep, I wish it were me in that coffin.

There is a gentle knock at the door and without a reply from me, they enter. I feel someone sit next to me on the bed and a hand is placed on my back. It's Jess. She strokes my back like a mother comforting a child and I hear her sniffle. "You need to try and eat something." She whispers.

I don't bother to answer her. Tears begin rolling down the side of my face forming a puddle on my sheets. I feel her lean close to my ear and I can barely hear what she says. But when I do, I smile. "How about a drink then?" I nod.

She jumps up and hurries to the kitchen. I sit up and await my drink. I look over at the picture on my bedside table. Evan, with the little fedora and black necktie. That was the best photoshoot I have ever done. Jess is back already with two short crystal glasses full of ice and a clear liquid. She hands me my glass and I take a huge drink. Wow, that is straight vodka. I inhale and cough as it burns the inside of my mouth and throat.

"God, Jess! You could have mixed it with something."
She looks at me and shrugs.

"Well, I know you need to get drunk so bottoms up." She holds up her glass and I take another huge swig but this time the warmth feels good flowing deep down into my belly.

It doesn't take long for me to feel totally drunk. I haven't eaten much of anything and I'm exhausted from crying so much. I needed to lose myself for a little while. Jess always tries to make me feel better. I decide I should sleep, or I'll be sick.

"Will you lay with me until I fall asleep?" I ask Jess.

"Of course. Anything for my sister." She lies down next to me and we both stare at the ceiling. She starts humming a soft tune. I can't quite make out what it is. It works in distracting me because it's all I can think of now.

"What is that? I know I have heard it before." It's beautiful.

"It's On Eagles Wings." Oh, that's right. This song always made me so sad. It's fitting today.

"Keep humming, please." I take some comfort in the fact that if there is a heaven then my little boy is there. Jess continues the beautiful melody and I feel the overwhelming need to pray. I need answers that I believe only God can give me. I offer a silent prayer for answers, for peace, for sense in all this pain.

Chapter 22

Stand

I don't know how long I have been in this bed for. I haven't talked to anyone in days, at least. My mother continues to bring me food which occasionally I pick at. I can feel that my hair is greasy and tangled. I haven't looked in a mirror since the funeral.

I feel like I need surgery to stitch my splintered heart back together. I miss him so much. I briefly think of Sam and wonder if he knows about the baby. I'm sure he does. Everyone around here knows everything. That's the pain in the ass part of a small town. I'm not thinking clearly today. I don't know whether it's a lack of food or the fact that I either can't sleep or can't wake up. I don't know what I need right now, but I feel just lost. I'm going crazy in this room, but I need to be alone and everyone keeps hounding me. Don't they understand that the only thing that could help me is to bring my son back? Bring him back and it will bring me back. Otherwise, I am lost forever.

While I lie there in my bed a thought comes to me and it becomes obsessive. My heart begins to race, and I can't shake away the idea. I get out of bed before I change my mind and get dressed. I comb my fingers through my hair not bothering to use a brush and tie it up into a messy ponytail. When I leave my room, my father is there. He stands from the table, surprised to see me out of bed. "Nettie, honey can I get you something?" He follows me as I scramble to the door. "Where are you going?" I don't answer him. I don't even look at him. I don't want to talk to anyone. I'm cursed. Anything I touch is cursed. I don't want to do any more damage to my family. Maybe it would be better for everyone if I didn't exist at all.

I snatch my purse from the hook beside the door and don't even bother donning a coat. As I slam the door behind me, I can hear my father yell from the door, but I run to jump in my car. I take off as fast as I can before he can follow me. In my rearview mirror, I can see him standing on the front porch with his hand pulling at his hair. He is confused and angry. I don't blame him. I would be too.

I'm not exactly sure if I'm going in the right direction. I have only been to my destination maybe one time and only driven by. I have never gone inside. I slow down knowing I'm in the vicinity and then I spot it. I pull into the enormous parking lot and climb out. I'm sure to lock my car as I go.

What the hell am I doing? I'm not thinking clearly, so I just go with it. I have completely and totally lost my mind, but I don't think anyone would question why. My life for the last year has been so wildly up and down, that I don't even know what to do anymore. I have nothing to live for and nothing to lose. So, fuck it. I walk in the double doors and I see a window to my right that is marked Check-In. I approach the window and address the older man in uniform behind the glass.

"Nettie Madison, to see a prisoner." I take a deep breath and exhale. "Samuel Knox please."

"I just need to see your ID Miss Madison and you need to sign in," he hands me a clipboard. "Thank you, dear. You can step over to those blue doors and I will buzz you in."

I move to the left side of the room now and as I hear the buzzer echo, I'm almost afraid to push open the doors but somehow, I do. When I walk through there are two uniformed guards who proceed to pat me down and search my purse. After removing my shoes and emptying my pockets I walk through the metal detectors and this is the last of my inspection.

258

"It will be just a few moments, Miss," he is very cold in the way he speaks even though he addresses me as 'Miss'.

It's not long before my name is called. I'm handed a plastic visitors tag and buzzed into yet another room. When I enter, I don't see him immediately. The officer instructs me to go all the way to the end of the room. There are 6 booths all divided with bright orange plastic walls and a stool in front of each, bolted to the floor. Glass separates the visitors from the prisoners with a phone to link their conversations. I count my steps as I walk to the end. Exactly 20 steps and I slowly turn to face him. He looks genuinely shocked to see me, but soon that shock turns to anger. I can see how the fire is building in his eyes. He looks nearly as angry as the night of the incident. I'm somehow incredibly calm. Probably because I have just plain lost my fucking mind. I sit down and look directly into the eyes of the devil himself. Evan looked nothing like him. Nothing at all.

I don't hesitate to pick up the phone and he sits perfectly still for a few moments, before slowly lifting his receiver from its place. I speak first. "I will kill you someday. Remember this moment. And remember that I have given you a warning. This will be the only time I will tell you. And I will never be here again. Don't forget this day."

259

He laughs out loud and leans forward so that I can see his breath on the glass. "What the fuck did you do to my son, you fucking whore?"

I know my face is burning crimson at this moment, I can feel it. I want to kill him, right now. I don't want to wait. I don't respond. I won't give him the satisfaction.

"You've got it wrong sweetheart. I will fucking kill *you*," he is so angry, but he speaks softly this time. "You put me in jail and then kill my child? I will come get you Nettie, don't you worry. I will bide my time, but when I'm outta here, you are going to be the first one I pay a visit to. And believe me when I do kill you, I will be sure to have my fun first. So, YOU remember that!" his volume escalates as he speaks, and by the time he is finished spit is sprayed on the glass.

I stand and lean in close to the glass as did he so that we are nose to nose. I hope HE hears me. "I look forward to it." Just then I slam the phone down as hard as I can, and he jumps. HAHA, he jumped! I fucking startled him. I cannot contain my smile. He is absolutely seething. I'm satisfied with my visit and turn to leave the room. The second I walk out the door I exhale loudly. Amazingly, I don't cry. I don't think that I have any tears left.

I meant what I said to him. He ruined my life and I will take his. The second he is released I will be ready, and I will fucking kill him if he comes at me. I want him to. Who could blame me for killing him, right? Evan's face flashes in my mind. Yes, I would do it for him.

*

When I finally arrive home after being gone for a few hours, my mother's car is now at my house and so is Jessica's. I don't want to deal with this right now. I'm a grown woman. Can't they just let me grieve? Before I can even get out of the car, they are all three at my door. I roll my eyes at them. They look angry and worried.

"Where the hell did you go?" my mother is screaming at me.

"I just needed to take care of something." I answer her in a monotone insincere way. I can't tell them where I was, or they will flip out. I walk right passed all of them and enter MY house. I drop my purse onto the floor and take off my shoes. Again, they follow me and begin pestering me with questions. Leave me alone already! I ignore them still and go to the bathroom locking the door behind me. I turn on the water to the shower to drowned out their desperation. I sit for a while before even getting into the shower and I just think. I need to tell my family to leave me alone for a while. If they keep smothering me, I'm ultimately going to hurt their feelings. I just don't need to be babied right now. I have every right to be angry, depressed, destructive and just plain stupid. I still won't dare to tell them that I went and saw Sam. They just won't understand.

There is no need to tell them anyway since I don't plan on seeing him ever again. Well, not until I kill him. I don't doubt he will come after me. Whenever that may be. I hate him. I hate him more than I have ever hated anyone in my life. I hope he gets brutalized like I was by him. He will never know the extent of pain he has caused me and my family. Even if he did, it would only feed his sickness. He is not human. He is something else, something dark.

I'm going to need to get my shit together eventually I suppose, but right now I don't want to think about anything. I take the longest shower of my life and when I finally decide I'm ready to face my family, I do just that. My father is sitting on the floor right outside of the bathroom and I can hear my mother and Jess whispering in the kitchen. My dad looks up at me with those sad eyes.

They look golden today, I think, but then again it's dark in here. I lock eyes with him but don't say a word. I don't care if anyone else is sad right now because I feel worse than they do. I quietly turn and walk into my room and put on some clothes. I don't even know what I grab, I just need to get out of here for a while. When I immerge from my room my father is still in his spot and I decide I should say something.

"I'm going out," I say quickly as I sidestep past him.

"What do you mean you are going out? Where? Why won't you talk to any of us?" he looks devastated.

"Dad, I just need to get out by myself, to think…" I hesitate, "to not think, I don't know. I just need to get out of here, or I'm going to lose my mind. You need to get Mom and go home. I don't need you both hovering over me every second. Just let me be destroyed for a while, okay? I need it!" I'm shouting at my own father and for a moment I feel like a child who is about to be scolded.

He says nothing and turns his gaze to the floor. His hands are stuffed in his pockets and I can tell he wants to shout at me as well, but he controls himself.

When I turn to continue down the hall, my mother and Jessica are standing there silent and in shock. I have never spoken to my father like that in my life. I pass both of them without a word, gather my things and walk out the door. Where am I going? It doesn't matter.

I just need to get out of here. I drive for a long while before I decide to stop into a bar for a drink.

It is still early, so there aren't many people here. A couple sits in the corner looking entirely too intoxicated for the time of day and the bartender is chatting it up with what I would imagine, is a regular at the far end of the bar. I choose a seat at the opposite end of the bar, to avoid speaking to anyone.

The bartender takes his time but then finally comes over to get my drink order. I decide on a vodka tonic. It will be strong enough, but not too strong. I still need to drive home. It smells like cigarettes and booze in here. It reminds me of the night Sam came to my home. I wish I could go back in time and eliminate that night from my life. Everything would be fine right now, had that night never been. I don't know where to go from here. Where do I start to put some sort of life together? I don't want to do a damn thing right now. I don't want to work, spend time with my family, or even wake up in the morning.

Before I know it, my drink is gone, and I opt for just one more. I lift my hand to the bartender and point to my glass. He quickly refills it and I thank him. I lift the cold glass to my lips and once it's there it doesn't leave until it's empty. The liquid warms my chest and I exhale. I'm feeling the tingling sensation from the alcohol spread through my body. I should go. I can't sit here, or I will continue to get drunk.

I climb into my red Honda and sit for a moment. I pick up my cell phone and see that I have ten missed calls. I don't even bother to check and see who it was. I know that it's my parents. I decide I should go home simply because I'm feeling so tired again. I wouldn't mind another drink at home. So, I stop by a local liquor store and get a few bottles of wine. It's not long before I'm home and when I look at the clock, I realize I have been gone for only about an hour and a half. When I pull into the driveway this time it's dark, and I see only Jessica's car. I'm surprised my parents aren't here too. Although, I did ask them to leave. I wish Jess didn't stay. When I walk into the house, I head directly to the kitchen and she is standing at the island, wine glass in hand. I open the cupboard and retrieve a wine glass for myself, pouring the remaining wine from Jessica's bottle inside. I take a large swig and sit down opposite her. She looks devastated, but I'm too selfish right now to have any sympathy for her.

"Where did you go?" she asks, but I don't think she expects me to answer.

"To a bar. I had a few drinks. I needed to get out of here," my tone is icy, and I don't even recognize myself.

"Oh, well do you want me to stay with you tonight?"

"No, go home. I want to be alone." I take another bottle of wine and walk back to my bedroom. I close the door gently behind me and lock it.

It's quiet in my room. I notice that my bed is made. My mother must have cleaned while I was gone. Just then I hear the front door close. I walk to the window and pull back the sheer curtains. Jess is almost to her car. Her head is down, and she looks as though she is wiping away tears. I let the curtain fall back across the window and I make my way to the bed. I debate on whether to watch a little TV. No, I think I will just drink. I open the next bottle of wine. It's a cheap chardonnay with a twist top and not even a cork. Cheap, but it will do the trick. I don't even bother to pour it into a glass.

"Bottoms up," I say to the empty room.

I spend the next several days this way. In a fog of alcohol and sleep. Dodging calls and knocks at the door. Only occasionally sending a text to report I'm not dead... yet.

Chapter 23

Tough Love

I'm startled by a knock on my bedroom window. I hesitantly flutter my eyes and see Matthew standing outside. He looks annoyed. "Open the door," he mouths. I look around the room and realize I'm on the floor.

"Go away!" I shout. Ouch, my head is pounding. I look down at an empty bottle on its side next to me. I climb up into my bed and pull the comforter over my head. Yuck, I smell like alcohol. It's seeping through my pores. Once again, I hear a stronger knock, knock, knock.

"I'm not leaving until you let me in, Nettie! And you know I mean it!"

I know he is telling the truth and I flip the blankets onto the floor like an angry child. I'm so annoyed. I stomp my feet to the front door and unlock it. After opening it, I don't bother to say anything to him, but make my way to the kitchen and my wine. I can feel him following me. I grab a bottle of wine and begin to open it when I'm startled.

"Are you kidding me? It's ten o 'clock in the morning. When was the last time you have even showered? You look like shit!" he is infuriated.

"Matt, I can do whatever the hell I please, I'm an adult!!" Before I can get another word out, he bends and grabs me by my thighs and hoists me over his shoulder.

"Put me down! Are you crazy?" I shout.

The bottle leaves my hand and shatters into the kitchen sink. Matt doesn't listen and carries me down the hall into the bathroom, and I hear the shower turn on. Suddenly he drops me, and I crash into the bottom of my tub in a spray of icy cold water.

"Get yourself together, God damn it! I know you are hurting but you need to snap out of this! Shower and meet me back in the kitchen. I will have something for your skinny ass to eat." He leaves the room without another word and I know he is right.

I look down at my fully clothed body and realize how much weight I have lost in such a short amount of time. I take a few deep breaths trying to calm myself. I stand and adjust the water temperature. I gently peel away each soaking wet layer and hang them on the curtain rod. As I let the warm water cascade over my face I begin to cry. My life lately is a complete and total blur. How do I start

to get back to some sort of normal? I haven't worked. I haven't had

any sort of social life and my parents have had to take over the

responsibility of my bills, because frankly I just don't care. I haven't

even talked to Jess about any of her wedding plans. What a great Maid

of Honor I have been.

Just then I remember someone mentioning a support group at

the hospital. Maybe I should look into that? I don't even want to leave

this house. I haven't even been to Evans grave since the funeral. I

think that's something I need to do, soon.

I hear a gentle knock at the door, and I'm snapped out of my

daze. "Hey, hurry it up in there I have breakfast ready for you."

I think I really needed Matthew's tough love today. I can't

be babied any longer. It obviously isn't helping me at all. Now that

I'm thinking about it, I'm absolutely starving. I can smell bacon

coming from the kitchen. I turn off the water and step out of the

shower. As the steam clears from in front of me a see a blur of

myself in the mirror. I use my hand to wipe away the fog. I'm

absolutely horrified at what is in front of me. I don't even recognize

this woman. I have deep, dark circles under each of my eyes. Even my cheeks are sunken in. I scan the rest of my body and notice that each individual rib is visible. Both of my hip bones jut out from my sides. If this is what everyone else has been looking at lately, then no wonder they are so concerned. I can't bear to look at this pitiful, sad woman any longer and I grab the towel covering my body. I take my time brushing out my knotted hair and sneak across the hall to my bedroom to dress. Matthew has seen me in much less than a towel before, but that was a very long time ago. I half-smile at myself remembering a happy time in my life. I instantly feel guilty for the grin.

After throwing on whatever was clean in my dresser drawers I tiptoe to the kitchen. Matt is sitting at the table with two place settings and he is eating already himself. He looks up with sad eyes as I enter the room.

"That's a little better," he whispers.

"Thank you. I needed someone to make me wake up a bit." I join him at the table and pick up a piece of toast and just a few pieces of bacon. I don't think I could handle eating too much.

"Can you do me a favor today, Matt?" He nods without hearing what it is. "I remember someone saying something about a

270

support group for parents who lost a child to SIDS," I pause filled with so much emotion the lump begins to form again in my throat. "Can you get the information for me? It's worth a try, right?" I meekly shrug my shoulders.

"Yeah, it's worth a try. I mean this as gently as possible, but I don't think you could possibly be any worse off than you are now." I know he's right. The only way things could be worse is if I were dead. And what is sad, is that it's something I welcomed.

"I want to go to the cemetery too." He nods. "I want to go to the cemetery by myself." I correct.

"Ok, I understand. I'll get the information you want while you go visit Evan." My heart twists at the sound of my son's name.

"Thank you," I murmur.

I take a few more nibbles of my food and begin to feel a little nauseated. I excuse myself from the table, deciding next I should call my parents. I'm sure they are the ones who sent Matthew over here. I know they are worried about me. I pick up my cell and see that I have ten missed calls and five voicemails. I'm not surprised. I dial my mother's cell first and she picks up after just one ring.

"Nettie? Honey is everything okay? Are you okay?" she sounds

panicked.

"Yes, Mom. Matt came over. I just wanted to check-in. I'm

out of bed today. I'm going to the cemetery and he is getting me

information on the support group thing." I try not to be short with

her.

She audibly sighs. "Oh good. I'm just glad you are feeling

better." Better? I don't think so! I just need to try something different

than what I'm doing.

"Alright, I have to go. I'll talk to you later. Love you." I hang

up before she can respond.

After gathering my things, I see my camera in the corner. I

don't know why but I decide to take it with me. When I step outside, I

notice the change in the weather. It's fairly warm. It dawns on me that

I have no idea what the damn date is. I assume it has been over a week

since Evan passed, but I really have no idea. I glance at the calendar

on my phone and realize that today is March 5th, Evans due date. I

begin to weep already. I have had and lost him before he was even

supposed to be put on this earth. I feel like I have been absolutely

cheated.

272

The drive is a short one and I cry the whole way. I have very mixed feelings about coming here. I hope that it helps me and doesn't send me into another downward spiral. When I arrive, I make a slow turn into the parking lot. I get out and for a quick second, I don't remember which way to go. The day of the funeral was such a blur to me. I scan the graves and see a tiny spot with no grass. Oh, there he is. As I make my way over, I'm careful not to step on any other graves. I don't want to be disrespectful.

When I finally approach, I realize that the headstone has been placed. I lose it immediately. I sink to my knees and place my hands over the cold stone. "Why? Oh, Evan, I miss you so much. I love you so much. I wish you were here with me." My words are inaudible. It's a mix of crying and begging. When I wipe away my tears, I read the headstone.

Evan Tate Madison

Not long with us on earth, but forever in our hearts.

January 18th -February 24th, 2019

I drag my fingers across the grooves of each letter. I get out my camera and take a few photos. I don't even know why but it makes me feel calm. Like I'm collecting pieces of him. I snap a few shots of the treetops above his grave. I hope he is up there in heaven. He wasn't here long but he certainly made an impact, on all of us. Just then it dawns on me. Not only is everyone worried about me, but they are mourning the loss of Evan as well. My parents lost their grandchild. I haven't even given that any thought. I need to be more aware of how they are feeling about all of this as well. I close my eyes before leaving and wait until the tears subside.

"I will be back my little warrior. Mommy loves you. My whole heart." I bend down and kiss his name. I should have brought him some flowers. Next time I will. I need to visit him regularly. I know it's just his body here and not his soul, but it was a comforting visit.

When I arrive home, Matthew is still there and is looking anxious as I walk in. "Oh, good you're back. I found out that there is a meeting tonight if you want to go. I was afraid you wouldn't be back in time. You were gone forever."

Was I? It seemed like only an hour or so. When I look at the clock it's three in the afternoon. Holy shit I have been gone for three hours. "Um, I don't know if I'm feeling up to a meeting so soon Matt, but thank you."

"I don't think so. You asked me to get the information and I did. I will take you there and bring you home. It's only an hour and you don't have to talk, just see what it's about, alright?" He sounds pathetic.

"Fine," I snap. "What time is it?"

"In one hour. So, go get ready and I'll make you a quick sandwich or something." I don't tell him that I'm not hungry, because I have a feeling it won't matter to him at all. I was going to wear what I have on, but I suppose I should at least put jeans on. I am once again in sweats and a t-shirt. I pull my hair up into a loose ponytail and put on a comfortable pair of jeans with a black V-neck cotton shirt. I open my compact and dust my face with a little powder and some blush. God, I am so pale. I look like death.

When I'm ready, I meet Matt once again in the kitchen and force down a few bites, before putting my hand in the air as though I surrender. I can't eat anymore. This is the most I have had to eat in days. He doesn't protest and instead stands and grabs his car keys from the kitchen counter and without a word, holds my hand and we walk to the car.

The support group is at the hospital in one of their meeting rooms. As we approach, I begin to get butterflies in my stomach. I feel like I'm in high school about to give a very important presentation or something. I almost feel as though I could be sick. As if reading my mind, Matt reassures me. "You don't have to say anything, remember. Just sit and listen. If you want to keep coming back great and if you don't, that's alright too," he speaks gently and kisses me on the cheek. "Now go," he gives me a little shove in the door. "I'll be in the car. See you in an hour."

I scan the room briefly and get myself a cup of coffee from the back of the room. I notice that people are wearing name tags, but I don't read any of them. I keep my head down and make my way to where the chairs are lined up. There are six rows with five chairs in each. I choose the very far back left corner. An older gentleman approaches me and introduces himself as the counselor that runs the group. I'm barely listening to him. I'm just looking at his crooked bright yellow teeth. He has a gray comb-over with no more than ten hairs left to cover his baldness. I try and judge the color of his eyes, but they are hidden by tinted glasses. I look down at his feet and he is wearing a pair of very dirty sneakers. Odd, he has dress slacks on. I nod dismissively at him and he moves along, but not before handing me a name tag which I don't apply.

Everyone takes their seats and I have yet to look anyone else in the eye except for Yellow Teeth. The meeting is underway, but not much translates. I'm completely tuned out. I have my eyes to the floor and slowly scan the feet of the people in front of me. There is a woman wearing way too expensive and slutty stiletto heels. Then there is the Flip Flop girl, not quite warm enough for that. A man with very clean, all too anally clean in fact, white Adidas with black stripes on them. I notice he has jeans that cover most of his shoe. He must be young. A few rows behind him I notice very petite white orthopedic looking shoes and powder blue polyester pants. It must be an old woman, but again I don't look up. I'm almost afraid to put a person with the shoe. We have all been through the same trauma in some way or another. Even though I haven't met any of them I feel a connection and I don't want to feel their sadness.

Before I know it, the meeting is over. I only know this because my new acquaintances stand in unison. I decide not to say anything tonight, but I quickly make my exit, picking up a flyer on the way out. I think I want to come back here. I don't even know why.

When I exit into the parking lot, I see Matthew sitting in his car playing around on his phone. He doesn't see me until I open the car door and I think I startle him.

"Hey, how did it go?" He looks as though he is holding his breath.

"Good, I mean I didn't really do anything but sit there. I think I would come back," my answer is clipped but I don't know what else I can say about it.

Matt takes me home and once again I'm alone. I heat up a small plate of leftovers that my mother has made and get myself my nightly, or daily rather, bottle of wine. I only eat a few bites and decide to limit myself to one glass of wine. It has made me sleepy enough that I could try and turn in. As I walk down the hallway, I pause at Evan's door. Nothing has been disturbed since the day he left me. I gently climb into his crib and start up the mobile. I can still smell him. I wonder how long that will last? I hope for a very long time. I'm staring up at the spinning sea creatures. It makes me feel a bit dizzy on account of the wine. I have a few things I would like to do tomorrow.

I need to call Jessica. I want to talk to both of my parents. And most importantly I want to buy a gun.

Chapter 24

Recovery

I'm in a gun store and have no idea what the hell I'm doing. The clerk approaches me gingerly, knowing I do not belong here. He clears his throat before speaking. "Um, is there something I can help you find Ma'am?"

"Oh, I don't exactly know what I'm looking for. Maybe you can help me? I'm just looking for something for protection. I want something for my home that I can learn to use easily." I'm talking incredibly fast. I feel a slight spike of adrenaline. I'm totally crazy.

"Well, there is paperwork that needs to be filled out first, so that you can be issued a license. Might I suggest going to a shooting range? Try out a few different firearms. They can help you find out what fits right for you personally."

"Ok, that sounds like something I would like to do. I mean I need to learn how to use one anyway," I say matter of factly. That sounds like just what I need. To shoot something.

I collect the paperwork from the nice man and head to the address he has written down for me. I have yet to call anyone today,

up again. I repeat this process until I look down and the box is empty. I immediately hit the button that I was instructed would get me Hank's assistance. When he enters the room, he looks a little confused. "Problem dear?"

"No, I'm just out of bullets," I'm panting and sweating.

"Ah, okay that was fast. I'm going to have to start charging you now, okay?" I nod quickly. Just get me some more bullets! I'm getting anxious. When he brings me more, I begin my therapy yet again. Firing and firing and reloading again. Before I know it, this box is empty as well. I look up at the target and press the button to bring it toward me. There is barely anything left of the black and white sheet. I pull it down and put another in its place. I press the call button again and Hank enters this time with two boxes of ammo and without a word, places them next to me. He smiles at me and shakes his index finger like a parent warning a child. I'm a bit addicted to this Hank, yes. I get what you are trying to tell me. Slow down. Once I have finished off the other two boxes, I'm proud of the progress I have made with my aim. I decide I should finish for the day. I still have some things I want to do.

When I walk out of the isolated room, I see that it's dark outside. Already? I look over at Hank and he shakes his head. "I don't think I have ever had someone in there that long, let alone a beginner. You must have a lot of anger in you, young lady." You have no idea, Hank.

"How much do I owe you, Hank?"

"Don't worry about it. But if you plan on doing that next time you will be paying." Wow, that is nice of him.

"Thank you," I whisper. He must get a lot of angry people in here. He seems to know that I really needed this.

When I arrive home my father's car is in the driveway. Jesus, I need to get my key back from them. When I walk in, he is sitting in the living room with a glass in his hand. He doesn't usually drink but it looks like he is tonight.

"Hi, Daddy," I sit next to him on the couch and offer a weak smile.

"I was worried. What have you been doing? Your mother said you called her yesterday." His eyes are that sad gold color again.

"I was just out. I went to a support group last night and I'll keep going every week if I feel up to it. I offer the most information I have since Evan's death.

"Well, that's good. As long as you aren't holed up in your room for days at a time," he sighs. "Do you want anything to eat?"

"No, but I will join you in a drink." He opens his mouth to protest and then closes it again. I open another bottle of red and realize it's my last bottle in the house. I'll have to go get some more tomorrow. This will have to do for tonight. I pour myself a glass almost to the rim and have half of it gone before I join him. We are both silent for a few moments enjoying our drinks. He is the first to speak.

"I'm so sorry that you are going through this. I just want you to be happy. I know it seems impossible right now, but believe me, you deserve happiness and you will get it. God never puts on us more than we can handle." I have heard these words from both of my parents my entire life. I used to believe it.

"I know Dad." He doesn't believe me. "I appreciate you and Mom paying my bills and when I'm working again, I will pay you back I promise."

He lets out a quick laugh, "No, you won't. We don't want you to. You take all the time in the world. We just want you to be healthy and happy. I mean it."

"Where is Mom anyway?" I say trying to change the subject.

He shakes his head in frustration. "She has thrown herself into work. I hardly ever see her," he looks so sad.

"I realized the last few days that you and Mom have lost something important too Dad. I just can't be supportive of you right now. I'm too lost myself to try and make anyone else feel better," tears threaten, and I have another sip before he notices.

"I know Nettie, I know." The ice in his glass clinks as he takes the last sip. He leans forward and places the empty drink on my coffee table and then sighs.

"I'm going to go home," he looks at me and smiles. "Call me tomorrow please, and just check-in."

"I will." I don't move or walk him to the door as I normally would, and he quietly leaves.

"Alone again." I tip up my glass emptying it and pour myself another. I feel like I made a little more progress today. All I can think of is how empowered I felt today with that gun. I'm going to be a hell of a shot by the time I come face to face with Sam. A warmth spreads from deep inside me. Anger, excitement, and pain. All rolled into one. I can't wait for that day. I imagine it in my mind. Him standing in front of me with those cold red eyes, the gun pointed right between them. Maybe I won't shoot him in the head. Maybe I will make him suffer first, like he has made me suffer. Would that make me a monster too? No. I shake my head. That would make me human. A woman violated and ruined. A mother robbed of her only child.

Broken and left alone. That's how I want to see him before he goes. Broken and alone. I replay the fantasy over and over again in my head. Each time it changes. Each time it ends the same. Him dead and me standing over his lifeless body, smiling. Relishing in the fact that I have won.

Chapter 25

Hello, My Name Is

I arrive at the hospital for my second support meeting and this time I'm looking forward to it. I know it will be quiet time for me not to have to deal with anyone else. As I make way into the room I look straight at the floor. I'm not ready to talk yet. Not only do I want to stay silent around this group, but I don't need one of these people cornering me, either. Luckily, the seat I occupied last week is still available and I sit quickly. I don't bother with the coffee they are serving, it tasted terrible. I opt to bring my own this evening.

I make myself comfortable and sip on my tall hazelnut blend. It is divine. After a beat, I hear the director begin his same speech from last week and I settle on what I think will be my weekly routine. I people watch. Well, I suppose I footwear watch. The woman in the all too sexy spiked heels is there again in the same spot, only today instead of black heels she is wearing bright red leather slingbacks. I move my eyes to my right and again see Adidas Man. Same shoes as before and it looks like the same jeans as well. Once again, the whites on his shoes are impeccably clean. This week though he is sitting back a row further than he was. I continue to look around the room and notice that Orthopedic Shoes isn't here, but instead, there is a pair of brown men's dress shoes. Wingtip oxfords, it looks like. I noticed that the director is finished speaking and Hooker Heels rises. I start playing music in my own head to make myself relax. Soon she is finished, and Adidas takes his turn. By this time, I'm on my third song and I'm imagining that I'm relaxing on a beach somewhere all by myself with only the music in my head and a drink in my hand.

I'm brought back from vacation by weak applause and I realize our time is finished. I hear everyone speaking at once. They are going through their goodbyes. I don't know if I will ever speak to these people or not. I don't really care right now. Maybe in the future, I'll find some friends here. We'll see.

After my meeting, I look at the clock and realize I can get in an hour or so at the shooting range if I hurry. I walk in and greet Hank with a smile.

"How are you tonight Hank?"

"I'm well, dear. And yourself?" I can tell when he looks at me that he thinks I'm crazy or damaged, or both. I have been here every day since my first time. I'm addicted. I feel complete and total control and power when I'm here.

"Fine thanks." I know the drill by now I enter through the doors and find my spot. Hank passes me the revolver. I haven't bought it yet because I can't decide if this is the right fit for my intentions. I'm getting so used to it, that I may want something more powerful.

The hour flies and before long there is rough and tough Hank over the intercom announcing that they are closing. I bring my target to me and notice that my aim is getting much better already. I see a few strays but overall, I would say he is dead. A slow smile spreads across my face. I don't know who this woman is that is taking over me, but I like her. I like her better than the weak pathetic victim I was just months ago. I think I could get used to her.

The drive home is a quiet one. I plan on calling Jessica when I get there and make plans to meet up. She will be married in a few months and I need to tell her I don't intend on being in her wedding. I don't want to ruin her day. I will be there of course; I mean she is my very best friend. I just don't have the patience to fake a smile for an entire day. I don't know if she'll understand, but I hope she does. I need her to be here when and if I ever get back to being a normal social person. When Sam is dead and gone. I want to spend time with my old friends again. I want to be with my family, and I want to somehow have a normal life if there is such a thing.

I prepare for my phone call by first having a glass of wine and then pouring another. The phone rings and rings and just as I begin to hang up, she answers. "Hello?" she sounds pissy already.

"Hey, it's me," I whisper.

"Yeah, you have your own ringtone remember?" her response is short, so I had better get to the point.

"Jess, I am so sorry we haven't spoken more and that I haven't returned your calls. I know you are probably busy with the wedding and I want to make it up to you. Can I make you dinner at my place this weekend?" she pauses, and I realize I have my fingers crossed and I'm biting my lower lip.

"Yeah, sure. How about Friday night? Colton has to work late so we weren't planning anything anyway." Oh, thank goodness.

"Great! And bring all your wedding stuff okay? I want to know everything that you've picked out so far." My mom is her

293

wedding planner but every time she has brought it up, I cut her off. I think it's only right if Jess shares this with me herself.

"Alright, I will. I miss you," her voice is much softer now.

"I know, I miss you too." We both hang up without another word.

We have always had this relationship that we never need to say we're sorry. We just go along with our day to day knowing that we will always be a part of each other's lives no matter what. We are sisters. I don't want to disappoint her. I can put on a happy face for one night to make her feel important. It's one of the happiest times in her life and I need to be supportive. Isn't it strange that the happiest time in her life is the most miserable of mine?

For the rest of the week, I go about *my* normal day to day stuff. When I can peel myself from my bed, I only go to the shooting range. The second I'm home I drink enough to go to sleep and the whole thing starts again. Sometimes I sit outside and stare at the sky. When the moon and stars are bright, I find myself praying and talking to Evan.

It's rare that I sleep a whole night without a nightmare. I notice the more I have to drink, the less they creep in. They are always the same. I'm losing the baby over and over again. I'm holding his limp body in my hands and trying to save him. That is the worst one. If it's not that, it is Sam on top of me tormenting me and I'm paralyzed under the weight of his body. I'm powerless in my sleep but when I'm awake, I dream of the ultimate power; saving the world from the devil. I have begun to form this sick obsession with killing him. A sick but satisfying obsession.

I look around my dirty house and decide to make a half hazard attempt to clean before Jessica gets here. I know she won't care what the place looks like, but it's truly disgusting. The dishes are piled in the sink and there are clothes trailed all through the house. I should light a candle too. Something is beginning to stink in here.

I do a quick sweep over the place not getting into any deep cleaning, but at least I run the vacuum and get the dishes done. Apparently, it has taken me longer than I thought it would because when I look at the clock, I realize I have no time to shower. Ah, fuck it! I showered yesterday. I run to my room to at least change my clothes and then do inventory of the kitchen to see what we have to drink and eat. Well, wine to drink of course and I have no food because I haven't been to the grocery store. Shit! Why didn't I go to the store while I was out? I promised her dinner! I snatch up my cell and dial the number of my favorite local Chinese restaurant. Delivery in twenty minutes. Perfect. She doesn't need to know that was a last-minute choice. It's her favorite Chinese place too.

Before I can place my phone back on its charging dock, there is a soft tap at the door. When I answer Jess has a sullen look on her face. I don't know if she is angry with me, sad, or indifferent. I take the initiative and pull her into an embrace. I hear her sniffling. "You know I can't stay mad at you."

I back away and give her the best smile I can manage. Showtime! I'm going to have to act my ass off. "So, let me see the wedding stuff. I ordered Chinese instead of cooking I hope that's okay?"

"Yeah, that sounds great. I have been craving Chinese." She moves her hand across her belly and makes a growling sound.

We both settle into our comfort zone immediately. Well, she does, and I pretend to. She flips through a binder, that is ridiculously too large, full of wedding ideas. Jesus, good luck to my mother with this wedding. Pages and magazine clippings are spilling out everywhere. Lord help her, she is the most disorganized person on the planet. I have no idea what she is going on about. Something about her dress and the bustle, whatever that is and there is a problem with the neckline? What the hell is there some sort of wedding language I need to decode now too? I just keep nodding along and agree with whatever she says. This seems to be the easiest route to take. It's not that I'm not interested. It's just not at the top of my list right now.

Soon the food is here, and we are sipping on our wine and digging our chopsticks into the cardboard containers. There is a brief silence and I decide that now is the time to spring on her that I don't want to be in the wedding. "Jess," I am hesitant. I know she is going to be upset. "I know that this is such a special day for you, and I wouldn't miss it for the world, but I just... how do I put this? I'm afraid if I'm in the wedding and I'm having a bad day it will ruin yours. I want to be at your wedding, but as a guest only. Is that okay with you?" I hold my breath waiting for some sort of reaction. Anything at all but I can't gauge her at the moment.

"I guess, I mean that makes me really sad," her bottom lip begins to quiver. "I always imagined you would be a part of my wedding. You're my best friend. I want you to be beside me." Her head is down, and she has yet to make eye contact with me.

"I know and I'm so sorry. I just have been a complete and total question mark. I don't think I can bare a fake smile all day. I mean, not that I won't be happy for you," I think I stuck my foot in my mouth.

"No, I get it. It will just take me a little while to get used to it." I can almost feel the distance between us widen. Oh, I don't want to lose my best friend. She is quick to change the subject and we go on with awkward small talk for a bit more.

At only 8 o'clock she makes up some sort of excuse for needing to leave and I let her. I'm beginning to tire of the phony, happy Nettie. We give each other a brief and now uncomfortable hug before she leaves. I pause a moment after closing the door and lean my head back. I exhale loudly when I hear her car door close. Alone at last. I pour my drink and decide to have a bath.

While I soak, I fantasize about how satisfying it will be to have Sam out of my life. For good. I play the scenario over and over in my head and it's soothing. I'm comforted by my imagination. I'm startled when my phone rings, and I attempt to reach out to grab it off of the counter. It's too far. Oh, well. Whoever it is I can call them back. The water is beginning to cool around me. I step out of the bath and wrap my terrycloth robe around me. I'm reminded of the day I went into labor. I wish we could rewind to that day and I could hold my little man again. I miss him so much. I'm hugging myself now in comfort. I'm interrupted by my phone again. How obnoxious. If I'm not answering maybe, it's for a reason. "What!" I snap.

"Nettie, darling," It's my mother. "It's Daddy". My world stops.

Chapter 26

Close Call

"Mom what? What about Dad?" I'm in a complete and total panic.

"They think he had a heart attack." Ok, what does that mean is he okay is he alive? Before the words can come out, she answers me. "He is at the hospital. I don't know anything yet. The guys from the dealership called me and said all they know is that he collapsed, and they called an ambulance. I'm on my way now. Do you want me to pick you up?"

"No, you are already on your way I'll meet you there," I hang up before hearing her response. I rush to get dressed and grab my purse on the way out the door. He has to be okay, he just has to be. God cannot do this to me too. Fuck! I'm going to lose my mind here. I don't even remember the drive to the hospital, but here I am. I rush into the front desk and merely say my father's name.

"Nettie!" My mom comes in right behind me. How in the hell did I manage to beat her here? A nurse interrupts before I can respond to my mother.

"He is on the fifth floor. Cardiac monitoring unit. Room 512"
This is all the information we receive.

Both of us scramble to the elevators and I press the button
that reads 5. My mom grabs my hand tightly as the elevator rises.
Thank goodness we are alone. I can hear both of our panicked
breathing as the elevator settles on our destination. The doors open
and we rush out. There is a large nurse's station, and we get a few
quizzical looks but don't bother explaining ourselves.

"There!" I shout. Room 512. The door is open. When we rush
in, we both let out a much-needed sigh of relief as Daddy is sitting up
awake in his hospital bed.

"Jesus Daddy! What the hell happened?" My mother is
already kneeling at his side with her face buried in his chest.

"Shhhh Mary I'm fine really." He looks at me, giving that
half-smile of his. He has a tube connected to his nose and wires
coming out from underneath his hospital gown. There are monitors
on either side of him. I would imagine these are keeping track of his
heart. So, he did have a heart attack.

"Dad, are you alright? Was it a heart attack?" I'm still
freaking out. He doesn't look like himself.

"No, they don't think it was a heart attack. They are monitoring me for the night though just to be safe. I'm sorry if I worried my girls." He sounds out of breath by the end of his sentence.

"So, I don't understand: if you didn't have a heart attack, what did happen?" I'm so confused.

"Well I was in the showroom at the dealership, talking to a few customers and I all of a sudden felt like I couldn't breathe, and I had a horrible pain in my chest. Apparently, I passed out because next thing I know I woke up here." Oh, thank God he woke up. "The doctor I spoke to a few minutes ago thinks I may have just had some sort of anxiety attack. I told him about all the stress I have been under." All because of my problems my strong father has been brought to his knees. My eyes begin to well up and I try and take a sobering breath.

"I'm just glad you are okay old man. I don't think we could have gotten along without you. But, I guess this means you need to stop worrying so much about other people and focus on yourself," I try being the parent.

the actual bills when I come to familiar handwriting. It's from Sam. Just as I'm about to rip it into pieces, I stop myself. I'm not as afraid of him as I used to be. I wonder what he has to say. I fight with my subconscious for what seems like forever and I finally decide to open it. As I slip my pinkie into the corner and begin to open it, I feel my heartbeat quicken and my palms begin to sweat. Alright, so he still makes me a little scared. I freeze when I read his words. I can hear him hiss each one to me. Something so simple, yet so scary.

My Darling Nettie, Tick, tick, tick.

Xoxo

Sam

Sick asshole! Doesn't he get it? I want him out. I want him out, so I can make sure I never see him again. I want him six feet under. And frankly, I don't care if we are both dead. As long as he pays for what he has done to me and my family. He has no control over me anymore. I have control. I need to repeat this to myself. This will be my mantra. "I have control!" I rip the letter into as many tiny pieces as I can and throw it into the garbage. When I do, I realize that

307

this is the first letter I have gotten at my new place. How the hell did he know the address? Why am I even surprised? He seems to know everything.

This has been yet another long day and the letter was just icing on the cake. I cannot wait until he is dead, and my nightmare can end. Speaking of nightmares, I pour myself a glass of red in hopes of keeping them at bay. Before falling asleep I say a prayer, "Dear Lord, if you are up there, I just want to thank you for taking care of my father. He is the most important man in my life, and I couldn't handle another loss. Please protect us and keep us safe from harm." I think you owe us that.

Chapter 27

Till death do us part

"I can't believe today is the day!" Jess is facing the mirror in her ivory wedding gown. She looks stunning. I have never seen her so happy.

"You look incredible Jess, really. I'm so happy for you," I wrap my arms around her from behind and give her a squeeze. I'm so glad that I have decided not to be in the wedding. I have been so emotional today. I've taken frequent trips outside to catch my breath and readjust my happy face. I lift my camera to break the tension. *Click, click.* I catch the bride off guard, and I know it will make a beautiful candid shot. I'm not the official photographer for the wedding, but I cannot help but make my own album for my best friend. She sticks her tongue out in annoyance and I snap yet another one. We both begin to giggle and soon comes her machine gun, out in full force.

"Five minutes!" My mother pokes her head through the door in announcement and she is gone again. Very professional she is today.

"Alright Cinderella, I will let you get to your future husband.
I'll see you out there." I give her a quick peck on the cheek. I need to
get out of here or I will burst into tears. As I walk out the door, I can
hear her sigh.

"Ready honey?" I hear her father whisper.

I make my way through the hallway lined with six beautifully
dressed bridesmaids in yellow chiffon. Each girl is holding a bouquet
of white lilies. The stems are wrapped in matching yellow fabric. My
mother is so very talented at what she does. The chandeliers above my
head are draped in flowers as well. Intertwined with the flowers are
small crystals, that sparkle at every turn.

I walk through the large cedar doors and I'm amazed at how
many people are here. The pews are completely full of guests. As I
make my way down the center aisle, I can smell the fresh flowers that
cap each row and smile with pride for my mother and for Jessica. I
notice my dad sitting on the right side about five rows back and I slide
in to join him. He puts his arm around me for a moment and gives me
a quick reassuring squeeze.

Colton is standing at the front of the church with his
groomsman, one of them being Matt. I know most of them because I

have known Colton for so long. He looks nervous. Really nervous. He catches my eye and I give him a soft wave and a grin. He returns the smile and rolls his eyes at the same time. I can see him let out a breath. *Click, click.* Perfect shot. I think it's only right that Jessie gets to see him before she made her grand entrance. Startling me the music amplifies and all eyes move to the back of the room. I stand in anticipation of seeing Jessica. My best friend. My rock. She is going to start her new life today. I'm feeling such pride at this moment like I am her parent. We have spent so much of our lives talking about the day we would be married and have children. We've dreamt about double dates and family vacations together. Our kids would go to school together and be best friends, just like us. I wonder if that will ever happen for us. If I'll ever have a family of my own. My heart begins to ache, and tears soon fill my eyes.

Jessica is almost to our isle now and I smile, trying to pretend that the tears I'm shedding are from happiness. I think she bought it. I glance toward Colton once more and he has tears streaming down his cheeks. He looks like a blubbering mess. I laugh out loud without warning and then manage to get it under control. Thankfully the music is loud, and no one noticed my inappropriate outburst.

311

The ceremony goes on without a hitch. It's touching, really. These two people I have known for ages and seen together numerous times. I didn't realize the depth of their feelings until today. As they say their vows, it's like no one else is in the room. It is just the two of them and they are pledging their love to one another. I know that he will treat her good. It's almost a relief to me that I have less of a friendship responsibility now. I know I'm so closed off lately. I can't pretend to be the person I used to be. She is in good hands for life.

Suddenly the room erupts with applause and I join the rest of the guests in cheers and laughter. Jess and Colton turn to face us and holding hands they raise them in triumph. They kiss and smile as they make their way back down the aisle. I can hear her giggle all the way to the back of the church. One by one, each row is excused, and we make our way through the receiving line at the church entrance. When I come to Jessica, her look changes, she looks somber. Oh, it's the pity look. I haven't seen it from her in a while. I give her a reassuring smile and we embrace for what seems like forever.

"I really am happy for you. You know that right?" I whisper in her ear.

"I do. I really do. I know you'll know only happiness one day too. Do you know that?"

I shake my head no. I feel the familiar lump grow in my throat again. I don't know that. In fact, I adamantly disagree with that. I pull away from her before I crumble to pieces. I quickly move to Colton and spend only a moment congratulating him. I put my head down as to avoid eye contact with everyone else and move straight to the door. When I reach the fresh air, I take a long deep breath as if breaking the surface of water. My face is buried in my hands as I weep. I can feel my father standing next to me, but he says nothing.

After I let myself release some of my pain, I gradually get it together. I wipe underneath both eyes and gently stroke my dress to release the wrinkles. I look at my father and nod. He wipes under my eyes again. I must have some lingering mascara. He holds out his hand for mine and in silence, I place my hand in his. We take our place in line with white rose petals in hand. A few minutes later Jess and Colton emerge from the church, grinning from ear to ear. The crowd begins showering them with the soft, perfumed flowers. They climb into the black stretch limo and pull away, waving out the window as they drive away. I laugh as I look at the back of the car. Written in white are the words

Just Married…Finally.

No doubt done by the wedding party. It's about time. The rest of the guests make our way to our own transportation. The reception will be held at a hall not too far from here, it's a grand ballroom and surely my mother has it made it look like a royal gala. I can't wait to see how everything comes together. I snap a quick photo of the car as it drives away. I decide once I'm at the reception, I'll only take a few photos and then make myself enjoy the wedding as a guest, not as a photographer. Well, I guess I can't even call myself that. I haven't worked for so long.

After today I realize I do miss it. I don't miss the boring shoots, but I miss capturing everyday life. Maybe this is something I should try and incorporate back into my daily routine. I laugh out loud at myself. Normal is far from what my life has become. Drinking, shooting, meetings and solitude are anything but normal.

"What's so funny?" my father asks.

"Oh, nothing I was just thinking." I blush with embarrassment. I forgot he was here. He shakes his head not pressing me anymore. The ride to the hall is full of boring conversations. I feel like my father is afraid of silence with me. I think back to his hospital scare.

He has since been put on a daily medication for anxiety as well as the "as needed" drugs. He had a few more times where he almost began to panic, and the doctors decided it would be best to have a daily depression and anxiety medication. He has been doing well. At least that is what my mom and he keep assuring me. I wish he would slip my mother a pill sometimes. For my sake, not hers. She is smothering most of the time, or tries to be.

When we arrive, there are cars piling into the parking lot. Even more so than there were at the church. Geez, there must be three hundred people here. So much for a small wedding. I'm amazed when we enter. It is spectacular. In all the years my mother has been a party planner, I have never seen anything like this. It looks like a million-dollar affair. The tables are draped with ivory linen tablecloths, accented with pale yellow napkins to match the bridesmaids. In the center of each table stand a tall glass cylinder that is etched with delicate diamond shapes, so that the candle inside lets off a magical sparkle. Encircling each is a ring of flowers, matching the décor of the rest of the room.

My father and I make our way through each table to find my mother. She is in the far corner near the 5-tiered exquisite cake, giving someone instructions. This is what she does best. When we approach, her tone changes and she looks so happy. This is her niche. She is in her own little world when she's doing this, and it's wonderful to see. My father and I both give her a huge bear hug and congratulate her on a job well done.

"Really? I didn't want it to be too much. I feel like this has been the most pressure I have ever had doing a wedding because it's Jess! I mean talk about not wanting to disappoint your client. I think she is happy with everything, don't you? Oh, I hope so." My mother is practically gasping for air after her rant. She seems like her old self for a moment. She is positively glowing. I feel a little relief inside, that maybe my friends and family are beginning to heal some from the trauma we've all suffered. I'm a bit envious of them. Moving on with their lives and having some happiness. I shake the feeling off and realize I should be happy for them. It gives me a tiny bit of hope that maybe someday, I will be there too.

I bring myself back to the present. My father and I take a seat at our assigned table and sip on our water. I'm in desperate need of a drink. I think my dad can sense my irritability because he offers to go get us a few cocktails. When mine arrives, I suppress my need to drink it down at once and take a much more appropriate ladylike sip. Our salads have arrived, even though the bridal party has yet to. I'm sure they are taking pictures and it makes me sad. I hope I don't look back on this day and regret that I wasn't in those pictures with her. I take another sip of my drink, this time not so ladylike, but no one notices.

The table we are seated at is referred to, I suppose, as the single table. I recognize only one person sitting here and that is Jessica's cousin Rachel. I'm sure she doesn't remember me. The last time I saw her she was in braces and overalls. She was annoying as a child. From the looks of her now, she has grown into a lovely young woman. Everyone else at the table is unknown to me and frankly, I'm offended my mother sat us here. I pick at my salad and make small talk with my father. Soon the main course has arrived, and it smells heavenly. A petite filet with a side of redskin mashed potatoes and a vegetable medley. I'm not very hungry, but I don't want to offend anyone, mainly my mother, so I put a dent in each of them. It really does taste decadent.

As soon as our plates are cleared there is an announcement that the bride and groom have arrived. The chatter around the room has slowly dulled and everyone is looking to the door. The bridal party is announced couple by couple and they finally come to the couple of the hour.

"Ladies and gentlemen, for the first time as husband and wife, Mr. and Mrs. Colton Daniels." The room erupts into screams and applause. Jess looks absolutely radiant. She and Colton are all laughs and kisses as they make their way to the front of the room. Standing together they face the crowd. I hear the clinking of glass and Colton's best man takes the microphone to make his toast. I stare at her in amazement of how far she has come from childhood to an adult. For some reason I have always felt like an older sister to her. Lately, the roles have been reversed but seeing her like this takes me back.

After the best man speech comes the maid of honor. As my replacement, she chose her college friend, Amber. I have to say, it stung a little. Even though, it was all my doing. Amber is a petite little red head who looks like she is still in high school but with big fake boobs. She has an annoyingly high-pitched voice as well. I suddenly feel very jealous and critical of her. I would have had a much better toast for Jessica. It would have been witty and sentimental, something she would have remembered her whole life. In fact, I had gone over and over it in my head before I decided to back out. I hope she can forgive me. Now for the rest of her life, she has to listen to little miss teenager tell her how wonderful she looks and how wonderful her husband is and how wonderful their lives will be together. God, doesn't she know any other words. No one is listening to you, fake boobs, sit down! I'm admittedly being a bad sport about this whole thing. It's my fault and mine alone that I'm not standing up there. I polish off my drink just as she finishes her, not so moving toast. Geez, she even has tears in her eyes. How fake can you be?

"Everything okay?" My father inquires. My irritation must be noticeable.

"Uh, sure. Just moved by the toasts that's all." He smirks at me sensing my sarcasm. I smile and tilt my head sideways in the most annoying way and give a runner up pageant clap.

Just then, a man in a black and white waiters uniform passes by and I order my father and I another drink. When I look at his glass.

It's only half empty. I had better slow down a bit. We still have three

hours to go here. That is if I stay the entire time. I feel like I'm ready

for another breather. The man next to me smells of cigarettes, which

makes my stomach churn. I excuse myself and head outside, which,

ironically is full of smokers. I make my way to the side of the building

and find a lone bench. I close my eyes and relax for a few moments.

Just then I hear someone whistle. When I open my eyes who other

than Matthew is standing in front of me, looking as dapper as ever in

his tuxedo.

"Aw, look at you all dressed up in your penguin suit. It

reminds me of prom," I give him a gracious smile.

He opens his coat and twirls showing it off. "No

compliments necessary. I know I look good," he says with a cocky

smirk on his face.

"Well, I'm in need of a drink so why don't you take this girl

in and get her drunk." He looks serious all of a sudden. "What?" I ask.

"Nothing, I just want you to take it easy tonight, that's all."

I can't believe he said that. What does he think I would get drunk

and do something stupid at Jessica's wedding? Who does he think

he is!

320

"Well, thank you very much, Dad! I think I can handle myself. I'll see you later," I stand and turn toward the front of the building stomping away in my new black mary janes. What a dick! I hear him mumble some sort of half-assed apology before I turn the corner. Making my way angrily through the smokers I head into the building and straight to the bar. I order a shot of whiskey and take it down quick. God, that burns! I raise my hand to the bartender for one more and throw it back as well. Oh, I should have ordered a chaser I feel the warmth rise for a moment and then thankfully it goes back down. I hope no one saw me take two. The bar isn't too crowded, being that it's the beginning of the night.

I make my way back to the reject table and my father is still sitting there. He pulls out my seat for me as I approach. I smile and sit next to him without a word. "You okay?" I nod in reply and turn my head away from him. I can tell that my face is flushed from the alcohol already. It looks like they are about to cut the cake. I'm ready to get out of here already. All this happy is beginning to make me miserable. My other drink arrives, and I'm careful to nurse it this time. I don't want my father to know that I'm getting drunk. How as an adult, can I still care that my parents know I'm drunk?

Finally, all of the formalities are done, and the music begins to get fun. Jess comes over to get me and I'm totally buzzed. I don't know how good of a dancer I'll be. She pulls me by the arm, and we make our way to the dance floor. A group of women and just a few men are out there now. I do my best to follow the beat and so does Jessie. We have only been superstar dancers in the privacy of our own homes. For some reason, our moves don't look as good next to other people. Before I know it, four or five songs have passed, and I'm sweating and winded. A slow song comes on and that is my cue. I make my way over to the bar and order another drink. As I tilt my head back for the first sip, I realize that I'm not just buzzed I am totally drunk.

I make my way to the bathroom as quickly as possible and hide in a stall before anyone sees me. I grab some tissue and wipe the sweat from my forehead, face, and chest. I need to drink some water. I peek between the cracks of the stall door to be sure I'm alone. I cup water in my hands and take a few sips. When I glance up at the mirror, I'm embarrassed. I'm visibly drunk and sloppy. I piece of toilet paper is sticking to my cheek. As I remove it, Matt's somewhat of a lecture replays in my head. I probably should go home.

"Are you feeling okay?" Matt is standing right outside the women's bathroom. I have been avoiding him all night. He is more relaxed now. No jacket or vest and his tie are hanging open.

"No, actually I want to go home."

"Do you want me to give you a ride?" I can tell he is thinking I told you so. but trying to hide it.

"No, my dad is here so I will tell him I'm ready," I snap.

"Well, actually I saw him helping your mother with something. Really, I can take you Nettie, it isn't any trouble."

"Fine. Just let me tell my parents I'm going and give Jess a hug." He nods and moves so I can slide by him.

Jess seems disappointed that I'm leaving but she is understanding. My mother and father are actually dancing with one another. They look so in love. My father looks up at me and I point to the door and mouth *Matt* so he knows I have a ride. He gives me a small wave and I return it.

Matt is waiting by the front doors and I walk past him exiting. I can hear his footsteps behind me. We ride back to my place in silence. I feel like I'm beginning to get the spins. When we pull into my driveway Matt asks if I want him to walk me in and I decline. I'm now embarrassed that he was right. I should have taken it easy tonight. "Matt, I'm sorry I snapped at you earlier. I know you were just trying to help. I shouldn't have had so much to drink."

"No, I'm sorry. It is none of my business. I just want what's in your best interest. I mean, I love you and care about you." All of a sudden, I feel my cheeks flush. "Oh, Nettie no, no, no. not like that. I mean of course you were my first love, but I don't mean like I want to date. I'm sorry that came out wrong."

"No Matt, it's me who is sorry. I was thinking you were saying something you weren't and believe me I'm not offended. I feel the same way about you. I love and care about you too, but I'm strictly in the friend zone." He looks as relieved as I feel.

"Ok, good." He puts his hand on his chest and giggles. I suddenly feel like I've sobered up a bit. I lean forward and give him a gentle kiss on the cheek.

"Thank you, friend. Great, amazing, handsome friend for bringing me home safely." He blushes.

"You're very welcome equally great, amazing and beautiful friend. Anytime."

I step out of the car and incredibly I make it into the house without the slightest stumble. I bend down pulling off my shoes, as I make my way to my bedroom. Without so much as unzipping my dress, I plop face-first onto the bed and stay there until morning.

Chapter 28

Time

The next six months are a complete and total blur. My days are filled with solitude. I have barely spoken to Jessica since her wedding. I don't know if it's because of my socially awkward behavior, or her busy married life. Unfortunately, the thought has not consumed me much. I have been focused on one thing and one thing only, my revenge. I spend nearly every day at the shooting range and have become a pro. I have upgraded from that .38 special to a beautiful .357 Magnum. I decided to stick with this one because I feel most comfortable with it. Hank has become a close friend. Even though I only see him at the shooting range. He jokes that because I'm there so much, I single-handedly am paying his salary. He is probably right. Luckily, I can use my credit card to pay for my addiction.

Finally, in the last few months, I have been able to start paying my bills again but barely. I have been selling some of my photographs. Mostly I have been doing candid photos. I have kept my camera with me at all times and if I see a moment that I feel needs to be captured, I do it. I have had a few shots of mourners in the

judgment to have him. My whole existence was turned upside down. I guess I just want to know…" tears are streaming down my cheeks before I even realize. "Will it ever get any better?" I'm full out sobbing now and I can't speak anymore. I can hear my own sobs as well as sniffling from some other group members.

"Yes, it will. The pain doesn't go away…ever. But it does get better." This voice is the most comforting voice I have ever heard. It's Adidas and I don't know if it's what he said or the sound of his smooth voice, but I want to match a face with the feet. Slowly my eyes move up his body to his face. When I look up, he looks familiar to me though my eyes are clouded with tears. I wipe them away with my hands and as I focus, I see the most beautiful chocolate brown eyes I have ever seen, again.

"Lincoln?" I whisper. Oh my God, it's Evan's pediatrician. All this time he has been a few feet from me. Why then didn't he ever approach me? I don't understand. And what is his story? I have never heard him. Suddenly, Director Comb Over interrupts my pure shock.

"Nettie, we are out of time I'm sorry. If you need anything this week feel free to call." What an asshole. I wipe away my tears feeling like an idiot. See, this is why I don't talk much.

The group breaks up and begins to leave, but not Lincoln. He remains in his seat with a kind smile on his face. I walk over to him and take a seat directly in the row in front of him. I turn around so that we are face to face. God, he is the most beautiful man I have ever seen. His hair is a bit disheveled, but in a good way. We both sit for a beat, not saying a word. I can feel warmth spread down my cheeks and I'm crying again. Finally, he speaks.

"Hi." That's all, just hi?

"Hi." Is my reply. Good comeback idiot! "Why haven't you ever spoken to me before?" I finally ask.

"What do you mean? I was wondering why you haven't spoken to ME. I thought maybe you just didn't want to be bothered. Or that I must have made a terrible impression on you." I giggle at him. Just the opposite I think to myself.

"No, I um, well to be honest. I haven't even looked at anyone in this group. I felt like I needed to be disconnected a little, I guess," I shrug my shoulders.

"Oh, well I guess that makes sense, it's strange, but makes sense," he hesitates. "I don't mean to be forward but can we maybe go get some dinner. I mean finally after almost year you have acknowledged that I exist and, well you seem like you need more time

than you got here," he looks around the room and I see what he

means. Everyone has picked up and gone already and it's just the two

of us.

"Sure, I'd like that." Wow, what a change in my day. A normal

depressing fucked up day in the life of Nettie Madison is ending with

dinner. And not just dinner, but dinner with gorgeous, sexy and

apparently sensitive Dr. Lincoln Connors.

He holds his hand out to me and I take it without hesitation.

Why do I feel so comfortable with this man? He smiles when our skin

touches and so do I. I feel a connection with him. I wonder if he feels

the same. He has been in the same room with me every week for

nearly a year and I had no idea. From the way he spoke, he wanted me

to talk to him.

We walk instead of drive to a nearby sandwich shop. I order a

bowl of soup and he gets a sandwich. We both opt for coffee since it's

cold tonight. We both eat in silence for a while and what's strange

about the situation is that I feel completely comfortable with the

silence. I occasionally glance up at him and each time he is looking

directly at me. He has the gentlest eyes I have ever seen. I suddenly realize that I have rudely not listened to his story in group. I finally speak first.

"Lincoln…"

"Linc, please," he interrupts me.

"Linc. Your daughter. You spoke about her the first time we met. She died of SIDS as well?"

He looks confused. "I have spoken about it in meetings, numerous times. Yes, she did. When she was nearly a year old."

"Oh, I'm sorry I should explain. I don't usually listen in group. I simply started going for the comfort of knowing I wasn't alone, but I didn't want the added depression of everyone else's story," I blush in pure embarrassment. "I apologize. I know that sounds very selfish."

"No, it's not selfish at all. I didn't speak for a while when I first started going. You have to get comfortable with everyone, I guess. And you don't go for them you go for you," he pauses then sighs. "So, you don't know anything about me?"

I shake my head no. "Sorry."

"Stop with the sorrys," he lets out a small giggle. "Well, do you want to know the whole story? I mean I don't want to depress you on top of your own story."

My "*story*". That sounds so cold. "No, I feel like I need to. I mean if you don't mind, of course?"

"No, not at all," he takes a deep breath and starts. "Well, my wife and I had our only child a little over three years ago." Oh, wife. Damn! "We named her Madelynn, after my wife's mother." He adds. "She was perfect, amazing actually. I know everyone thinks that of their own children, but she really was. She slept through the night almost immediately. She only cried when she was hungry. A perfect baby," he sounds so happy when he speaks about her. I want to ask what she looked like, but I don't want to interrupt him.

"When she was eleven months old, I was watching her while my wife went for lunch with a few friends. She was taking a nap in her crib and I decided to lay down myself. I must have zonked out because the next thing I know, my wife was screaming bloody murder." I visibly see him shudder at the thought. I am reminded of my own screams the morning I found Evan. "It was too late by the time my wife found her. There was nothing that could have been done. As a doctor, the rational part of me knew it wasn't my fault, but as a father, I thought the exact opposite. Now after group, I can say it wasn't my fault." I can tell he is trying to convince himself of this fact. He stops talking and looks down into his coffee cup.

"I'm so sorry, Linc." I want to reach across the table and squeeze his hand, but I feel like that would be inappropriate given the fact that we are really strangers.

He clears his throat and continues. "It doesn't get much easier telling the story. Like I told you in there though…" he points in the direction of the hospital, "it does get easier. It's still painful for me every day," a tear finally lets go and falls down his cheek. "But I can function now. I can go to work. I can see my friends. I can do happy things without feeling guilty about it."

"What about your wife. How has she coped with it?" He looks surprised by my question.

"Well, she didn't cope well. She blamed me. I blamed me. She left shortly after Maddy passed away. She couldn't stand to look at me anymore. She had my eyes; the baby," he wipes his tears away with the back of his hand. God, he has beautiful hands. "She hated me, and we divorced only three months later." He looks so broken. This time I do reach out and grab his hand giving it a gentle squeeze. I see him blush as I do.

"That must have made it twice as hard on you. Not having her to lean on," I whisper.

"Yeah, it was the worst year of my life. But about six months after that I started coming to the meetings and it really did help. To talk about it. To talk about Maddy and Lynn."

"Lynn?" I ask.

"Oh, my wife." Of course. "But you know not everything in the group is depressing. I mean, we talk about the good things that have happened since tragedy and it really does give hope for a future. You should really listen next time," he gives me a small wink.

I smile for the first time in a hell of a long time. A real smile. I feel shy all of a sudden and feel the need to speak.

"So, tell me. What are some happy things that have happened to you since then?" He looks at me and I can tell he is thinking.

"Well, I have a job that I absolutely love. I have a wonderful and supportive family. And I have been making some really great friends lately." I hope I can be added to that list. I think we can be friends. More than friends, I hope. Then it occurs to me that he doesn't know my whole story. Or does he? He was at the hospital when the baby was born. I wonder if anyone told him. I decide not to ask now. If he doesn't know, I'm in no way in the mood to explain.

I look up at the clock and it is getting late. Not that I have anywhere to be tomorrow. I just don't want the subject to turn to me.

"Well, I appreciate you sitting with me and telling me about all you've been through. Even with Evan's anniversary coming up, I feel like maybe there is some hope for me in the future. Thank you." He gives me that gorgeous, warm smile again.

"Anytime Nettie, really." I love to hear him say my name. His voice is comforting as he does. He has a strong but soothing voice. "Give me your cell phone." He catches me off guard, but I hand it over to him. He punches something in, and I hear a beeping sound. "There." He hands it back to me. "I put my number in. Anytime you need someone to talk to, day or night you can call me okay?"

"Yeah, thank you again. I will." I hope I do. I want to see him again. And not just at the meetings. Just then he stands, and I follow suit. Oh, I guess we are leaving. Suddenly I don't want to go. He leans toward me and for a moment I have no idea what he is doing, and I reach my arms around him and give him an awkward hug. He giggles and as he does, I realize he was reaching for my coat. How fucking

338

humiliating! I feel my face turn bright red. "Oh, my God. I'm so sorry that was wildly inappropriate. I just thought you were...I don't know what I thought. I'm so embarrassed!" I throw my hands over my face. I want to crawl into a hole! I hear him laughing and he grabs my hands.

"Don't be embarrassed. It's not inappropriate I was just going to help you get your coat on first." He places it back on the chair and this time slips both of his arms around my waist and pulls me into a gentle comforting hug. I embrace him back, wrapping my arms around his strong shoulders. For some reason, this doesn't feel strange at all. It feels wonderful. His wavy hair tickles my nose before we let go. As we pull back from one another our eyes lock. I feel that butterfly feeling that I felt the first time we met. He has such kind eyes. I want to see him again.

"Well, I hope we can see each other again," I say before I chicken out.

"Me too. And not just at group," he grins that sexy grin again. He read my mind.

He helps me to put my coat on and we both walk out together. We exchange a quick goodbye. We begin walking in opposite directions to our cars. I want to turn and look at him so badly but fight the urge. When I near my car the need has overwhelmed me, and I finally risk a quick glance. Just then he turns to look at me as well. He smiles a wide smile this time and I realize he has a dimple on his left cheek. I hadn't noticed that before. I smile back and he waves before getting into his own car. I give a small embarrassed wave and get in mine.

The entire way home I cannot stop thinking of him. I haven't been this giddy in a long time. I haven't been this, dare I say it, almost happy since before I lost Evan. This is what he meant by it gets better. I wish we had stayed longer. I want to hear his voice again. I start to feel almost anxious about it. I enjoy everything about him. His looks, his voice, the way he loved his daughter, and the way I felt when we hugged. I felt so safe and so comforted. We have such a natural connection but not only that we know what the other has been through. No one can possibly know the pain of losing a child unless they have lost one themselves. It's a feeling that is completely indescribable. I wonder when I will see him again.

Once I arrive home, I'm still going over our conversation. What a bitch his wife was for leaving him when he was is so much pain too. I'm going to have to tell him about my situation eventually. I'm surprised he didn't ask me tonight. Then again that makes me wonder yet again if he already knows. But if he did, he must be crazy for approaching me. If he knows how totally damaged I am, you would think he would try and steer clear.

As I lay in bed, his face is still burning into my brain. That beautiful dimple and the smile he gave me right before we left. Something sweet to dream about, I think. This is silly! What if he just intends on being friends? Although, he did say I could call anytime. I shake my head. He only said that to be supportive. Like if I was having a bad day or something. Well, every day is a bad day, right? So, I guess I could call him tomorrow. I roll onto my side with a grin on my face. "Sleep Nettie, just sleep."

Chapter 29

Getting to Know You

I wake at my usual time and I am drenched in sweat. This time I was in an open meadow and I could hear a baby crying. I knew that it was Evan, but I couldn't see him. I was startled by footsteps behind me and when I turned, Sam was there running toward me. I turned and tried to run from him, but I felt as though I was moving in slow motion. Just then, Evan appeared in front of me. He was wrapped in his blanket lying on the grass, and I knew I needed to get him before Sam did. Suddenly, Sam wrapped his hand around my mouth from behind. That's when I woke up.

I stay in bed for a while, staring up at the ceiling and decide it's a lost cause. I'm again thinking of Linc. I wonder what he is doing right now. Well, sleeping, hopefully. It's after two in the morning. I make my way to the living room and decide to read instead of watch TV. After a few minutes, I realize the effort to forget about Linc is fruitless. I pick up my cell and decide to text him. I know this is stupid, but I feel this uncontrollable need. I take a deep breath and scroll through my contacts. There he is. I smile when I read his name.

Lincoln Connor; call him!

Oh, my God, he put that in my phone! Well, I guess I'm going to do as instructed. I hit call instead of a text. Surprisingly he does not sound like he has been sleeping when I call.

"Hello?" his voice is so rich and smooth.

"Um, Lincoln. This is Nettie, from group." You are such a fucking idiot. Of course, he knows who you are! You just left him not five hours ago!

"Hi, are you alright? Is everything okay?" Shit, I shouldn't have called.

"Yeah, no I mean, I'm okay I just couldn't sleep and thought I would take a chance that you would answer your phone." I wait in anticipation for his reply.

"It's no problem at all, Nettie. I'm actually just having a coffee." Coffee? I look at the clock on the living room wall. It's 3 a.m. "I have rounds at five," he explains. Oh, yes, he is a doctor. Well good, I don't feel like such an ass about calling him so early.

"Good, I'm glad I didn't wake you. I should apologize anyway. It was rude of me to call in the middle of the night like this. I just felt like hearing your voice." Did I just say that?

"Well, I'm glad you did. Call I mean. I have been thinking about you since I woke up." I can hear the smile in his voice. Oh good, so I'm not crazy. These feelings I have for him are mutual. "What are you doing right now?" He catches me off guard. What does he think I'm doing? I'm at home in the middle of the night.

"Well just sitting here, not being able to sleep. See I have these nightmares sometimes. It's kind of hard to go back to sleep after having one." I feel the need to explain my erratic behavior.

"Can I pick you up?" Huh? Why? I thought he had to go to work. "I have time for breakfast if I skip the gym." I blush at the thought of seeing him again.

"I'd like that," I say shyly.

"Good. It's a date. Where do you live?" He called it a date. I'm beaming on the inside. I give him my address and he agrees to pick me up in ten minutes. And we hang up.

Oh, shit ten minutes. I run to the bathroom and turn on the light. "Fuck!" I look terrible! I brush my hair as fast as I can and pull it

344

into a tight smooth ponytail. Reaching for my make-up bag I pull out only the essentials My concealer, mascara, blush, and some lip gloss. I do my best to make myself presentable in the short amount of time I have been given. I throw on a pair of jeans. Just as I'm digging through my closet to find a sweater, there is a knock at the door. Shit, shit, shit I'm not ready. I grab the first shirt I find and throw it on. It'll have to do. After smoothing my hair once more with my hand I make my way to the door. I take one last deep breath before I open it. When I do Linc is standing there with that gorgeous grin on his face. He looks as handsome as ever. He is clean-shaven and his hair still a little damp. I want to scold him because it's so cold out, but he looks so damn good. He has on a long wool coat and black leather gloves. His neck is wrapped with a matching black scarf.

"It's really cold, you know," he interrupts my evaluation of him.

"Oh, sorry. Come in," I giggle and step back so he can move into the room. I close the door behind him and get my coat and scarf on as well. "Ready," I say to him.

"How do you look so adorable this early in the morning?" I'm so uncomfortable with compliments, but I maintain eye contact.

345

"You mean this late at night?" he shrugs his shoulder at me.

"My day is just beginning. And beginning well at that," he smiles, just enough so that his dimple shows. "Breakfast?" he holds out his hand for me and I don't hesitate to take it.

He is so charming and sweet. On the way to breakfast he tells me about a few of the patients he will be checking in on today. He lights up when he is talking about these kids. He describes a few and luckily none of them are in for anything more serious than pneumonia. He stops talking for a moment and shakes his head.

"What is it?" He looks so sad all of a sudden.

"My job. I love it, but sometimes I do lose patients. I think of how lucky I am to be around kids all day but that just makes me miss my own. And the parents." He focuses again on the road and doesn't say any more about it. I think about the doctor who had to come out and tell me that Evan was gone. To think that Lincoln has to be the one to do that. He seems like the type of person that would take his work home with him. He looks so young right now. So handsome.

"How old are you?" the question just flies out of my mouth.

"How old are you?" he snorts at my audacity.

"You should never ask a woman that!" I giggle "I'm proud to say I'm thirty." I stand up very straight to reinforce my pride. And he giggles again. He has a beautiful laugh. It is deep but soft and very infectious.

"Well, since you told me I'll tell you. I am thirty-two, not thirty also but thirty-two," he holds up his fingers to me and emphasizes the number two. I notice his sculpted hands again. Long slender fingers and perfectly smooth and soft. I am staring at him. "What? Do I have something on my face?" I can't help a loud laugh that escapes.

"No, sorry. I didn't mean to." How can I not stare? "You're just…funny."

"Funny? Funny ha-ha or funny strange?" He is trying to sound offended, but I can tell his mood is light.

"Don't worry, I meant funny ha-ha." I feel relaxed and nervous with him all at the same time.

"Ok great. Funny ha-ha I'm okay with. So, do you have a preference where we eat?" he asks, changing the subject.

"No, wherever you want, is fine with me. I'm not picky." He has a childish grin on his face.

"Good, because I only go to one place." We pull into the dirt parking lot and I can't help but laugh. "What's so funny? Have you eaten here? It's my favorite."

"Yes, as a matter of fact, I have." I look up at the sign that reads Mona's and sigh.

"Oh yeah? Do you like it? I have been coming here almost my entire life."

"Me too." He looks surprised.

We climb out of the car and I'm startled when he grabs my hand. "It's icy, I don't want you to fall. Don't worry, I'm not getting fresh with you," he winks at me. Damn, I wish he was. I nod at him and we make our way inside. I search the room for Jen, but she is nowhere to be found. She probably doesn't work this shift.

As I look around the room, I don't recognize any faces. A woman by the name of Zel seats us. What a strange name. Linc seems to know her well. He must come here a lot at this time of night. He is very sweet with her, almost flirty even though she is old enough to be his grandmother. She is a pretty woman. She has very dark brown hair and her eyes are a beautiful soft blue. After we are seated, she

348

takes our drink orders and we both get coffee. I need a coffee the size of my head right about now.

"Zel this is Nettie, a friend of mine. She has been coming here for a long time too." She looks confused.

"Never this early in the morning. And I haven't been here in a really long time actually." She smiles politely at me as she fills my coffee cup. "Um, I know Jen really well. Does she work this morning?" Her face pales in an instant.

"No, I'm sorry to be the one to tell you, but Jen passed away. It's been about five months now." My heart aches for her. She was such a nice woman. I should call my mother. Surely if she had heard she would have called me.

"I had no idea. Wow, I feel terrible." I look over at Linc and he is looking at me sympathetically.

"I'll give you two a minute to look at the menu." I think she is about to cry.

"Are you all right?" He gently places his hand on mine.

"Yeah," I shake my head. "I'm just surprised that's all. I can't believe I hadn't heard. She was a great lady. Every time I have been in

349

here, for as long as I can remember, she has waited on us." My eyes tear a bit and I wipe them before they can fall.

"I don't think I knew who she was," he said. I smile at him. Oh, he would if he had met her. She was very hard to forget. The waitress is back again. She looks as though she has composed herself. Oddly enough we both order chocolate chip pancakes and a side of bacon.

"Are you doing this on purpose?" I ask partly joking but partly serious.

"What do you mean?" he returns a mischievous grin. "Have you ever thought we might just have a lot in common?"

"Mmm-hmmm" I shift in my chair. I do think we have a hell of a lot in common. This must be the reason I feel so comfortable with him. I feel like I have known him all my life. I can't shake the way he looks at me sometimes. I don't think anyone has ever gazed into my eyes the way he does. Like he is really listening to me and not just waiting for his turn to speak. I like him. I like him very much.

After the most fun breakfast, he asks If I want to join him for rounds. I can do that. Well, anything to spend more time with him. I agree and he takes me across town to the hospital. I'm a little hesitant at first because I haven't had many pleasant experiences here, except for Evan's birth, of course. He senses my apprehension and once again holds my hand. I feel like I'm a teenager again and on a first date with the most sought-after boy in school. When we walk through the doors, he takes me into the doctor's lounge. He takes off his black suit jacket and replaces it with the white lab coat that he was wearing the first time I saw him in. He then reaches into his locker and pulls out a stethoscope, draping it over his muscular shoulders. He looks so professional. So together.

"Ready?" I nod. This is exciting. He visits his first few patients and I watch cautiously from the doorway. He is so amazing with these kids. He is sensitive and funny. They seem to adore him as much as he does them. The parents are smitten with him as well. He was made for this job and it's obvious. After about an hour he says a few words to one of the nurses and turns his attention back to me, "Do you mind if we make one more stop?"

"Of course." There must be a colleague he needs to speak with or something. I follow him to the elevators, but instead of stopping he continues to walk. We go through another set of double doors and then to the end of the hallway. The walls are yellow with suns and rainbows all over them. We approach a room and he holds a finger up to his mouth and his dimple appears.

What is he doing? He looks like a kid himself. He peeks quietly into the room and I tiptoe behind him.

"Boo!" Holy shit! I jump about two feet in the air and so does Linc. A little boy in a hospital gown, about ten years old, just scared the hell out of us! He is attached to an IV and has no hair on his perfectly round head. His hand is on his stomach and he is laughing hysterically. Tears are running down his face. What is going on here? "Hahaha Dr. Connor you are going to have to learn that I can hear your clumsy feet coming from a mile away!" Linc leans forward and playfully puts his dukes up.

"You think you can pull one over on me huh? Now you started a war!" We are all laughing now. Finally, Linc excuses himself and properly introduces us. "Cam this is Nettie, Nettie this is Cameron Drake. My favorite former patient." He lights up as he speaks. He must really love this kid.

"It's a pleasure, Cameron," I nod, and he blushes.

"Wow, you are really pretty." Then I blush. "What are you doing hanging out with this guy?" Linc shoots daggers at him with his eyes.

"Well, nobody else wanted to do anything at five a.m. Just this guy." I point my thumb at him and roll my eyes at the same time. When I look at Lincoln the daggers are now flying in my direction. I flash my famous too much teeth, please forgive me, smile. He can't contain his own grin and focuses his attention back at Cameron. He is a handsome young man. He has a twinkle in his eye too. So full of joy. He must be a very strong kid. They talk and joke for a while before another doctor comes in. He and Linc exchange pleasantries but he doesn't introduce me. Linc bids goodbye to Cameron and gives him a warm hug.

"See you tomorrow?" Cameron asks him on the edge of his seat.

"Yes, see you tomorrow." Lincoln replies. I wave to the little boy as we walk out of the room and I hear him yell.

"Nice to meet you, lady! You're welcome back anytime!" What a little flirt he is!

"Is he like that with all the ladies? Awfully bold for such a young kid." Lincoln looks so happy right now. I can see why he loves what he does. I don't want to ask how sick Cameron is. I'm afraid I won't like the answer. Lincoln doesn't offer any detailed information. All I know is that he has lymphoma. I don't know how bad it is, or if he will get better or not, but I don't want to upset Linc. I'm sure we will talk about it again. I hope we have many more talks.

"Well, I guess I need to take you home now. I would love to spend the day with you, but I have patients at the office now." The feeling is mutual. I want to spend the day with him too.

"Sure, I should get some things done today too." After a nap of course. I'm so exhausted. I only slept a few hours.

On the drive back to my place, there isn't a moment of silence. We talk the entire way and realize we have a lot more in common. Neither of us has siblings. His parents are still happily married as well, which seems unheard of these days. We love the same movies and music. And he has one of the most important qualities I love in a man, he cracks me up! He has the best sense of humor. I haven't felt this good in so long. I'm finally feeling like a human being again. I feel like

354

something inside of me has woken up after all this time. I'm falling for him already and oddly it doesn't scare me at all.

When we arrive, I'm hesitant to get out of the car. I don't know whether we will say our goodbyes here or if he'll walk me to the door. Just then he opens his door and I know it's the latter. He walks around to open my door and helps me out of the car. When we reach the door, I'm secretly hoping he will kiss me. What am I thinking? We practically just met. Our eyes lock for a moment and I feel like he can read my mind. He begins to blush a bit and I can tell he is nervous. He slowly leans forward planting a soft kiss on my cheek. I close my eyes and take in the soft feel of his lips. The smell of his skin is divine. I can't pinpoint what cologne he is wearing, but I know I have smelled it before. When he backs away from me, I can't help the silly grin covering my face. I don't know what to say. I don't want him to leave.

"Can I call you later?" he acts like a teenager. A thirty-two-year-old man is uncomfortable talking to a girl.

"I would love it if you would," I suddenly have butterflies in my stomach again anticipating his call and he is still in my presence.

"Good. I'll call you tonight. Around eight?" I nod. His grin begins to grow as well, and I know I'm not alone in my feelings. He likes me too. Without another word he gets into his beautiful BMW

and leaves. I miss him already.

Chapter 30

Much Needed Love

It's 7:50 and I'm sitting at my kitchen island willing the phone to ring. This has been a horribly long day. I did my usual after resting up this morning. The only difference is that I cannot get Lincoln out of my mind. I have been giddy all day. Even Hank noticed my change in mood. He joked that I must have gotten lucky because no one's mood changes that quickly. Well, I did get lucky just not in the way that he was implying. I shake my head. No, I'm certainly not ready for that step, but I hope I will be someday. My cell phone ringing interrupts my stray thoughts. I snatch it up a bit too quickly.

"Hello?" Oh shit! I sounded too anxious. Play it cool Nettie. No need to throw yourself at the man.

"Hey, what's up?" It's Jessie. Damn, why is she calling now?

"Oh, hey. Nothings up here. What's up with you?" I lack in hiding my disappointment.

"Were you expecting someone else? You picked up the phone before it even rang." I think she has me figured out.

"No, I'm sorry. I was expecting someone, but I would much rather talk to you." Good, that should do it. Can't hurt to butter her up a little bit.

"Well, I was just calling to check in with you. We haven't seen each other in a while, and I wanted to see if you wanted to have a girl's night?" That sounds like it could be a lot of fun. I suppose we do need to make up for some lost time. I have been completely emotionally unavailable for a long time.

"That would be great Jess. Just let me know when and where."

"How about this Saturday at my place? Colton is going to be out of town all weekend with the boys for some fishing trip or something. We can have a few drinks and just catch up."

"Perfect, I can't wait," I sound a little too enthusiastic, but what's funny is I'm not pretending.

"What's with you?" What does she mean? Does she think I'm being sarcastic? "You sound, I don't know happy. What gives?" God, does she know me too well. No sense in lying to her about it.

"I think I met someone," I say bluntly

"You met someone? Wow, when? Why didn't you tell me?"

"No, it's just recent and it's actually an odd story. I'll tell you all about him this weekend." Just then my phone beeps and it's another call. "Speak of the devil Jess I think he's calling. Can I let you go?"

"Yes, yes by all means. You better be prepared to give me every little detail! I'll talk to you later." She hangs up before I answer my other call. I take a quick breath.

"Hello?"

"Hey." Oh, his voice makes me melt.

"I'm glad you called," I didn't really expect him not to.

"I said I would. I never say anything I don't mean." I wish he was here. "I miss you."

What? He misses *me*? He is very forthcoming. I don't think I have ever met a man who hasn't played some sort of game with my emotions.

"You do?" My heart is beating a mile a minute and my palms are sweaty.

"Sorry, I should have kept that to myself." I can hear an embarrassing giggle. "It's just well, I do. I had a great time with you this morning. And you have to remember that I've been pining away for nearly a year over you." Pining for me? What the hell! This is so exciting! Even though I just started talking to him it's like we've known each other forever. I was hoping these feelings weren't just on my end of things.

"No, it just surprised me, that's all. The truth is I have been thinking about you all day. I miss you too," I cannot contain my smile, in fact, my cheeks hurt from my enormous grin. I can hear him audibly sigh.

"Oh, thank God, I thought I was going to scare you off!" No way. Not happening. I'm falling hard and fast myself. And I'm not easily frightened...anymore.

We talk for hours with ease. This is the first night in a long time that I can remember that I don't feel the need to drown my sorrows. We talk about everything under the sun. He explains more about the boy in the hospital, Cameron. He is intense when speaks about him, and I can tell he cares for him immensely. Apparently, Cameron has been battling cancer for some time now, but Linc is hopeful that he will beat it. Just when I think there isn't anything else for us to possibly talk about, something random comes up and we talk and talk. His tone changes with each subject. When we talk about his family, he is very serious and warm. I can tell he loves them very much. He has the same care for his patients as he talks about them, as well.

He speaks a little bit about his ex-wife, but I don't push the subject. I don't want to make him uncomfortable. He asks me about Evan's father, and I freeze. This is the first time I have been truly uncomfortable in this conversation. I debate on whether to get into this now or later.

"Well, it's a very, very long story that I will eventually tell you about. But for now, can we not? I'm sorry. You have been so open and honest with me I just..." He interrupts me.

"Hey, I don't want to make you talk about anything you don't want to. If it's a touchy subject, you don't need to tell me anything. It's none of my business." Touchy is the understatement of the universe.

"Thank you, I appreciate that. I will tell you though, sometime." He is smart, charming, loving, caring, and funny. On paper and in person he is a perfect man. I hope he sticks around for a while.

"Well, I hate to do this Nettie, but I do have to be up in about three hours." I look at the clock. Wow, we have been talking longer than I thought. "Believe me, I don't want to hang up this phone, but I know I will be dragging tomorrow if I don't."

"It's fine. I'm tired too." I don't want to hang up. I don't want to hang up.

"When can I see you again?" Now, I think to myself. I want to see him now.

"What about this weekend?" I don't want to wait that long.

"This weekend it is. Can I call you again tomorrow?" Woo hoo! I feel like jumping up and down. I hope we make a ritual of our nightly talks.

"Yes," I say simply trying to hide my, over the moon excitement.

"Good, same time then. Have a good night, Nettie."

"You too. And Linc, I noticed you too, ya know. When we met before. In fact, I remember checking to see if you had a wedding ring on." I laugh out loud at myself. I sound ridiculous.

"Did you? Well, I'm glad. I haven't been this giddy in a long time."

"Me either. Good night, Lincoln." I don't want to hang up.

"Goodnight."

When we hang up all I want to do is pick up the phone and call him right back. I know I can't, but I want to. I want him to be here. Shit, I'm going to have to cancel on Jess for this weekend. She is going to be pissed. I think about going to bed, but I'm not even tired. How am I going to sleep after such a wonderful conversation? I try to sleep because it's late, but I can't. I make my way onto the couch and turn on some old reruns. I have no idea what time I finally fall asleep, but when I do, I'm thinking of him.

The next morning, I call my mother to see how she and my father are doing. I haven't spoken to her in a while. I feel like I have some making up to do with my family. They were there for me so much and I have been, well, a bitch to them. When my mother answers she sounds like she is in a pretty good mood.

"Darling, how are you? I'm so glad you called me. I didn't want to bother you, but I wanted to hear all about it. So, tell me, you met someone. Who is he? What does he look like? How did you meet him?" I'm going to kill Jessica! She had to have called my mother as soon as we got off the phone last night. Geez, I don't want everyone knowing about Linc. I wanted some privacy for a while. Who's to even say things will work out with him? Maybe I don't want him to meet my family.

"Well, first of all Mother, you just asked me about a thousand questions. Secondly, I'm pissed that Jess would tell you about him!" I am sure she will have a coronary if I don't tell her every detail.

"How do you know that Jessica is the one who told me?" Oh, please. Don't try and get yourself out of this one.

"Well, let's see... because she is the only person I told."

"Oh." Yeah, Oh!

"Listen, Mom, I don't know what this is yet. I just know that I met a very nice man and I like talking to him, that's all." That's not all and I know it. There is much more to this I can feel it in my bones. He is special.

"Well, good for you then. Jessica said you sounded very happy. Don't be mad at her, she was just excited for you. We all are." We? So that must mean Dad knows too. Argh, sometimes my family is so infuriating. They need to mind their own business. I'm completely over our conversation and end it before I say anything to upset her.

When we hang up, I send Jess merely a text acknowledging that she has a big mouth. The text I receive in reply is a half-assed apology and a winking smiley face. She isn't sorry. She is a gossip.

I decide today I'm going to do something different. I place my phone on the speaker charger and start some music. I put on my 90's station. It is perfect cleaning music. I deep clean my house for the first time since the baby. Organizing and throwing out a much as I can stand to, without getting anxiety. My mother has been having a cleaning woman come every week. Not that I don't appreciate it, but I need to start to do things on my own again. Since I'm on a roll, I decide to head to the grocery store. I spend a good two hours there. The cart is so full that I can barely push it myself.

"Three hundred and eight dollars and thirty-seven cents." The teenaged cashier says through her gum chomping teeth.

Holy shit! I hand her my credit card and load up the cart again with the bagged items. I wouldn't mind cooking tonight. I wouldn't mind cooking for Linc. God, why can't I stop thinking about him? I wonder what he is doing right now. His beautiful eyes flash into my mind. Those mesmerizing deep chocolate brown eyes. I feel like I have hit the jackpot with him. I hope I'm not just building him up in my head. And I hope that I don't get hurt. God knows I cannot deal with any more hurt.

Once home I put away my groceries and realize I have gotten way too much. My mother has been stocking my pantry for me, but she only gets the things that she wants. Now, I have no room to put things away. Oh well. I take comfort in the fact that at least I have felt well enough to resume some of my pre-Samuel activity. The pieces of my life will come back together. The last few days have been proof of that. Lincoln's words come back to me: *"Yes, it will. The pain will never go away…ever. But it will get better."*

I can be better. Just because I have been dealt a shitty hand at life so far, doesn't mean that I can't change it now. I can't change what has happened, but I can move forward or try to at least. Alright, I need some therapy time now. Enough being normal for one day. As I make my daily trip to the gun range, I find that I'm not as anxious to get there. My fantasy has not changed. I want to take out Sam the second I have a chance and I know that I will. He won't be able to stay away when he gets out. He wants to kill me too. I cannot let my guard down for a moment. He is a monster and he will try his damndest to get at me. I have received about one letter a month from him since the only one that I opened. I have resumed the normal, pretend they don't exist game. I must fight the urge every time to open it. I really should use them as motivation. Although, if I hated him any more than I already do, I would probably be completely mad. They would have to lock me up as well. Yeah, I should just continue to avoid them altogether.

As I'm shooting all the stress releases from my body. Shooting to me is like going to the spa for my mother. I think briefly about when I want to tell Linc about Sam and the assault. I really need to. Especially the way things are going. I don't want things getting physical until I talk to him. He needs to know that I'm wary of intimacy right now. Not that I was ever really that great at it before. Maybe I should bring it up this weekend. The last thing I want to do is scare him off. I'll have to give it some more thought. I can't wait until he calls me tonight. I have a smirk on my face when I feel a tap on the shoulder. "Shit!" I quickly turn and standing behind me, is Hank. I still have my gun in hand.

"Sorry I didn't mean to startle you, but I was yelling, and you didn't hear me." He has both hands up in the air.

I lower the gun and take my headphones off. "You scared the shit out of me Hank! What's the problem?"

"Oh, nothing I just wanted to let you know we are closing early tonight for maintenance. You have a half-hour." He points to the clock behind him.

"Okay, no problem. I'll wrap it up."

When I leave I have a strange feeling. I'm not quite as satisfied as I would normally be after leaving there. I realize maybe it's because I haven't been so hung up on my anger the past few days. I can't wait to get home and talk to Lincoln again. I can't imagine what we could possibly have left to talk about, given that we spent most of last night enthralled in conversation. I don't mind sitting in silence with him either. I wonder what we'll do this weekend. My mind begins to wander to things I haven't thought of in so long. I want to have some sort of closeness with him. Some sort of physical connection. Yes, I need to tell him sooner than later about my situation. That's all there is to it. If he can't handle it then he isn't the man for me. I wince at the thought. I hope he can handle it.

My phone rings at a little after eight. "Always so prompt." I say softly. I really love this about him. No games.

"I do what I say, and I say what I do," his voice is hushed.

"Is everything okay you sound quiet?" he takes a deep breath.

"Can I come over?" My heart begins to race with anticipation.

"Yes, of course." I try to contain my excitement, but I don't think I did a very good job.

"I'll be there shortly," his voice doesn't give much away and when we hang up, I just stare out the window, waiting. I'm chomping at the bit to see him. It's not long before I see his car pull into the driveway and I light up. I meet him at the door, and he has a dazed look on his beautiful face. Oh, no what is wrong?

"Are you alright?" My pulse begins to quicken.

"Yeah, yeah I'm fine. Better than fine actually." Oh? What is he talking about?

"Cameron, the boy you met at the hospital?" I nod. "He's in remission." He cannot contain his beaming grin. It stretches from ear to ear and his dimple is deep. He looks like a child on Christmas morning. I give him a quick smack on the shoulder.

"You scared me!" Then without thinking I throw my arms around him and squeeze him tight. He doesn't miss a beat and wraps his arms around my waist. As he does, he lifts me slightly so that just my toes are barely touching the floor. I can feel him nuzzle his nose into my hair. "That is wonderful! I'll bet you are just ecstatic!" I pull away from him expecting a response. When I do, he is looking at me with such intensity in his eyes and I know he is going to kiss me. He leans forward and pauses a moment I think waiting for permission and I nod. His mouth curves into a satisfying grin and slowly he leans forward, and our lips meet. I feel the butterflies overwhelm me and I'm lost in his kiss. He is by far the best kisser I have ever had the pleasure of being in a lip lock with. His hands move gently up onto either side of my face and he pulls away softly. He plants one more quick, gentle kiss on my lips. I force my eyes open. For a moment we are completely silent and lost in a gaze.

"Wow," I whisper.

"Yeah, wow," he mimics.

"I think I should tell you about Evans...um, biological father." His eyes change and he looks almost stunned. Not exactly the response he was expecting I suppose. I feel like I need to tell him before I lose the nerve.

"Ok," he says with confusion.

"Maybe we should sit," I wave my hand to the couch and he makes his way over, taking his coat off as he does. Silently I go into the kitchen and pour each of us a glass of red wine. As I hand him his he looks up at me bewildered.

"Oh, it's that bad that I'm going to need this?" You have no idea.

"Yes." He takes a long drink, as do I. Here goes nothing. "A few years ago, I was walking home from work with a friend of mine." I hold up my fingers and make air quotes when I say the word friend. He waits for me to continue. "It was someone I had known since high school. And well, he attacked me." I look down at my hands not wanting to see his reaction. "He beat me up, bad. He also, um, raped me," I cringe at the word. "He could have killed me. He nearly did," I take a deep breath and will myself to continue. He doesn't say a word and I'm thankful. If he did, I may fall apart at the seams. "Evan was the result of that attack," I look up at him and he looks angry. So angry, and sad. Oh, yes, the pity look. I should have expected that. "Long story short, he is in jail and I decided to have the baby, despite how he was conceived. I felt as though it was meant to be. I was so in love with Evan. He was my world, and then…"

371

"Oh, God Nettie, I'm so sorry," He slowly reaches to put his hand on my knee, and I don't resist him. "I shouldn't have just kissed you like that. I didn't know." Oh no I didn't even think of that.

"No, no, no I wanted you to. I mean, I wouldn't have let you if I didn't want you to," I place my hands on his. "I just wanted you to know that I haven't been with anyone since. This is new to me. I never thought I would want anyone to touch me again." His eyes soften and I notice a small furrow in his brow "What?" I say.

"I just didn't know you felt that way." I can feel my face redden.

"I think it's pretty obvious that we have, well, chemistry, for lack of a better word."

"No, it was obvious to *me*, I just didn't know it was obvious to you," now he is the one blushing. "Remember, I have been looking at you for months and months, just waiting to talk to you." He is so sweet. I wish he had done it sooner. But if he had, would I have been so receptive? Maybe the universe just knew I would be ready now.

"I just want you to be patient with me. I'm broken." His eyes are sad again. "Talking with you, being with you these last few days

372

have woken up a part of me that I thought I would never know again. I want to thank you for that," he flashes me a smile but that sad look is still in his eyes.

"I feel the same way about you," he brushes my face with the back of his hand. "May I?" he asks shyly.

"Yes, please," and he kisses me again. This time very slow and sweet. Cautious almost. I couldn't have dreamt up a better man if I tried. For the first time in a very long time, I feel lucky.

Chapter 31

Two Months Later...The Anniversary

I'm exhausted when I wake. Infomercials are still playing on the television. I glance at the clock, it's 5 am. One of the worst anniversaries of my life. A day that I cannot forget. I have been having nightmares and it's no surprise. Today is exactly two years since my life was changed forever. Since Sam put his imprint on my life. Whether it was for better or for worse, it doesn't matter. The start of a rollercoaster of emotion and change. I wish that someday this date will be erased from my mind. I know I can wish all I want but, it will never happen. Sam's face flashes in my mind. The look he had on his face when he raped me was terrifying. I miss Linc. I wish I would have had him stay here last night. He offered, but I knew I would have a rough night. I didn't want him seeing me like this.

We have seen one another every day for the past few months. I'm head over heels in love with him, although I have yet to say the words to him. I want to call him. He will be doing his rounds.

I should wait a while. I don't want to worry him by calling this early. Oh, but I miss him so much. I just want to hear his voice. He has been an angel, sent to me. Piece by piece he has slowly put me back together. We have spent time with my family together. Even Jess, Colton, and Matthew have met him. He has passed their tests with flying colors. They love him just as much as I do. He has brought me back from the dead. I owe him my life.

Just then my phone buzzes. I didn't realize I had it on vibrate. I look at the caller ID and it's my mother. I can't believe she would call this early. "Hi, Mom."

"Oh, honey I hope I didn't wake you." Well, I should be sleeping. I wish I was sleeping.

"No, I was up. Just for a few minutes though, Mom. What is it?" I obviously know why she is calling. I just feel like giving her a hard time.

"Well, I was just calling to tell you I was thinking of you today." I roll my eyes even though she can't see me. "Daddy and I just want you to know that if you need anything today, you can call us. Are you seeing Lincoln today?" She can't help being nosy. I don't mind.

"Yeah, after he is done working, we are having dinner together," my face cracks into a slight smile. Maybe I can change the way I look at this day. Turn it into something positive.

375

"Mom, can I call you later? I haven't even had my coffee yet."

"Sure, sure. I'm sorry. Don't forget to call if you need anything alright honey? I'll talk to you later. I love you."

"I will. Love you too Mom." I really need coffee. It's too early in the morning for deep conversation.

I'm sitting on my back patio and the sun is just coming up. The sky is almost completely pink. Only a few slight streams of orange. It's beautiful. Breathtaking. Before I sip my coffee, I grab the camera to capture this beautiful morning. I settle in and take a nice, deep, relaxing breath. It's a little cooler than I imagined it would be this morning, but it's nice. The air smells so clean and fresh. I can smell a hint of freshly cut grass. I like sitting out here so early in the morning. It's so quiet. Only the birds to break the silence of the morning. I lean my head back on the chair and close my eyes, taking in the sounds and smells of the morning.

I repeat the mantra that I have heard so many times in group, "I cannot change what has happened to me, but I can change the way I react to it." From now on I will make my own happiness. I will not allow that one day dictating my entire life or the lives of the people around me. It's not fair to them or me. Sam got what he wanted, ME.

But I will only let him have the physical time he took and no more of the emotional. He cannot win. And he won't.

*

"Good morning Hank!" My voice echoes through the room.

"You're here early," he states glancing down at his watch.

"Actually, I was waiting for you to open. I have been up since five." His eyes widen. It's nine o'clock and they have just opened this very minute.

"Couldn't sleep, eh?" I shrug my shoulders at him. "Well, have a good day." He gives me a wink as I enter the familiar cold all too massive room. I'm in serious need of stress relief.

As I aim and shoot at my target, I'm into a smooth and steady rhythm. I hope Linc stays with me tonight. Since we have been together, he has stayed at my place a handful of times. We have yet to actually "sleep" together, we just sleep together. I'm reminded of the first time he saw my bedroom. He was very confused about the minimal pillow situation. That was one uncomfortable conversation. We were having a great night together until I had to explain to him in detail my attack. At least I got it over with and now he knows everything about that night. He knows about the scars and the other women. He knows about the fact that Sam occasionally sends me letters. Now that I'm thinking of it, I haven't gotten one in quite some time. Maybe he has given up on trying to torture me from the inside. Doubtful.

I have become completely at ease with this gun. I have two firearms now. One is safely at home just in case and the other is here so that I can practice. Ha, who am I kidding? I don't need practice anymore. I'm a crack shot. I just come for the fun of it now. And of course, to let off any aggression. This is another thing Linc and I have recently discussed. He doesn't like the fact that I come here or the fact that I have a gun at home, but he understands why. He prefers that I take some sort of self-defense class instead of resorting to guns. That might be alright too, but at least I know this way if Sam comes back for me, I will shoot him dead. I failed to mention that part to Linc. My intentions will remain just that, mine. I don't need to tell him anything. Especially because I have a good couple of years to break that news. If we are together. God, I hope we are together, forever. I love him. I'm going to tell him soon. Life is too short not to be with the people you love. Lincoln and I know that all too well.

I don't spend my normal amount of time at the shooting range but instead, choose to take a long drive on a gorgeous day. I find myself parked outside of Lincoln's office. When I go in his secretary, Amelia is in her normal spot behind the glass. When I approach, she doesn't look up from her People magazine and instead slides the glass door open and hands out a clipboard.

"Fill this out, please. The doctor will see you shortly." I stifle a small snort. "Oh, sorry Nettie. I'm in a trance here. I'll tell Dr. Connor you're here. Is he expecting you?" She looks embarrassed. Amelia is a woman I would guess to be in her late forties. She isn't sore on the eyes, but I can't help but notice, that her ass hangs over the side of the rolling chair she occupies constantly. In fact, I have never seen her off that chair. She simply rolls from one side of her tiny room to the other when she needs something. The word, "lazy" springs to mind, to describe her.

"No, I just thought I would stop by. I was in the neighborhood." I hope she can't tell that I'm lying. I just need to see him. I miss him.

It's not long before Linc comes through the door and ushers me back to his office.

"What's the matter? Are you okay?" He looks worried. He is so handsome. I don't say a word to him, instead I smooth both of my hands over his stubble and pull him into a gentle kiss.

"I'm okay now. I just needed to see you," I kiss him again, lingering a bit longer this time.

"I missed you too." He has a knee-weakening smile on his face. I love this man. I should just say it. Blurt it out right now.

"I'll let you get back to your very important patients." He looks around at his empty waiting room and laughs. "It's a slow day, ok?" He leans closer to me and plants small kisses first on my forehead, then the tip of my nose and finally my lips. I giggle. I like this side of him. It's exactly why I wanted to see him. I knew he would lighten my mood.

"So, are we still on for dinner tonight?"

"Yes, please. And I want you to stay with me." He looks a little surprised given that last night I asked for space.

"I would love to," he kisses my nose again. "I'll see you tonight then."

"Tonight." I'm blissfully happy.

*

I'm waiting for Lincoln to arrive as I smooth through my hair and check my make-up one last time in the mirror. He called me earlier and said he had to go to the hospital for some sort of emergency and that he would be late. I still wanted him to come over no matter what time he got here. It's nearly eleven o'clock. So much for going out to dinner. I've made the effort to clean the house today. I bought new bedding for the occasion in hopes that tonight will be different. I have somewhat gotten over my pillow phobia. I have been able to sleep at his house with them, but they are always knocked off the bed by morning. I'm just used to sleeping without them at this point. My room is beautifully warm and inviting. I have candles on either side of the bed. I don't know if they will get to burn tonight being that is getting so late. I shouldn't expect anything to happen but if it does, I think I will be okay with it.

There is a knock at the door and my heart leaps into my chest. I'm so excited to see him. When I open the door, he is looking handsome as usual with a pair of dark grey slacks and a white dress shirt that he was wearing earlier, but this time, no tie. He smiles, his heart-melting smile and his dimple shows.

"I love you!" I blurt out. His smile spreads from ear to ear and he snatches me up in his arms kissing me hard on the lips.

"I know, and I love you. I love you so much. I have been waiting for you to be ready to hear it," he is still holding me and whispering against my lips. Without thinking I wrap my legs around his waist. He pulls his face away from mine just enough to look into my eyes again, awaiting my permission.

"Yes," I whisper. I can feel him hold me tighter as we make our way down to my room. Halfway there he stumbles with me in his arms and we both fall to the floor. I'm unable to control my laughter and after he gives me a quick once over to be sure I'm not hurt; he bursts into laughter himself. After a few minutes, we both grow quiet laying on the hallway floor.

We don't make it to bed. He makes love to me right there on the cool hardwood floors and it is perfect. He is gentle and loving and I have never felt so cared for or so cherished in all my life.

We are crumpled up on the floor together surrounded by pieces of clothing. Damn this floor is so uncomfortable. "Can we please move to the bed. This floor is killing me." He arches his back and winces. We both hop into my bed and face one another.

"New sheets, and pillows," he whispers. "Miss Madison, were you expecting to seduce me?" I shrug.

"Well, not expecting, hoping maybe," I smile at him. "Why didn't you tell me sooner that you loved me?"

"Because I was afraid to scare you off," he is avoiding eye contact. I grasp his chin so that he looks up at me.

"Why would you scare me off?"

He smirks and takes a deep breath. "I have wanted to tell you I loved you since our first unofficial date." Oh? How could he?

"We didn't even know each other," I whisper.

"I knew *you*. Remember I watched you for months at those meetings. I saw the sadness in you, the beauty. I listened intently to you. I had feelings for you then, but when we sat down together...I realized that I hadn't built you up in my head. You were the woman I thought you were, and I fell for you. I could have told you that day that I loved you and I would have meant it." I can tell he is being truthful. "Wait here." He jumps out of bed and I hear him in the hallway, and he slides back into bed being careful to cover himself as he does. What the hell was that about?

"What's with the odd grin?" I'm totally confused.

383

We are lying facing one another and he leans up on one arm. His eyes burning into me. "I love you more than I thought I could love someone. I know you think that in some ways I saved you, but no. Nettie you saved me. I was walking through life going through the motions, never really, truly living. Never believing I would find love again, nor believing that I deserved it. You made me feel like I can be happy again," he lifts his hand and on his pinky finger, he has the most beautiful ring I have ever seen. It is a round diamond, with smaller round diamonds encircling it. Not only that, but tiny diamonds lace the band as well. It's stunning and I'm stunned. "Will you let me spend my life making you feel the same way? Will you marry me?"

"Are you serious?" I think he may have gone crazy.

"I have been carrying this around for a few weeks, waiting for the right time. I knew you loved me. I just wanted you to be ready to say it. I don't want to know life again without you in it. Please say yes."

"Yes!" The word flies out of my mouth before I know it. This man has breathed new life into me, and I don't want to spend a moment without him either. Are we both completely and totally insane?

"Oh, thank God! I love you so much!" he grabs my face and kisses me hard. He is giggling as he does. Then it dawns on me. Oh, no. I do not want the anniversary of that assholes attack to be the night I got engaged. How do I say this delicately "What is it?"

"Today it's just... I don't want this proposal to be tainted by the anniversary."

"Oh, well..." he looks at his watch and grins. "Well, yesterday was the anniversary of that horrible day, that will now be known as the night we first said, 'I love you' and the first time we were together. *Today,*" he emphasizes, "will be the day we got engaged." He shows me his watch and it's after midnight. I can't contain my grin.

"Perfect. Slowly replacing the bad with the good. I love you."

"I love you more." He kisses me again, forehead, nose and ending at my lips. "Sleep or eat?"

"Eat." I say with certainty. He slips his boxer briefs on and I toss on a t-shirt and we both head to the kitchen. Tonight, ended up being a better night than I could have possibly imagined. I'm here in this moment with him and I'm happy. I never thought it would be possible.

Chapter 32

Tick Tock

My cell phone wakes me, and it's a number I don't recognize. Linc is not next to me but I can smell coffee and bacon so he must be cooking us breakfast. I answer the phone anyway.

"Long time no talk Ms. Madison," I recognize the voice, but I can't pinpoint it. "It's Detective Montgomery, Nettie." Oh, shit this can't be good, can it?

"Sorry, I didn't recognize your voice, it's been so long." Why is she calling me now? "I wanted to let you know that you are being asked to speak at a hearing next week."

"Hearing? What kind of hearing?" I can feel the familiar prickle of anxiety spread down my arms.

"Samuel Knox is up for parole," she says simply.

"Wait. That is impossible! He has only been in there for two damn years!" I have never been so angry! I can't even see straight.

"Nettie, calm down. I know this is a shock. Apparently, he has been behaving like a fucking angel and his lawyer found some sort of loophole. If you ask me, I think someone has been paying to pull some strings, but I can't prove it." This is not happening. Lincoln comes running into the room. I was obviously screaming. He sits next to me on the bed and puts his arm around me. I put my finger up as I listen to Det. Montgomery continue. "This doesn't mean that he is going to be released. It's just a hearing and you get to speak. I want you to tell them every detail of what he has done to you and how it has affected your life, your family, your career, everything! I don't want you holding anything back. I want him to look like the total prick that he is!" I think she may hate him as much as I do.

"So, when is this hearing," I look over at Linc and it clicks in his head why I'm so upset. He is shaking his head no.

"Next Thursday at nine. You will be getting some paperwork in the mail about it. I just wanted you to hear it from me first."

"Well, thank you for the consideration," I cannot help my sarcastic tone. This is a bunch of bullshit. What kind of justice system do we have? I hang up on her before she can respond.

"What the fuck was that about?" Linc is furious, I can tell.

"Sam is up for parole and I need to make a statement to the board, Thursday." This is so fucked up.

"Well, there is no way they will let him out. That's insane. He nearly killed you!" He is shouting now.

"I'm not worried," I say matter of factly. I'm sure this will not be the first hearing over the next couple of years. It's too soon. He won't get out. Although the timing is fucking perfect, isn't it? It's like he knows when things are starting to get better for me and then here comes Sam, a man behind bars to slap me back down again. Well, not this time. I'm happy and he will not ruin it for me, for us.

*

I'm nervous as hell, going into the courtroom. Luckily, I have found out that I do not have to come face to face with Sam. My lawyer has informed me that I simply need to give my statement to the parole board and leave. There are only a handful of people in the room, seated at a conference type table. Linc is right beside me. I reach over and he grabs my hand, giving me a reassuring squeeze. I'm seated across from a man who introduces himself as the judge. He begins with a few "simple" questions; my name, relationship to the inmate. Relationship, what a fucking joke!

Then the million-dollar question. Why do I believe that the inmate should or should not be granted parole? I go off on a complete

388

mirror for a minute and notice that my cheeks are beginning to regain their shape. My eyes still have a trace of dark circles, but I look much better than I have in a very long time. I feel better too. My hazel eyes even look like they have a slight sparkle to them tonight. And it's all thanks to my fiancé. My amazing, wonderful, Godsend fiancé.

I hear my cell ring and choose to ignore it. I need to hurry up if I'm going to be ready in time for dinner. I don't want to be late. After putting my hair up in a turban type wrap, I apply my makeup. I have never been much for makeup, but I feel like getting dolled up tonight. I look fresh-faced and happy when I'm finished. I bend over drying the underside of my hair, being careful not to mess up the job that I've done on my face. When I flip my hair up, I nearly jump out of my skin. Linc is standing in the doorway ogling me. I shut off the dryer and grip my chest with my hand.

"Jesus, you scared me!" he has a mischievous grin on his face.

"I was just enjoying the view." He giggles. Before I know it, he scoops me up into his arms and carries me to the bedroom. My cell phone begins ringing again and I turn it off throwing it to the floor. I don't want any interruptions when I'm with this man.

After our tryst, I try and tame my unruly hair and fix up my makeup. Linc has dressed again and looks as gorgeous as ever. He runs his fingers through his hair and that is all he needs to be perfectly presentable. How nice it would be to be a man and not have to worry about hair products and makeup and simply look good all the time. Well, at least this man does.

"How long do you need to get ready?" he asks looking at his watch.

"Not long I just need to get dressed and we can get going. Did you get the wine?" He looks embarrassed.

"I completely forgot. I couldn't wait to get home to you," he grins a please-forgive-me smile.

"It's, fine we can stop on the way."

"No, I'll just run up the street while you finish getting ready, that way we won't be late."

"Alright, I'll try and hurry. I'll be ready when you get back," he kisses me on the lips, and we melt into each other. Oh, maybe we can just skip going to Jessica's and stay home. I swear he can read my mind because he shakes his head no at me.

"Shit, I know, my phone was off," I hear sirens now in the distance. I'm oddly reminded of the movies. Why is it that the cavalry shows up after the intruder is already taken care of? Just then the door bursts open and it's Lincoln. He runs to me throwing his arms around my waist.

"Oh, God are you alright?" he looks down at the ground, a bloody man lying face down on the floor. He squeezes me tighter this time. With his thumb, he wipes the blood from my lip and kisses me carefully.

"I'm fine…now." I hug him back and we all slowly make our way outside onto the front lawn. It's a swarm of cops, all with guns drawn and Leigh is explaining what has happened. I'm wrapped in Lincoln's arms as an ambulance arrives. Why? When they wheel Sam out on a stretcher my eyes meet the detectives. She shakes her head no. No, what? He's not dead? He's not going to make it?

Linc kisses me on the forehead and gives me squeezes.

"Don't worry." He whispers. "The amount of blood in there. If he is still alive, he won't make it to the hospital." I breathe a sigh of relief.

"I love you," I breathe. "I love you, my whole heart."

399

Epilogue

It's July and this would be the year that Sam would be getting released. My, how life has changed in five years. I'm happily married, and I'm 12 weeks pregnant. Linc and I found out yesterday that we are being blessed with two babies. This I know, is a sign from God. We are not going to find out the sex of the babies, but I know deep down it's one of each. My parents are over the moon. They have already been spoiling the twins, and they aren't even here yet. Linc and I will have our own little family soon enough. He has been the most amazing husband. I feel so safe when I'm with him. We decided to get a place all our own and I'm glad we did. It's neither mine nor his, it is ours and we have made it quite a home. Jess and Colton live nearby with their baby girl, Sophia. We see them often, and I have never seen her happier.

Lincoln's practice is still going amazingly well, and I have started my own photography studio. People hire me to come to them for the day and basically stalk their family to get some great live action shots. I love doing it and I was finally able to pay my parents back what I owed them. Sitting here on our back patio sipping on my iced tea, I have never been more grateful. Lincoln and I make a weekly

outing to visit Evan's and Madelyn's graves and bring fresh flowers. It

has brought us even closer than we were before.

I have even met his ex-wife. He was resistant to the idea at

first, but I needed to know what she was like. In fact, I really like her.

We won't make a habit of being friends by any means, but it was nice

to put a face with the name. We share the same loss after all. There are

no secrets between us, Linc and I, and we like it that way. I love him

more than anything, my husband. I love him, my whole heart. Finally,

after all this time I believe my parents when they said that everything

happens for a reason. They were right. I'm exactly where I am

supposed to be. I'm grateful for everyone in my life. And I live every

day with the strength knowing that I can get through anything. I have

experienced the lowest of lows and risen to the highest of highs. Life

can only get better from here, right?

Made in the USA
Coppell, TX
01 March 2022

74280418R00236